AU
CONTRAIRE

ALONNA WILLIAMS

www.blueginghampublishing.com

Copyright

CONTENTS

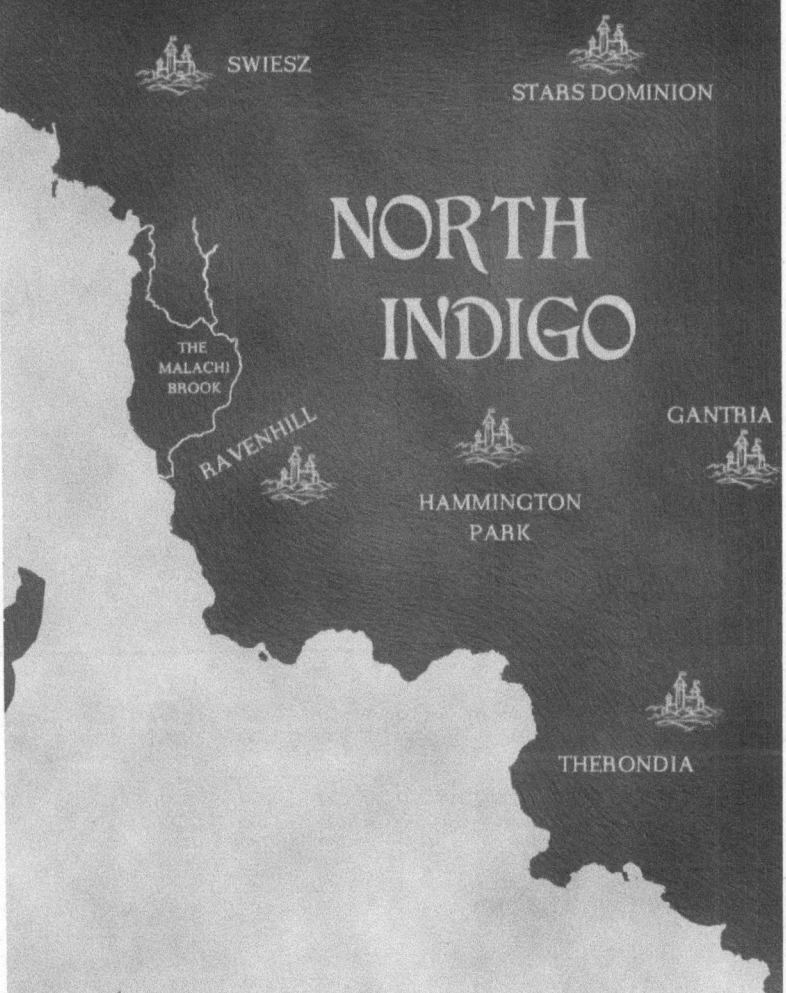

Une

Ravenhill, North Indigo, 1795.

North Indigo is a very prominent country and Ravenhill, a prosperous city. Most notable in the city was the Kensington Family, a family of bankers who had grown their wealth over the past generations. Five years ago, Reginald Kensington, the patriarch of the family, had passed away. He left behind three sons to care for their aging mother, Elise, and their grandmother, Genevieve. Gladstone was the eldest at the age of thirty-one years, Pritchard, the second-born at the age of twenty-eight, and lastly, Arlo, the youngest, at the age of twenty-one.

The brothers were a lovely sight to the country. Gladstone being well-built, standing tall and strapping. His dark hair, blue eyes, and chiseled face were elegantly charming—all of the ladies of Ravenhill wished they could have a chance with him, but Gladstone was often engulfed in his work, especially after the death of his father, though he always tried to be attentive and benevolent to those around them.

Pritchard was the quiet one—while he took the banking

business seriously, he had his own plans in mind that involved traveling to the surrounding countries and starting a new business venture on his own, as he was curious to see if he could make it on his own. Like his older brother, he had the light blue eyes, and the lighter brown hair of his mother. He was much thinner than Gladstone, the gangly one of the three. Sharp features along with a tall, slender build, made him appear a little villainous, but like the eldest, he did his best to be just the opposite of that.

And then there was Arlo, the youngest, with his father's green eyes and dark hair. The one thing the three boys had in common was their no-nonsense behavior; they had inherited that from their father and it tended to show in their expressions and actions—while, as it was stated, they were never aggressive to their neighbors, they had very little interest in the games and gaudy parties of North Indigo. Although after the passing of Mr. Kensington, Arlo had quietly drifted off into a prodigal state. They all received a portion of their inheritance, as was the custom in the country when one of the parents had passed. A portion would come after the second parent's death and another would come after they had married. Arlo had taken the portion that he gained after Mr. Kensington died with the same wish as Pritchard, that he would make his own name apart from the Kensington banking company, and squandered it having rushed into too many business deals that ultimately fell through. Now, with a new venture in mind, he came to request a loan from his older brothers.

"Arlo, you were given enough money to invest in something else and you decided you'd waste it all taking a foolish chance. And now you stand here, having the audacity to request money from Pritchard and I," Gladstone hissed. It was odd and rare for his family to see him so enraged; his cream skin reddening with every word. "How could you basically betray father like this?"

Arlo stood from his seat, ready to lash out at his elder brother, but Mrs. Kensington interrupted, standing between the two. "There is no need for an argument," she ordered. "We're a family and this can be worked out."

"You act as if I went and squandered it without a purpose; I had goals in mind just like Pritchard," Arlo defended. "And do not deny my loyalty to my father!"

Gladstone scoffed, rolling his eyes and taking steps around the living room. He leaned his hands upon the large blue chair in front of the fireplace and shook his head. "If you need money, you'll have to earn it."

Arlo crossed his arms and shrugged his shoulders. "All right. What would you suggest I do? Work for you?"

"No," Gladstone replied. "I already know I'll go too easy on you. Fortunately for you, arrangements were being discussed last week, and now that you feel the need to make up for your mistake, I think that they should be finalized."

"What sort of arrangements?" Arlo carefully asked, shifting his eyes from his brother to his mother.

Pritchard entered the room and stood beside Gladstone. "You know of the Wilhelms of Therondia," he said, focusing in on their younger brother.

Arlo gave another disconcerted look to his mother before returning his attention to his brothers. "Yes, I know of them," he sternly replied. "Was it not one of them that nearly ruined the bank two weeks ago? Dancing around like a fool?"

Pritchard sighed. "Anyhow, the youngest has shown no interest in having a season, no matter how much her family is pushing it. She's a performer with the family company, a ballerina, and she has a dowry of five-thousand and three hundred stire, along with a yearly allowance of one thousand stire; and the Wilhelms are a very wealthy and hardworking family."

Arlo turned to Mrs. Kensington and began to laugh. "This is a joke, isn't it?" he asked. "You don't really expect to marry me off to the whimsical oddballs of Therondia, do you? They reek of new money and play too much, and you think that this is the best way to get back at me for a small mistake?" he complained. "What you should be doing is suing that wretched family for every cent that they own after what happened to the bank!"

"Firstly, throwing part of your fortune away like refuse is not a small mistake; it's a grave one, which shows that you're not very capable at handling money. Yes, you're very responsible in many areas, but this is not one of them. Secondly, this is the agreement we've come to with the family."

"The girl is sweet, charming, and on the shy side," Pritchard stated, earning him an eye roll from his little brother. "I know if you had it your way you wouldn't choose a Wilhelm as a bride, but—"

"I wouldn't choose a bride at all. You think I'm bad at handling money now, you just wait and see when I have another mouth to feed and a woman to please," Arlo snapped. "You know how ostentatious those Wilhelms are, you've heard about them."

"We've *heard*," Gladstone interjected. "That doesn't mean that it's true. Now please, enough of this. The decision is made."

"Heard? You've seen it, Gladstone! We're fortunate that everything our ancestors, including Father, worked to build was repairable after the damage that was done to it!" Arlo complained. He turned to Elise. "Mother, are you allowing them to go through with this? I have to marry this unbearable Wilhelm girl and subject myself to some immature and bizarre entertainment company?"

"I'm sure she isn't unbearable, Arlo. And I think that a connection with the family would be very lucrative for us," Elise softly stated. "They are not just an entertainment company, they're the largest entertainment company in North Indigo, possibly the entire continent of Eroth."

"Is that a reason to marry? Give your life over to someone you don't care about?"

"You always said that if you married, it would be for business reasons and not love," Pritchard reminded him. "Now here's your chance. After you marry, you'll receive another portion of your inheritance—which Gladstone and I will monitor."

Arlo heaved a sigh of regret and resentment. "I hope she's in this for the same reason because it's going to get very lonely for her once she becomes my wife," he warned.

"I think you need to go meet her and the family and court her before you decide that you hate her," Gladstone told him.

Arlo gave it some thought. He despised the idea—all the stories he had heard about this family was proof that they were total opposites of him and his family. Being married into the Wilhelm family seemed like a cruel and unusual punishment. But, on the bright side, he did know of their wealth, despite them being "new money" that didn't make them any less rich. And as Pritchard had stated, he always planned to marry for financial benefit if he had to be married; it couldn't be too great a sacrifice—marry the girl, be connected to a filthy rich family, and go on about his business daily, pretending she didn't exist. After all, if she was shy and charming, she'd surely stay out of his way after the wedding. "All right, fine. I will meet her and I will court her; but if I can't bear her, I will walk away."

Gladstone sighed at the obstinate attitude of Arlo. "All right, then," he finally said. "But if you do and you end up in another mess, trust that Pritchard, Mother, and I will not be there to fish you out. Clear?"

"Clear," Arlo arrogantly nodded.

Deux

The manor of the Wilhelm's was nothing too fanciful as many who knew the family would expect it to be. In all truthfulness, it was like any other manor in the country; a white-washed brick structure, ginormous and graced with many windows, along with a courtyard that trailed up to the entrance.

The Wilhelms were embraced by most of the elites, despite being known as "new money." Five years ago, they had jumpstarted an entertainment business—it was something that many hadn't thought of in such a quiet and docile country as North Indigo. But, nevertheless, the business took off; many came to marvel at the stage plays, operas, ballets, and so on that were owned and operated by the family. They were called 'The Whimsical Wilhelms of North Indigo" and while many looked down on the way they acquired their wealth, it was clear that the acts and performances that the company offered brought many smiles to the faces of the country's citizens.

Elonnie Wilhelm was the youngest of four at the age of nineteen. Her three older siblings were each only a year older than the next, her brother Chris, her second eldest sister, Meag, and another sister Elle. She wasn't married like the elder three, but often spent much of her time reading, writing, and keeping an eye on her little cousins; playing with them, reading to them the stories she'd write about fantastical worlds, princesses, princes, dragons, and more. She was a dancer in the family company—a principal ballerina with a heart mostly for the step-dancing that entertained many.

She walked down the lovely courtyard with her best friend, Étienne, who was visiting from France and happily embraced the sunny spring day that wasn't a common occurrence in North Indigo.

"Lundi," Étienne instructed, her French accent prominent.

"Lundi," Elonnie giggled, often unable to contain her laughter at the simplest things.

"Très bien, Elonnie," Étienne commended as she clapped her hands.

"Thank you! I mean...merci," she replied. "If only I could retain it all," she sighed.

"You will," Étienne gave a smile, "just continue practicing."

Elonnie and Étienne hadn't grown up together, they had only met when the company took a show to France a few years back. But still, they had become close friends and many found it humorous that the two resembled one another. Both with dark brown skin, dark brown eyes, and curly hair. Étienne was about a hair taller than Elonnie, with a bit of a looser curl pattern. Both were dressed in traditional day dresses, Étienne's a blush color, adorned with daisies, and Elonnie's a solid mint green. As was the tradition in most parts of North Indigo, Étienne kept her long, wavy hair tied into an updo, while Elonnie let hers hang down, although many encouraged her to wear it up. Unfortunately, the girl just found the updos of North Indigo too boring and felt a freedom with her hair down.

"Elonnie! Time for tea!" Elonnie's grandmother, Sue, the mother of her mother, called from the porch of the manor.

"Yes, Nana, coming!" Elonnie called back.

"Will you be joining us, Étienne?" Sue inquired.

Étienne smiled, shaking her head. "I must continue my packing if I am to head home in the morning," she replied. She turned to Elonnie, giving her a tight squeeze, and headed off in the opposite direction to her carriage.

After seeing her carriage off, Elonnie ran as fast as she could back to the manor and was stopped by her grandmother. "Slowly, child," Sue instructed. "We'll not have any more incidents," she stated, shifting her eyes down to the girl's scarred knee.

"Sorry, Nana," Elonnie replied.

Sue cupped her grandchild's chin and kissed her forehead. "Get yourself ready for tea, we have news to share with you."

Elonnie could feel her heart racing—especially after the scene she had caused in the Kensington Bank.... Also, the last time there was news to share, she had learned that her brother was getting married and she feared that meant she'd never see him again. And it was the same case with her sisters.

She calmed down a little, thinking of how fortunate she had been.

Her siblings and their spouses often returned to visit the manor, being that they lived not too far from it. Along with that, every one of her siblings' spouses were wonderful additions to her family and she never regretted the fact that they had become part of it. Surely, the information she was about to receive couldn't be all that bad. "Yes, Nana," she said, walking into the house and heading to her room.

Upon entering her bedroom, she smiled at the clothing left for her on her bed. A bright yellow, long-sleeved evening gown. She looked beside the dress and saw a small box with a note on it, which read:

"Exciting news on the way, you should dress in something exciting, with the perfect accessory to complement it! -Love, Aunt Sonia."

Eagerly, Elonnie opened the box to reveal a charming necklace of sterling silver with a pendant of ballet shoes. She released a quiet squeal, always finding joy in her aunt Sonia's gifts. Now she wondered what the news could be; perhaps the company was ready to put on a new ballet. That would be amazing—only, she had recently hurt her knee; hopefully it wouldn't be too much of an issue, as it was nothing internal. She sat on her large bed which was in the center of the room and continued thinking. She loved to be in her room, it was simple and elegant, but still had the touch of whimsy that the Wilhelms loved.

The room had walls of white, with many accents of mint green and light blue; the bed coverings were mint green, while the curtains were light blue, draped back, showing the large windows that let in the perfect amount of sunlight. Elonnie had many ballet inspired trinkets in her room, such as a vase in the style of a pointe shoe that held fake mint green flowers. Across from the vanity was an elegant bookcase that was combined with a desk where she penned many of her stories. The bookcase was filled with a number of fictional books and fairytales and just a few educational books, mostly for dance education.

She took the ballet shoe necklace out of the box and put it on, then readied to take a bath so that she could hear this exciting news.

❧

THE LOVELY SMELL of tea filled the charming living room and Elonnie felt at ease about everything; she could smell the 'Merry Berry' tea steeping, and this added to her anticipation—she loved the fusion of the strawberries, blueberries, and raspberries. It was her favorite tea; a touch of lemon and honey made it just right.

She took her seat in her favorite chair—a teal rocking chair—and tried her hardest to remain patient as her aunts and the rest of her family scrambled around, getting prepared for the evening. She sat back in the rocking chair and looked up at the golden ceiling of the room; it was a match to the surrounding walls and merged well with the burgundy carpet. She turned to the fireplace on her left and was captivated by the crackling flames. Although it was spring, North Indigo's evenings had remained quite chilly.

"Elonnie," a small voice said, walking into the room. Elonnie's heart filled with warm love seeing her little cousin, Alex. She knew he was coming to hear a story, as he always loved to hear her tell him her stories. His brown eyes looked over his red glasses as he walked over to her and climbed into her lap. He was only six, yet still, he was a compassionate kid. The fire lit up his sandy skin and big brown eyes as he wrapped his arms around his cousin. "Can we talk about the moon men?" he asked.

Elonnie laughed. He always loved to hear about the

moon men; men who lived on the moon and sometimes made their way down to earth to see how the humans fared. "I wish I could, little one, but I have an urgent mission I must see to before we can," she explained. "But tomorrow, I promise."

"Okay," Alex laughed, revealing his two missing front teeth.

Elonnie's aunts, Sonia and Rhonda—sisters of her father —and her grandmother entered the room, offering gentle smiles as they took their places in the room. Sonia and Sue took their seats on the couch across from her, while Rhonda stood behind the couch. "How was your day?" Sonia inquired.

"Très bien," Elonnie proudly responded, sitting up straight. "J'ai beaucoup appris."

Sonia grinned, proud of her niece; she prepared to speak, but a servant entered the room with a tray and gave them each their mugs before leaving. "I'm glad you're taking your French seriously."

Rhonda walked around the room, her arms crossed and a serious look on her face—the family often compared Elonnie to her aunt Rhonda as she had picked up many of her mannerisms. She had always admired her aunt's long soft and shiny hair and serious demeanor, although she herself was more jittery. "I think you're going to like our news, Elonnie," Rhonda stated.

Elonnie gulped. "I don't have to do a season, do I?" she asked, almost pleading.

"No." Sue shook her head.

Elonnie's eyes brightened, looking from face to face. "Are Elle and Benji here?" she inquired regarding her eldest sister and brother-in-law.

"Not yet, but they'll be visiting soon," Sonia assured.

"What about Meag and Thom?" she asked. "Or Chris and Phabi?" She grinned.

"This hasn't anything to do with your siblings, although you did receive letters from each of them today," Sue stated. "As well as your parents. They'll be in Tamin for a short while."

"We're trying to tell you that," Rhonda started, "I hope you won't take this in a bad way but..."

"They're going to sue us because of the bank, aren't they?" Elonnie sighed.

"Erm, not quite. We've found a suitor for you, dear," she told her.

Elonnie could feel her heart beating rapidly; she didn't want to let her family down, and she knew that they had been trying to find her a perfect match as of late, but could they really know what the perfect match for her was? She had always had her own ideas of who she'd marry, if she ever did marry. She wanted a prince, as free-spirited as she was, that she'd meet under the craziest of circumstances and fall in love with immediately. She laughed to herself, knowing that was highly unlikely—but a girl can dream, can't she? "A suitor?" she meekly asked.

Sonia nodded. "I think you'll make a lovely couple," she excitedly said, sitting forward. "He's a gorgeous young man, about two years older than you. Dark hair, green eyes, tall, charming; if you saw him, I think you might fall for him in a second!" she told her.

Elonnie readied to reply, but the family dog, a joyful golden retriever, came trotting into the room and rested its mug upon her lap. Happy to see him, she gave his head a kiss and then returned her attention to her three family members. "Wh-who is he?" she nervously asked.

"One of the Kensington boys," Sonia squealed, unable to contain her elation. "The youngest."

"Kensingtons?" Elonnie gasped. "The Kensingtons of Ravenhill? The bank Kensingtons, whose bank I practically ruined two weeks ago?"

Rhonda, Sonia, and Sue nodded. "They've agreed that instead of pressing any charges, they'd like for you to be married to Arlo, the baby. I hear he's just as dashing as the other two and very focused and driven. I don't doubt you'll be among one of the most striking couples in all of North Indigo," Sonia said.

Elonnie panted as her eyes darted around the room. "But...I hear they're so...uptight," she stated. "And brooding. And boring. And—and why on earth would they think that this would be the answer? Surely, I would have thought that they'd want nothing to do with us anymore."

"I think your differences are what'll make you the perfect couple, in all honesty," Rhonda explained. "It's often good to put differing personalities together. They say opposites attract. As much as we adore you and your spirit, even you recognize that you need to be reined in a little every now and then," she said. "The family may be brooding, as you say, but they held back from spreading any harmful gossip about what took place in the bank, and refrained from pressing immediate charges against us. I would say that their offer is generous."

Elonnie sat back in her chair and took a deep breath. If her aunts thought she needed to be reined in, then surely this hoity-toity Kensington boy would think so. She wondered how such a thing could work and would he allow her to remain as she was, or would he want her to follow suit with his family's behavior? Again, she was lost in thought—perhaps this could be a good thing for her. She knew that the Ravenhill estate had to be filled with mystery and intrigue; maybe this would be the adventure she'd always wanted. One thing she did know was that, while sophisticated and prudent, Gladstone Kensington was known to be a gentle giant; she shouldn't expect Arlo to be any different.

She also didn't have many other options, perhaps if she had been a bit more cautious and ceased dancing in the bank when she was told to, she would have a right to reject the offer, but as her Aunt had stated, they were being generous. "I-I suppose it should be interesting," she replied.

"So, you'll accept without any argument?" Sue raised an eyebrow.

Preparing to accept, Elonnie froze. Was she ready to end her adventures as a single woman? Her respect for marriage was strong and she knew that once she was married, she was married for as long as she or her husband lived. "Yes," she courageously replied. "I accept."

Sonia and Rhonda grinned from ear to ear, making their way over to their niece and embracing her. "As hard as it seems, we know you won't regret it," Rhonda said.

"Do Mummy and Father know of this?" Elonnie asked.

"They do," Sonia replied. "Mr. Kensington will be here next week to meet you. I'm sure he's bubbling over with excitement!"

Trois

A deep frown was cast upon the face of the youngest Kensington; there was only one day left until he was to go and meet this Wilhelm woman. He already knew how this would end; his life was going to spiral out of control after he was tied down to this wild performer. He looked down into his bowl, not hungry for the porridge in front of him and now, being that he had sat there for so long without touching it, it was surely freezing.

"You should eat." Genevieve gave a smile, her deep-set blue eyes squinting as she grinned. She was aware of how this union would clash, but she felt that this was just what Arlo needed—she often felt that he didn't use his youth the way it should have been used; he was obsessed with business and banking like his brothers, but she thought all of them should have received the chance to do something wild and fun.

Arlo returned a half smile to his grandmother as he looked over at her. Her wrinkled skin was endearing, as was the long, grey hair she kept tied back into a bun and covered by a woven bonnet. "I'm not hungry," he replied. "I trust that it's amazing, though."

"You know, your mother and I were talking earlier—it's been so long since you've made a painting," she stated.

"Time is fleeting as you get older," Arlo shrugged. "I've more important matters to handle. Along with that, inspiration isn't that easy to locate."

After offering a slightly saddened face to Arlo, Genevieve looked over at her daughter and then took a sip from her teacup. "Have you gotten the chance to meet the girl?" she asked Elise.

Elise shook her head, spooning her porridge. "Not yet, but I've met her aunts. Such an...interesting family," she replied. "They are very attractive as well," she added, looking over at her son.

Arlo's frown grew deeper. That wasn't enough to stir his interest in this girl; he had seen many attractive girls before, many of which threw themselves at him the same way they did his brothers. If he wanted a pretty wife, he could get one. "Have you met her, Grandmother?" he asked.

"No, but I have met her grandmother. She had the most beautiful singing voice. It's no surprise that she's able to bring in a large crowd with her operas. I'd love to see one soon," Genevieve answered, grinning from ear to ear. "Maybe my new granddaughter-in-law will be able to offer me tickets," she chuckled in a whisper.

A look of disgust flashed across Arlo's face as a bit of a nauseous feeling came into his stomach. *This is really going to happen.* "You don't have to call her that," he assured his grandmother as he reached for his teacup, taking a sip of the straight black tea. He almost choked on it as it was so cold and distasteful. He sighed as he stood. "I should see that everything is in order before my departure," he told his mother and grandmother.

Quatre

The garden at the Wilhelms manor was lush and dew-covered; the sounds of the common wildlife filled the air as the flowers began blooming. Elonnie sat on a blanket with the little ones, relaying to them another story about the moon men. "The moon men can be quite dangerous when they become starved," she enthusiastically related to them.

Alex perked up, always happy to hear of the moon men. The little girl beside him (who was named Maddie and was six as well,) stared at Elonnie's face as she spoke—she was paying attention, but she wanted to hear a different story. Her round pink glasses on her face made her big brown eyes look even bigger and her hair was in two puffs—she was slightly taller than Alex, for now. The littlest one there was Bella; she was only two, so of course she hardly paid any attention to the story. She let her eyes travel around the garden as she scratched her black hair and took notice of the fluttering butterflies.

"When the moon men last came to earth, they stated that they wanted to feed...on..."

Maddie and Alex scooted closer, waiting for Elonnie to

reveal the secret, and this prompted little Bella to copy them.

"Little ones!" Elonnie exclaimed, jumping up and preparing to chase the children. They each scattered and Elonnie slowed her running so that the small-legged children could actually get away. Watching as they dispersed, all separating to different hiding spots, Elonnie laughed. She ran after Bella first, knowing she was going to the same hiding spot she always ran to. Climbing onto the ground, Elonnie crawled on her elbows as she came up to a white, antique garden bench. "Ha!" she exclaimed, expecting to see little Bella but instead greeted by black leather shoes. Her eyes widened as she shifted them up to see Arlo peering down at her with a look of disdain. "Oh dear," she whispered, jumping to her feet. "Erm, I'm sorry," she giggled, "I was just playing with the children." She took a moment to appraise him; my, was he a sight. Although she knew that his furrowed brow was a sign that he was displeased with her, she felt it made him more attractive. That, and the authoritative navy tailcoat he wore gave off such strong vibes from the stranger. She gulped, wiping her hands on her already grass-stained dress and awkwardly looking around as she tucked some of her wind-tussled hair behind her ear. "Can I help you?" she asked.

Arlo took a moment to process everything; he was barely on the property and he had already seen signs that made this entire arrangement a nightmare. A pretty girl, sure, but not worth the chaos. Was he really to marry into this family? Looking down at the mess of a girl, he believed that she surely had to be the notorious bank dancer. "Yes," he finally spoke up. "I'm here to meet Mrs. Sue Ridderleigh and her granddaughter," he told her.

Elonnie felt herself grow tense as she realized who was

standing before her. "Oh," she gasped, embarrassedly. "Y-you must be Arlo Kensington."

Arlo studied the girl judgmentally; her wild, free hair, grass-stained dress, and torn stockings were highly unappealing. "'Yes," he sneered.

"I'm, erm..."

"Don't say it," he said under his breath, now recognizing that this in fact was his betrothed.

"Elonnie Wilhelm," she told him.

"Of course you are," he grumbled.

"I, well," she looked down at her clothes again and hoped that she didn't appear as embarrassed as she was. "I'm sorry I look a mess right now," she told him. "I'll be with you in just a moment." She looked around the garden and smiled at seeing the gardener. "Harper!" she called and the middle-age man approached them. "Please take Mr. Kensington to the home while I fetch the children," she requested.

Harper smiled and nodded before gesturing for Arlo to follow him. After taking one more studious look at the girl, Arlo followed after the gardener. When the two were far enough, Elonnie released a mortified squeal and rustled a few grass blades out of her hair.

Walking with the quiet gardener, Arlo took one more peek back, but the girl was out of sight. He cleared his throat, ready to break the silence. "Is she always like that?" he asked.

"Miss Elonnie?" the gardener laughed, his slanted eyes growing smaller as he did. "Today she is in a better-behaved mood," he told him.

"May I ask what she thinks she's doing?" Arlo inquired.

"She's a very playful young lady; the little ones love

her," Harper explained. "I think you will too, should you get to know her," he nodded.

Arlo responded with a sour smile and the pair reached the front of the manor; as the young man examined it, he didn't find it any different from his home. That was a good sign, was it not? Only, he had already met the girl and she was exactly as he had expected her to be—unruly, misbehaved, and too lively. So, whether or not the family was normal, the girl his brothers had picked for him was not up to par with his standards.

When they entered the home, it was just as dainty on the inside as it was on the outside, despite the hustle and bustle going on. The sizable entry hall reminded him of the one at his home; there was a wide, beige staircase just ahead of them, each step covered by red carpeting, and a giant red, carpet boasting gold accents in the middle of the floor. There was an entryway on his left to the living room and one of his right to a library. The colors were a bit too loud for his taste. Reds, golds, and yellows; he much preferred, blacks, whites, and greys. Arlo could hear the sound of joyful chatter, laughter, and scrambling coming from around the corner ahead of him; most likely that led to the kitchen. And, boy, did it smell good in there, the smell of a summer stew filling the air, along with the faint smell of baked goods.

He now shifted uncomfortably, having been standing in silence beside the old gardener for too long. "Have you worked here long?" he asked.

"I have," Harper nodded, proudly. "The younglings call me 'uncle' now," he stated.

"I see, and—" he started. His words cut short as Elonnie came racing into the house along with the children unintentionally running into the young baron, sending them both to the ground.

She cringed when she realized what she had done, looking into the man's disappointed green eyes and scrambling to her feet. "I'm so sorry, Mr. Kensington," she shivered, shamefully looking down at her shoeless, stocking-clad feet. Hiding her left foot behind her right leg so that he wouldn't see the large run in her stocking, she offered him a helping hand. "I didn't see you there," she continued.

"Perhaps if you weren't going so fast," he nearly hissed, rejecting the help and getting up on his own.

"Right," she replied, lowering her hand. The sound of a thud followed by Bella crying brought their attention to the direction of the staircase. "I should handle that immediately," she stated, carefully scooting around Arlo to hurry up the stairs and attend to her little charge.

"I take it she often frolics barefoot outdoors?" Arlo asked in a patronizing tone.

Harper laughed out loud and then covered his mouth as he nodded his head. "Often," he replied.

"Who could ask for anything more?" Arlo grumbled satirically.

Rushing up the stairs, Elonnie raced into the play room, where Bella sat on the floor in tears as the other kids tried to console her. "What happened?" she gasped, glancing around the messy room. The colorful playroom was always messy; the pastel yellow, pink, and blue walls resembled a carton of sherbet, and toys were always scattered around the airy green carpet, serving as a hazard to anyone who walked in.

"She tripped over the building blocks," Alex told her.

"Aww, you poor thing," Elonnie whimpered as she lifted Bella off of the ground. "Twinkle, twinkle little star..."

she sang, and quickly Bella ceased her crying to begin singing along. "See," Elonnie smiled, "everything is fine. Now let's get you all cleaned up and ready for dinner," she told them, unable to hide her apprehension. "Perhaps you can soften Mr. Kensington into a smile—and if you can't, I haven't the slightest clue what can."

"Elonnie," Sonia called from the doorway. "Let me handle the children, you should ready yourself and get down there as soon as possible," she smiled. "A bath is already prepared for you."

Elonnie nodded her head, obeying her aunt and making her way to her room. She slowly walked over to her wardrobe and shuffled through the clothing. Smiling softly, she reached for a light blue day dress that had a cream lace belt sewn around the waist with pink flowers embroidered into it. She felt that this was her prettiest dress. Something about this stirred excitement in her.

Her heart raced as she lowered the dress and looked at herself in the mirror. Was she really ready for such a union? It didn't seem as if the young man was too excited about this whole thing, so why should she be? Shaking her head, she tossed the dress onto the bed and prepared for her bath. She wouldn't think the worst of this; this was going to be an adventure for her and nothing would put a damper on that.

There was a gentle knock at the door and Elonnie went to open it; her brown eyes filled with joy at seeing her friend again. "Étienne! What are you doing here?" she gasped.

"I heard about this arrangement and had to return instantly!" she exclaimed in a whisper. "Where is he? Who is he?"

"He's downstairs," Elonnie replied, "and I haven't the slightest idea who he is." She frowned. "I must say, I don't think we're off to a good start. I'm glad you're here...I only hope my brothers and sisters will come soon."

Cupping her chin, Étienne smiled. "Everything will be fine," she assured her. "Now, don't have me keep you from getting ready," she told her.

E lonnie returned downstairs, now dressed in the outfit she had picked out; she kept her long black curls hanging down and her hand was wrapped around the new necklace from her aunt as she and Étienne peeked around the corner into the living room where Arlo sat. "Il est si beau," Étienne gasped.

Elonnie bit her lip, watching as Arlo seemed to struggle with hiding his annoyance with the little ones surrounding him. "Mais trop sérieux," she replied.

"Bon courage," Étienne told her, offering an encouraging nudge.

Nervously, Elonnie stepped from behind the corner and stood in the entrance to the living room. Arlo shifted his eyes over to her and he admired the dress she had picked out; it was simple and elegant and flattered her figure, but his eyes then traveled down to her shoeless feet. Well, whatever—after all, she wasn't outside, right? He returned his attention to Alex, who leaned on the arm of his chair, pelting him with question after question. "I don't know what a moon man is," he stated, trying to remain patient.

Alex walked to Elonnie and pulled her into the room. "Elonnie can tell you all about them," he smiled.

Elonnie met eyes with her suitor and shyly blushed, messing around with her hair. "Erm, it's just some tales I tell them," she mumbled.

"I'm sorry?" he asked, sitting forward and slightly tilting his head to signal that he couldn't hear her.

"I said 'some tales I tell them,'" she spoke up.

"I see," he replied, sitting back and crossing one leg over the other. "You were much louder crawling around in the grass," he stated.

"Right, yes, about that...I'd like to apologize for knocking you over," she told him. "The, erm, the children love to play," she continued, walking into the room and taking a seat on her favorite chair across from him.

"As *children* should," he replied, glancing at the little ones.

Elonnie quietly sighed; this was not going well, she knew that. "I—I see you have tea already," she said, looking to the teacup beside him. "Can I get you anything else?"

"No, thank you."

"I'm sure dinner will be ready soon," she smiled. "I would have loved to have prepared it myself for you, but I had—"

"More urgent matters, I'm sure," Arlo nodded. "After all, the *moon men* can't wait, right?"

Elonnie frowned. He could have been saying it as a harmless joke, but his tone didn't come across that way, and the way in which he looked her up and down as if he was judging every inch of her didn't help. "I had to look after the children," she firmly said. "Their parents requested that I do so."

"Quel crapaud arrogant," Étienne grumbled to herself,

turning her nose up as she eavesdropped on the conversation. The sound of a throat clearing caused the girl to nearly leap out of her skin.

"Care to help me set the table?" Sonia asked with a smirk.

"Of course," Étienne nodded.

"Are you, uh, finished with your tea, Mr. Kensington?" Elonnie asked, nodding at his teacup.

Arlo looked at the teacup and picked it up from the table. The sweet aroma of the Merry Berry tea made him grimace a little. "Not quite finished," he told her.

"That's Merry Berry," she grinned, taking in the scent. "My favorite."

"I'm sure it is," he replied.

"Dinner is ready," Rhonda said from the entrance.

"Thank you," Elonnie and Arlo said in unison. Elonnie jumped up and waited for the baron to rise so that he could follow her to the living room. "I do hope you'll enjoy dinner; my aunts are among the best of cooks," she told him, locking her hands together in front of her as they walked. "Summer vegetable and chicken stew is one of my aunt Renee's best! You'll meet her in a little if you haven't already. I feel that cooking seasonal dishes brings the next season faster."

Arlo's attention shifted to Rhonda, who walked ahead of them. She was so quiet and calm. Judging by their looks, it was easy to see that she and Elonnie were of the same blood, but Elonnie wasn't half as composed as the older woman; in a case like this, he didn't expect her to be, but it would have been nice. "I'm afraid that's not how nature works," he finally said.

"I don't know. I think nature in itself is magic," she told him. A loud quietness embraced the room and the walk to the dining room felt like a long walk through a labyrinth.

Elonnie's brown eyes traveled over to Arlo and she swallowed—he was gorgeous and she knew that was true. Of course, this wasn't the only reason she was interested in the arrangement, that would be ridiculous; and she had never seen him previously, so she couldn't be sure of how he looked when she had accepted.

Something about the idea of her being whisked away into an arranged marriage to a man she had never met actually made her curious and excited. She had heard hearsay of the Ravenhill estate and the Kensington sons, but she had never been. Arlo was quiet and seemingly cryptic; she hoped that his standoffish behavior wasn't due to a disdain for her, but due to the fact that he was mysterious. No doubt, the Ravenhill estate had to be the same; she imagined it to be made of grey stones, with stained glass windows and long, magical hallways that she could take her lantern and run down in her nightgown at two o'clock in the morning. A smile lit up her face.

"Is something amusing, Miss Wilhelm?" Arlo inquired.

"No," she shook her head. "I, erm, can you tell me about Ravenhill?" she asked. "I picture it to be something dark and mysterious; like the kind of place that Don Quixote might live," she beamed.

"No," Arlo stated, shaking his head, "It's not like that. It's quite dark, yes, but in a dreary fashion; nothing that would excite a woman like you."

"Hmm," Elonnie thought. She had a grand feeling that what he said wasn't true. Sure, he was the one who had grown up there, but with a name like Ravenhill, things had to be exciting. "We're here," she said with relief when they reached the dining room.

Arlo stared at the unusual dining room, slowly turning his nose up. The table was a long rectangle, colored marble, black and white; each chair was rounded and designed with a card suite at the top of it, diamonds, spades, clubs, and hearts. The floor appeared as one big domino. He cleared his throat, subconsciously taking a step back and then turning to Elonnie. Speechless, he returned his gaze to the dining room.

"Awww, come in!" Elonnie's paternal grandmother, Marei, invited.

Arlo forced a smile at the elderly woman. She did look like the perfect grandma; her round glasses, grey and black hair, and soft gown. He glanced at Elonnie one more time, realizing that if her grandmother were nineteen, the two could be twins. "Good evening," he bowed.

"You have an older brother, correct?" one of the women asked, shifting her big brown eyes up and down the baron.

"Two, actually," Arlo nodded, completely missing the joke.

"That's Aunt Renee," Elonnie laughed. "That's her way of telling you she thinks you're attractive," she told him.

"Oh, I see," he nodded. "Thank you," he told Renee.

"And that's my best friend, Étienne," she told him, pointing to her friend.

"Nice to meet you," Arlo told her and received a judgmental frown from the girl who took a sip from her glass.

"Have a seat, please," Sue told them.

They fully entered the room and found seats across from Sue and Marei. Elonnie reached for her chair to pull it out, but Arlo took it from her and pulled it back for her to sit in, as a gentleman should. The gesture wasn't too common around the household, so Elonnie had to refrain from giggling and blushing as she sat down. "Thank you," she told him.

"Can we discuss the wedding?" another woman chimed in. Her face was also outstandingly similar to Elonnie's.

Arlo and Elonnie's eyes both widened—they knew what this whole ordeal was about but they didn't expect to jump into everything quite so soon. Arlo straightened in his chair, turning to the woman. "I take it you're the mother?" he asked.

"No," she shook her head. "I'm her aunt, Antoinette."

He blinked. This girl had many aunts. "Lady Antoinette," Arlo began.

"Aunt," she corrected.

Arlo gulped. "I, erm...I don't think that's necessary," he nervously chuckled.

"Aunt or nothing at all," Antoinette warned.

Taking a deep breath, he squirmed in his seat. "Aunt," he forced. "Antoinette. Miss Wilhelm and I should at least take time to get to know one another before we start wedding planning," he told her. "I know this is more of an arrangement, but still, I prefer things the old-fashioned way."

"I find that to be much more romantic," Elonnie agreed.

Arlo refrained from curling his lip and forced a smile to the best of his ability. He had no intentions of being romantic—it was only practical for him to do things the way his father had done them. "I like to do things by the book," he added.

"Do you believe in love at first sight?" Elonnie asked.

Arlo shifted with discomfort—what a bold yet ridiculous question. "It's impossible," he responded. "Love doesn't come from sight, that's quite superficial if you ask me. On the other hand, I think it comes from two people taking time to learn about the other. And compatibility is a major factor."

Elonnie shook her head. "No. I think that some people are made for each other. And once they finally see each other, then God makes it click in their heads and then they're in love."

"A bit of a childish belief, wouldn't you agree?" Arlo scoffed. "Judging by the design of the earth, I believe God would much prefer to take His time with things."

"Oh, Mr. Kensington," she giggled, "you got me there. But I believe that all must see things through the eyes of a child," she told him.

"And when do they grow up?"

Elonnie leaned closer to him. "Never," she joked.

Arlo would have rolled his eyes, but looking at her family surrounding him, he was sure they would have caught it and possibly attacked him. "How old are you, Miss Wilhelm?" he inquired.

"Depends on the day," Elonnie replied and of course the young man frowned. She reached for the stuffed olives upon the plate that the servant had just placed on the table and popped it into her mouth. "Nineteen according to time and nature," she added.

"I see," Arlo nodded. It was a good age—if only she acted it.

Upon finishing dinner, Elonnie quickly stood to assist the servants with clearing the table, initially confusing Arlo; of course, he wasn't used to this and he didn't expect it from a family as rich as the Wilhelms and a family with servants. He followed suit, standing and choosing to help her. Elonnie gave him a quiet, grateful smile before starting out of the dining room. "If you'll just follow me," she guided.

After leaving the dining room and entering the kitchen Elonnie peeked back at Arlo as she placed the dishes down into the sink. "Was everything to your liking?" she inquired.

"Yes, I suppose," he nodded. "I can't say I've ever had a summer stew like this one."

"Is that good or bad?"

Arlo shrugged. "Certainly not bad," he replied. Even with the background noise of the back and forth of the hard-working servants, a disconcerting silence engulfed the room. "I don't trust that this whole thing is agreeable to you," Arlo finally said to her. "I'm sure it's not your ideal circumstance, seeing as you'd rather fall head over heels for the man just by looking at him. Unless, of course, you think that we're meant for one another?" he asked.

Elonnie took the plates from him and placed them atop the other ones before she shyly wrapped her arms around herself. "Erm...well, this has been an interesting turn of events," she told him.

"And that means?"

"Because it's an odd circumstance...it could be that we are...meant for one another."

Arlo mistakenly laughed a condescending laugh. "You don't honestly believe that, do you?" he asked. "You can't live with your head in the clouds, Miss Wilhelm."

Elonnie quietly sighed. "It's just as bad to live with your head in the dark, is it not?" she asked.

"I think there's a medium in there somewhere. One that allows you to believe that, yes, love is real and possible, but certainly not at the sight of someone, nor is anyone *meant to be,*" he told her.

"You're wrong," she shrugged.

"Hardly," he retorted. "So, you think that you're meant to be with me simply because we're being forced into marriage, and not meant to be with someone who thinks and behaves like you?"

"Yes," she nodded. "That's the way the magic of the world works," she firmly continued.

Crossing his arms, he leaned against the wall. "And have you fallen in love with me?" he asked.

A warm cinnamon scent filled the air as Elonnie removed pastries from the large oven and placed them on the table to cool down. She turned to Arlo with a frown. "You haven't given me a reason to," she stated.

"Meaning your theory is incorrect," he affirmed.

Elonnie lowered her head and her shoulders; looking up at him, she began to shake her head. "Not incorrect," she replied. "It's just that this version is different." She lifted the tray of pastries off of the table and carried them back to the dining room.

Arlo groaned quietly. She was going to be a handful—his brothers couldn't have picked a worse match than this one. He met eyes with another one of the servants who gave him a scowl before they left the kitchen with a bowl of fruit. Finally, Arlo decided to return to everyone in the dining room.

Six

"*If you must know, I think this is the worst decision you could have possibly made. I doubt Father would agree with this arrangement, he'd think it was absolutely preposterous and you know this. Nevertheless, I will go through with it, all to benefit myself; and if the girl is hurt in the process, just take responsibility for your own actions.*

Your Brother,
Arlo Kensington."

After concluding his letter, Arlo prepared it for mailing. The room offered to him by the Wilhelms was more than charming; the giant bed with four pillars of pure gold, the warm white carpet gracing the floor, the large fireplace with a mirror above, also boasting pure gold. Still, he would have preferred to stay off the property, but they of course insisted. He took his letter and then made his way to the entry hall. The home was terribly quiet, causing him to wonder if he was the only one awake at the moment—it wouldn't have been too surprising, as he was an early riser.

"Good morning," a small voice said behind him.

Arlo turned around to see Alex standing there, still in

his pajamas. He kept a distance from the little boy, unsure of how to interact with him. "Good morning," he replied.

"Whatcha' doing?" Alex asked.

"Mailing a letter," Arlo replied. "Erm, is anyone awake?"

Alex laughed. "Me," he replied.

"Someone older?"

Alex nodded. "All of them," he said. "But most of them went to go working. It's just Elonnie and Nana and Grandma," he said.

"Where can I find Miss Elonnie?" he asked.

He walked closer to him and looked up as he nodded. "Elonnie is in the garden. Can I ride on your back there?"

"Don't you think you should dress in the appropriate clothing for going outside?" he asked.

"We always play outside in our pajamas on Sundays," he replied. "As long as we take a bath, we can put on new pajamas and play outside."

Arlo huffed, finding the ritual to be a grotesque one. "All right, I'll take you with me, but not on my back."

Alex held out his hand and, after a brief moment, Arlo offered the child his finger to hold on to. He rarely ever spent time around children, and that had a great effect on how he viewed and dealt with them; of course, it wasn't that he didn't like this little kid, he was only an innocent child. Arlo just didn't know what he should do with him.

After Alex took hold of his finger, they walked out of the manor to go out back to the garden where they found Elonnie, Maddie, and Bella sitting around the stone bowl of a fountain with their feet in the water. "Not just anyone can see a faerie," Elonnie whispered to the girls, "only the truest believers, with the purest hearts," she smiled. "Meaning children can always see them."

"And you too, Elonnie?" Maddie asked.

"Well, I do believe," Elonnie nodded.

"What about him?" Maddie asked, pointing to Arlo, who appeared behind them.

Turning around, Elonnie greeted Arlo with a soft smile. "Good morning," she said. "Care to join us?" she asked, making room for him on the fountain.

"I'm not really one for such an activity," he replied. "I don't think a lady should behave the way you're behaving right now."

Elonnie helped Alex onto the fountain and then turned back to the girls and shook her head. "I'm afraid it'll take some time for someone with such a closed mind to be able to see a faerie," she told them. She glanced back at Arlo. "That doesn't mean it's impossible though," she stated.

Discreetly, the young man rolled his eyes at the nonsense; he wasn't in the mood to deal with this at this hour in the morning. He faded into his own head, realizing that this would be the rest of his life, waking up to find his wife sitting in a fountain in her nightgown, telling far-fetched stories and fairytales. He groaned within himself before he hesitantly tapped her shoulder. "I was wondering if you'd be interested in a carriage ride around the city?" he asked in a grumbly tone.

Elonnie blinked, turning back to him. "That sounds like fun," she exclaimed, splashing out of the fountain. "I could show you around if you've never been. And there's a lovely patisserie in the square! The children would love to pick out—"

"The children?" Arlo interrupted.

"Well...yes, I thought they might—"

"No," he shook his head. "We're not—" He took her arm and pulled a tad bit away from the little ones. "We're not

37

taking them with us," he told her. "Surely your grandmother can watch them. I'm trying to get to know *you*, if you don't mind."

"You can get to know them too, they're—"

"I'm not supposed to marry them, Miss Wilhelm; now please, stop arguing with me," he told her.

Elonnie pulled her arm away and gave a pouty look. "I wasn't arguing, Mr. Kensington," she told him. "I'll just take them to set them up for breakfast and then I'll be ready," she said. "Come, little ones," she called for the kids. They climbed off the fountain and ran to her and the four started back into the home.

"Miss Wilhelm," Arlo called. He locked his hands behind his back as she turned to him. "I trust you'll be dressed in appropriate clothing?"

Elonnie looked down at her nightgown and then nodded with an annoyed look on her face.

☙❧

THE START of the carriage ride was cumbrous as both parties kept quiet, just watching the city of Therondia flow by; it was a nice city, filled with various shops, food stops and outdoor carts, well-dressed civilians and classy families strolling about. Arlo looked over at Elonnie as he brought the carriage to a hold, allowing a family to cross to the other side of the street. She was well-dressed, a better sight than he had seen this morning; clad in a long, cream-colored nap dress and clutching onto that special necklace. He frowned at her free hair; like most women, it should have been up.

Elonnie waved at the little ones who had taken the initiative to wave to her first and smiled. "It's such a lovely day to be out," she sighed, finally breaking the silence. "Don't you just love springy days? Or don't tell me, you'd rather it to be rainy and dark?" she tittered, folding her arms.

"I like a balance," he replied. "Naturally, I find sunny days favorable, but I enjoy the rain just the same."

"I do too," Elonnie admitted. "I love to stand outside and get drenched by it and after that, take a long, warm bath, followed by a hot cup of Merry Berry tea and a good story."

"Is your intention to catch a chill?" Arlo asked.

"No," Elonnie replied. "Hence the long, warm bath that follows."

"The risk remains," he grumbled.

Elonnie sighed, returning her attention to the city. There had to be a fun side to this man somewhere, she just needed to know how to unearth it. After all, he had said where they were going was a surprise—she found that to be romantic, even exciting. She slid closer to him and he peeked at her from the corner of his eye. Studying his face, she smirked, working up the courage to move a part of his hair behind his ear, to which he flinched. Elonnie laughed; she knew he had a vulnerable side somewhere, but she hadn't expected to see a part of it so soon. "You're very handsome," she told him. "Do you hear that much?"

"Life is more than just looks, Miss Wilhelm," he reprimanded.

"I never said it wasn't; I asked a question, to which I deserve an answer," she said.

"No one *deserves* anything," he stated.

"Oh, must you be so dreary?" she complained, sitting back. "And to think I've complimented you. It's like you're taking offense to that."

"No, Miss Wilhelm, I'm not taking offense to anything. Thank you for the compliment."

Elonnie began messing around with her curls; she sat forward and pointed to large metal gates to the right of them that were covered in rose vines. "That's the park," she told him. "I think you'd like to go one day. There's a lake and many feeders that the birds love to come to; they're not so afraid of humans anymore," she explained. "Even the Rivias. I suppose that only matters if you're a bird lover," she added, lowering her head. Her head rose in excitement as they passed a massive theater; even in the morning, people were lining up to purchase tickets. "That's one of our theaters," she told him. "A new play starts tonight, it's called 'The Whisper of the Phoenix,'" she told him. Of course, she didn't receive too much of a response from the man, causing her to sit back once more and focus on her city.

Arlo quickly took a glance at her; she clearly adored the city she was born in, and while it didn't stand out blatantly from the rest of the country, something about it did match her interesting personality. "And you have no issue leaving Therondia behind? I have no intentions of moving here," he told her.

Elonnie softly smiled as the wind gave a gentle blow, her mind back on the Ravenhill estate. "I'm quite excited to see Ravenhill," she told him. "I know you might think it boring, but it's clear that you and I see things differently."

"Do you believe that two people who see things as differently as we do should be a union?"

"I believe anything is possible," she replied. "I think that because love is so strong it can make even the oddest of couples become one. You see, I told you I believe in love at first sight, and I do; but I do also believe in letting love grow every now and then. I predict that by the end of the year, you'll be head over heels for me," she told him.

With that, Arlo let out a laugh; it was so loud it almost shocked Elonnie out of her seat. She didn't know it was possible for the man to laugh. "Head over heels? For you?" he chuckled.

Elonnie's brow furrowed as an offended scowl took its place on her face. "You don't have to be rude about it," she told him. "I do think you will, and I predict you'll buy me a puppy as well." She crossed her arms and legs.

"I predict you'll be very disappointed," he told her.

"Hmph. We'll see," she retorted, staring at the passersby. After a brief pause, Elonnie gave the man her attention once more. "Do you not think I'm attractive?" she asked.

"I never once stated that I—"

"Just answer," she rolled her eyes. "Not everything needs a long-winded reply."

"Mind your attitude," Arlo ordered, he gave her a swift look and then returned his eyes to the brick road ahead. "Physically, yes," he told her. "I'd be a fool to say otherwise."

Proudly, Elonnie smiled, although she didn't want to. "Why?" she asked. "What is it you find attractive?"

"I didn't think a girl like you would need validation from anyone, especially not someone like me," he replied.

"I don't need validation. I'm curious."

"We're here," Arlo stated, bringing the horses to a halt.

Elonnie took a look around and pursed her lips in confusion. *Towne Hall? What on earth are we doing here?*

Arlo concealed a smirk, seeing her displeasure. "You look baffled."

"Towne Hall isn't really the most romantic spot in Therondia," she nervously laughed.

"Did I give you the impression that this was supposed to be a romantic endeavor? If so, I apologize," he told her.

"I just figured the whole thing is to get to know one another, you do that at a park where you can take a stroll down the enchanting sidewalks, listen to the songs of the birds, and—"

"Maybe next time," Arlo interrupted abruptly. He climbed out of the carriage and walked around to assist the young lady out. "Besides, don't you enjoy a nice debate?" he asked.

"Debate?"

Arlo nodded. "North Indigo is due for a new monarch family to take the throne. Do you not care who's sworn in?" he asked.

"Politics?" Elonnie groaned, dropping her head back and rolling her eyes. "You must just be pretending to be this grey."

"No," he shook his head. "Not pretending at all."

"Well, if we're going to do this, then it's only fair if you attend a show I want to see," she protested.

"Oh, don't tell me you're a complainer," Arlo sighed.

"I haven't complained nearly as much as you have," she replied. "You just do it differently."

❦

ONLY A FEW MINUTES LATER, Arlo came storming out of Towne Hall behind Elonnie. He took hold of Elonnie's arm and pulled her back. "How dare you embarrass me like that?" he hissed. "Have you gone airheaded? How can you talk to someone who might be the ruler of your country that way?"

"Don't you call me airheaded! How about you call that disrespectful wretch airheaded?" Elonnie snapped. "If someone were to talk to you the way I was spoken to and disrespect your work and so on, I wouldn't allow it, seeing as I'm expected to be your wife. Maybe you don't want this to happen, but should it happen, I would very much appreciate it if you would please defend me when the need is there."

"You started it. You want me to defend you when you're in the wrong? At the same time, I just met you, you can't really expect me to just fall at your feet and do whatever you want me to do."

"Do you consider my work to be not hard work?" she asked, crossing her arms.

"Elonnie, be serious. Frolicking around in a pretty dress is not hard work," Arlo said underneath a chuckle.

Elonnie made her way closer to him. "Let's see you try it," she said. "Put on a shoe nearly as hard as stone and *frolic* around on your toes with a smile on your face for two hours or more and make it look pretty. And you tell me if it's not hard work! North Indigo seems to benefit greatly from what me and my family do, more so than they do from banking, that's for sure."

"And yet where would they be without a bank?" Arlo asked. "Where would your family be without the loan they took out from us to start the business in the first place?"

"Aren't you arrogant?" Elonnie said, turning away from him.

"I take it that it was you who nearly destroyed my family's livelihood a couple weeks back?" he asked.

Elonnie's brown eyes carried disappointment and rage

as she turned to look up at Arlo. "Take me home," she finally said.

"The day isn't over yet."

Again, Elonnie turned her back to him as she crossed her arms. "Well what else did you have in mind for the day, Mr. Kensington?" she asked.

Arlo clenched his fist and swallowed, showing a clear apprehension in his face. "Why don't you decide?" he asked, knowing he was setting himself up for a disaster.

Elonnie's face softened as she slightly tilted her head back in his direction. "Really?" she asked.

"I picked first, now it's your turn," he told her. "Although you did ruin my fun," he grumbled in addition.

"All right then," she smiled, fully facing him. "I want to go to the park."

Arlo shrugged. That couldn't be terrible; there was nothing outlandish about the park—it was just the simple beauty of nature, something that anyone would be a fool not to enjoy. "Very well then, the park," he nodded.

"And then let's see a play," she grinned.

"Now wait a minute. One or the other, let's not forget I didn't even get to see the end of the debate because you were getting lippy with the potential monarch of North Indigo."

"I was not. I was insulted, I retorted; for example, if I were to call you a stuck up, snot-nosed man who only got anywhere because of your father's legacy, how would you feel?" she asked.

"Why you rotten little..."

"You see," she placed her hands on her hips. "Now let's go before all the best spots in the grass are taken."

Before she could take off toward the carriage, Arlo

grabbed onto her arm. "We'll go to the park. But we will sit on the benches and we will not see a play," he told her.

Elonnie lowered her eyes and then looked up at him. "It's a historical play. Do you not like history?" she asked.

Arlo may not have known her all that well, but it was obvious that this wasn't a whole truth. "Historical about what?" he asked, arching his eyebrow. "Pirates?"

Elonnie tried to contain her shock. *How did he know it was about pirates?* "History is history," she replied.

"It's that bogus hobjockey about mermaid pirates, isn't it? Absolutely not."

"Siren," she corrected. "And it's not hobjockey." Elonnie shook her head. "They're real and with proof," she continued. "But I wouldn't want to sit and listen to you complaining the entire time, so I suppose we should settle on the park." She took a few steps closer to him and offered eyes of pleading. "Could we walk? It isn't so far."

Arlo took a look down the road, trying to calculate the distance of the park and where they stood; he thought for a moment. It was a lot easier to let the clopping sounds of the horse's hooves muffle out the uncomfortable silence, but perhaps the noise of the citizens would offer the same comfort. "I don't see why not," he finally said.

Elonnie let out a squeal of excitement before she wrapped her arm around the baron's. "It's always refreshing to take a nice walk on a spring day," she assured him.

⚜

ELONNIE COULD FEEL tenseness in Arlo's arm as they walked and that only caused her to latch on to him tighter. She knew it wasn't an ideal circumstance for him to be seen publicly with her and so soon, but he was the one who had offered to take her out, and if this was going to work he needed to get used to being seen with her. "You know, my friends find this to be just as strange as yours do," she spoke up.

"What in heaven's name are you talking about?" Arlo sighed.

"I know you're feeling uncomfortable because we're drawing eyes. Perhaps it could be because my aunt was right and we make an attractive couple," she said with a nudge.

"There's more to being a couple than being attractive," he complained, just as Elonnie had predicted he would and said it along with him in a mocking tone. He scrunched his face in annoyance as he looked down at her, to which she replied with a snarky smile. "I think they think it's all an oddity, that's all," he said.

"I doubt that," Elonnie replied. "And if they do, they like it."

"Go ahead and keep your head in the clouds," Arlo groaned.

"I will, thank you," Elonnie replied.

Sept

When the couple arrived at the park, the beautiful piece of land was crowded, which didn't come as a surprise on such a day and at such a time. Families had often made it a weekend routine to spend a good chunk of time outdoors during the warmer months, and today there was no rain, something the citizens of North Indigo often took advantage of. It was still a gorgeous sight despite the crowds. From the flowery bushes beside each white bench to the large rectangular fountain in the middle of the space and the lush green grass and singing birds of all kinds, it looked like something from a fairytale Elonnie would have loved to read.

Elonnie slightly frowned, seeing all the spots on the grass taken, but she let it go; after all, she was the one who wanted to walk there, which had lost them a great deal of time. Her eyes brightened at seeing her favorite oak tree and she turned to Arlo. "I know the best seat in the park," she told him.

"No," he replied.

Elonnie took a step back in offense. "You haven't even heard what I was going to say," she stated.

"One would think we've already been married for twenty years with how I can predict what you're thinking, Miss Wilhelm," Arlo chuckled. "You want to climb the tree. And in a dress? No."

Biting her lip, Elonnie took another glance at the oak before she lifted her head arrogantly and walked toward the white benches that lined up along the gate of the park. "I wasn't going to say that," she lied as she sat down. "I was going to say right here by the peony bush."

"Oh, of course," Arlo nodded, unconvinced, as he sat on the bench. He left enough space for two others to sit between them if they wanted to, and then sat quietly.

Elonnie looked at the empty space and readied to comment on it, but decided not to. "What's your middle name?" she inquired.

"Why does that matter to you?" he asked, crossing his legs.

"A peculiar middle name," she giggled and Arlo frowned. "I want to know every little detail about you," she told him. "When my parents are cross with me, they call me Elonnie Mary Wilhelm, so when I'm cross with you, I'd like to call you, Arlo Why Does That Matter To You Kensington," she shrugged.

"It's Darcy," he told her.

"Darcy," she repeated. "Arlo Darcy Kensington...that's lovely."

"Thank you. But I doubt I'll give you reasons to be cross with me; on the other hand, I can hear myself saying Elonnie Mary Wilhelm quite often."

Elonnie laughed, throwing her head back and covering

her mouth. "I don't think so." She shook her head. "And I suppose it would be Elonnie Mary Kensington," she added.

His eyes traveled down to the ground. "Right," he quietly replied. He turned, ready to ask a question, but his eyes widened and his cheeks reddened with mortification at seeing the young lady reaching into the top of her dress to retrieve a bag of seed. "Miss Wilhelm!" he gasped.

"It's for the birds," she defended upon seeing the scowl on his face and hearing the disciplinary tone. "I always bring food to—"

"Food does not go there! Have you no pockets?"

"I do, but they're occupied at the moment. Now would you stop making a scene?" she demanded.

"*I'm* making a scene? I didn't pull bird food out of my bosom, I don't think I'm making a scene."

"Lower your voice," she embarrassedly snapped, gazing at all the eyes that were now on them. "I always feed them on Sundays. There's nothing bizarre about—"

"I don't care that you feed them, Elonnie, I said...never mind. Like I said, I can see myself being the one who ends up cross at the end of the day," he grumbled.

49

Huit

Glancing around the garden of the Wilhelm Manor with excitement, Elonnie twirled her fingers around in her long kinky hair. She knew that soon her siblings would finally be arriving for the family garden party planned by her aunts.

She peeked over at Arlo, sitting in a chair across the way from her in the same moping manner as he often did, reading a sizable novel—she wondered if that was just the way he looked or if he just did not want to be there. She found that strange, as his brothers were soon to arrive. *How could one not be excited to see their family?* "Arlo?" she called.

He looked up from his book as she approached him. "Do you think you'd like to play a game of Wokkie Ball?" she asked, sitting in the grass beside his chair.

Arlo stood, offering her his seat. "I'm not familiar with such a thing."

"Oh, it's quite simple," she explained, remaining in the grass. "All you have to do is—"

"Miss Wilhelm, take the seat please," he requested.

"I'm all right down here, I love to sit in—"

"I was not asking," he told her. He observed the simple pastel pink gown with gold dots for a moment. "Your dress is far too...certainly, you wouldn't want to ruin your dress, would you?"

Elonnie stood, brushing herself off. She smiled at him. "Far too what?" she asked.

"It's not something you'd want to ruin."

"Do you like it then?" she asked, looking down at her gown.

"I don't dislike it," he told her.

Elonnie frowned—it would take a miracle to get this man to answer a yes or no question with yes or no. "I think you look nice just the same. Perhaps you should wear navy blue more often. As for the game, it's really easy; all you must do is position your whacking stick to strike the ball down the lane and into the standing bottles, with the goal to knock them all down."

"Now this sounds familiar," he realized. "The game the homeless children play on the streets of Odsia, correct?"

"What does its origin matter if it's fun?"

"I think I'll have to pass on Wokkie Ball, I'm afraid," he told her. He looked past her to see his family arriving and then turned her around to face them.

Elonnie felt her heart jump before latching her hand around his arm. What if they hadn't forgiven her for the bank debacle? After getting to know Arlo just a little more, it was clear he wasn't the sweetest thing, so could his brothers actually be the same way? "Is this, erm, your family?" she asked.

"Yes," he replied. "Elonnie, my mother Elise, my grandmother Genevieve, and my brothers Gladstone and Pritchard," he said.

Elonnie curtsied. "It's a pleasure to finally make your acquaintance," she said, letting out a slight warble of her voice.

"Acquaintance?" Genevieve gasped with a giant smile as she took the girl's face in her hands. "We'll be more than acquaintances, Miss Elonnie, at least that's what I hope for."

Elonnie almost instantly warmed to the endearing woman, her anxieties fading as she took both her hands. "Might I say, you are far lovelier than described," she told her.

Elonnie's chestnut skin almost transformed to cherry red as she bashfully grinned. "Thank you, Madam." She looked over at Elise and gave a smile. "You must be Elise," she stated.

"What an honor to welcome you into our family, Elonnie," Elise told her.

"Not quite family just yet," Arlo muttered.

"Arlo Darcy," Pritchard said with a reprimanding stare.

Elonnie turned to him. "Are you Gladstone?" she asked.

"Guess again," Pritchard smiled.

"Pritchard," Elonnie said.

"Correct, and only on the second try," he joked.

Elonnie laughed, now giving her attention to the eldest. "And so, you must be Gladstone," she said.

"Yes, Miss," Gladstone nodded. "I trust Arlo hasn't made too many negative comments about us to you."

"No, of course not," Elonnie shook her head. "I believe he saves them all for me," she teased.

"Is that so?" Gladstone frowned.

"Oh, I was only joking," Elonnie replied. "I, erm, I'm really thrilled to meet you all and I hope we'll all have a nice time this afternoon. My siblings should be—" She looked to her right to see her siblings now arriving at the home and her eyes brightened with delight before she raced in their direction.

"Elonnie! Don't run!" Arlo snapped. "How boorish of her!" he continued.

"Arlo, keep your temper," Genevieve told him as she gently stroked his hair. "She's excited."

"Were we not having a conversation?"

"Her siblings arrived. Fortunately for them, she adores them and greets them joyfully," Gladstone said. "In time, you'll get used to each other; just give it time," he instructed.

"We should probably greet them too," Pritchard said, extending his elbow out for his mother to take.

<hr />

As the day went on, everyone appeared to be having a splendid time; though exceptionally different, Arlo's family didn't clash with Elonnie's as badly as he expected them to, and even though the Kensingtons were quiet, they enjoyed the company and endless chatter on the part of the Wilhelms. Arlo didn't seem too joyful as he sat in his chair, watching Elonnie conversing with her siblings.

"Can you try not to look so angry?" Gladstone requested.

"If she wanted to have a tea party with her brothers and sisters, then perhaps she should have set that event up instead of this one," Arlo nitpicked. "Why exactly am I here again?"

"If you'd like to go join in on the conversation, I trust you'll be welcomed."

"She can come over here and invite me into it herself. She's my betrothed, after all, is she not?"

Gladstone sighed at his brother's attitude. "Please don't

behave like a spoilt child. Perhaps she was carried away by the conversation. She's not going to know that you're feeling left out if you don't go tell her."

"It should be quite obvious; if I were to do this to her, she'd throw a tantrum."

"As you're doing now? Watch how simple it is," he told him. Gladstone walked across the garden, then took a seat beside Elonnie and her siblings, joining the conversation with ease.

It wasn't enough to satisfy Arlo; and now seeing her so happily conversing with his older brother and paying him no mind only furthered his frustration. He looked at his side to see Maddie and Alex staring at him. "Go on," he told them. "Shoo, will you?"

"Arlo?" Elonnie said as she approached.

He focused on her—*finally, she'd show him a little respect.* "Yes, Miss Wilhelm?"

"Would you like to come sit with us?" she asked.

"And I wouldn't be intruding or anything, would I?" he asked.

"Would you like to sit with us, yes or no?"

"I don't see why not. I suppose it's only sensible that we spend *a little* time together if we're to be married, correct?"

"Why does your tone have to be so condescending? Have I offended you?"

"No," he said bluntly. "Shall we?" he asked, offering his arm.

Elonnie accepted and they returned to the table where her siblings sat.

KNOCKING on the guest room door that evening, Elonnie balled her sweaty palm up, holding a flower bouquet in the other hand. Arlo opened the door and gave her a confused stare. "May I help you?" he asked.

"These are for you," she said, giving him the flowers.

"I beg your pardon?" he asked, looking at the colorful bouquet.

"Well, it would seem I did something that bothered you at the garden party, seeing as you nearly shunned me and only spoke to your brother, and so I wanted to apologize."

"Should I not be the one to get you flowers?" he asked.

"You can get me flowers if you'd like," Elonnie smiled. "But I only like daisies."

"Oh?" he said as he leaned against the doorway. "Not every flower in every color?"

"Not this time, though daisies do come in an assortment of colors," she replied. She looked at the flowers and further held them out to him. "Are you going to take them?"

"I don't see why not," he shrugged, accepting the gift.

"M-may I show you something?" she asked him.

"Show me what?"

"Come," she said with a wave of her hand.

After giving it thought, Arlo followed her until they came to the doorway of her room. "Miss Wilhelm, I'm not setting foot inside your room, especially at an hour such as this."

"Oh, oh no, it's nothing like that," she assured. "Just through here to my balcony," she said.

"It's not worth the risk."

"Then will you come downstairs through the entry door?" she asked.

"Yes," he nodded.

Elonnie beamed. "Good," she said before hurrying

down the stairs with the baron following her at a much slower pace. She opened the door and stepped outside. "Look," she told him, pointing to the endless twinkling stars in the sky. "Isn't it beautiful? Isn't it magic?"

"Yes, it's charming; that's the beauty of simplicity," he told her. His voice made it evident that he wasn't half as excited as she. "Thank you and thank you for the flowers. Goodnight."

"Goodnight," she replied. Elonnie took a deep breath when he left her. The wedding was fast approaching and she truly hoped she wasn't making the biggest mistake of her life.

Neuf

T he day of the wedding had arrived, and while Arlo would have much preferred a quiet and small event between his immediate family and hers, it was obvious that the Wilhelms would have never settled for that. In all honesty, now having met the girl's parents, he wouldn't have been surprised if *they* had agreed to a small wedding; he didn't expect them to be so calm. But her aunts, of course, would never. They were scrambling around the home to make sure everything was in order; he started to feel like he was in the way. He had asked several times if he could assist them, but each time he received the same reply, that instead he should be somewhere relaxing before it was time for him to be married.

He started toward the library, hoping to find some solace there, but the room was filled with all of Elonnie's little cousins, so he tried the living room, and there were all her older male cousins, including her big brother. Of course, he knew that around them he'd have to be careful of every word he said, otherwise he might get attacked. Especially by her brother and her cousin Leon.

Over the past month, he had seen just how close she was to her big brother, to all her siblings. They weren't like him and his brothers; of course he loved his brothers, and as much as he was ready to snub them when they arrived for putting him through this, he was still excited that he was going to get to see them. But the Wilhelm siblings were a different kind of close, with their inside jokes and strong desire to be near one another. It was amusing, even endearing, but that's probably what comes from having such an odd family. He stepped away from the living room entrance and tried the upstairs with the intention of finding his bride; he stopped in the long hallway and shook his head, deciding he'd go back down there and spend time with the males of her family. Perhaps the other brothers-in-law would serve as a protection for him. After all, he knew Elonnie enough to know she'd overreact if he were to see her wedding dress before the wedding, and now she was most likely bonding with her sisters and gushing over her dream wedding and perfect marriage.

"I THINK I CHANGE MY MIND," Elonnie vacantly said to her sisters as she stared into the mirror expressionlessly while Elle finished her hair.

In the room with her were her two blood sisters, Elle and Meag, one tall and one short, both with curly hair styled into different updos, along with her sister-in-law, Phabi, whose golden hair was also pinned up, and Étienne, who had her hair pinned back. They all wore lavender gowns which had some similarities but were all different.

Phabi finished up the last few touches on the muff she

was sewing for her and looked up. "No, no," she encouraged, "Everything is going to be fine."

"Did you see him? Does he look excited?" Elonnie asked, turning around and annoying her eldest sister as she caused her to mess up on her hair once more.

"He can eat an elf if he's not excited," Meag sassed.

"Meag!" Elle reprimanded.

"How do you tell if he's excited?" Phabi joked with a laugh.

"I've seen it only once," Elonnie replied. "His eyes grow big and his mouth actually breaks into a big, wide-open smile and he has dimples. The cutest dimples, to be honest."

"What were you doing? Watching grass grow?" Étienne inquired, causing all the girls to laugh.

"Actually," Elonnie awkwardly started. "It was because he heard Lu Rally Hastings was going to be giving a speech about Odsia's independence from this country," she frowned.

"Eesh," Phabi groaned. "Lu Rally Hastings has one of the most boring voices in the country. You know, I'm curious as to how you, out of all of us, ended up with someone so bland. I thought I was bland, but Arlo makes me seem like a Taminite Carnivale."

"He is good to look at, though," Elonnie sighed, turning back to the mirror and resting her face in her hands. "I guess that's not a good reason to marry. But that's not why I said yes, I hadn't even seen him," she rambled, mostly to herself. Elle prepared to finish her hair but she again turned around. "You don't think he'll be mean to me, do you?" she asked.

"If he is, send for us and we'll make it look like an accident," Étienne instructed.

Elonnie snorted out a laugh. "I'll hold you to it," she said, finally turning back to the mirror.

Elle swiftly finished her hair, putting part of her curls up into a high ponytail and leaving the rest of them dangling down her back.

Elonnie stood and faced them to show the final picture; a long white gown with a sweetheart top and long, loose sleeves. "Am I going to the end of my life?" she nervously asked.

The girls frowned at her in reply and she made a face at them. In a few hours, she'd be Mrs. Arlo Kensington. She hoped she was getting the adventure she expected with this.

❧

AN HOUR LATER, she sat in her room alone, basically watching the time go by; she hoped that would make it go slower, so she could spend as much time as she could in her room for the last time. A soft knock at the door brought her attention away from the clock. "Come in," she said.

Genevieve opened the door with a warm grin on her face. "Aren't you a sight?" her future grandmother gasped.

Elonnie smiled shyly, though she was happy to see the woman. "Madam Genevieve," she greeted.

"Now, now," the older woman soothed; she pulled up a chair and sat beside her at the vanity. Cupping the girl's face in her hands, she looked her in the eyes. "No need for titles anymore," she encouraged. "Other than Grandmother, of course."

Elonnie grinned. Genevieve was so much different than Arlo; it was like the woman hadn't lost her smile since she'd met her, and she had a soft demeanor that made Elonnie feel comfortable in her presence. "You wouldn't mind?" she asked.

"Of course not," Genevieve shook her head. "Elonnie, dear. I have a favor to ask you."

Elonnie gulped. "O-of course," she hesitantly replied.

"As you know, my grandson is very...different from you. He's pretty serious most of the time; a sweetheart and lovely to look at, but he can be a bit dreary, wouldn't you agree?" She giggled.

Elonnie laughed, lowering her head.

"You don't have to be afraid to say it, I know already," Genevieve continued. She sat up and held out a hardcover journal to Elonnie, with the words 'Once Upon a Time' engraved on the front. "It's yours to keep, so long as you don't let him rub off on you too much," she told her.

"Madam Gene— I mean, Grandmother—I could never accept this," Elonnie breathed.

"Yes you can, and you will," Genevieve told her. "I want you to write something nice and exciting in here and I want you to keep what's special about you, do you promise?"

"What makes you say I'm special?" a confused Elonnie asked.

"Your family," Genevieve shrugged. "You and your family live to make others smile and I've seen the cheery manner in which you behave, even despite this big change coming, and all I can ask is that you rub off on Arlo instead of the other way around. Keep wearing your hair down and dancing and telling those stories. Keep picking plays over politics and keep your joy and innocence. Promise?"

Elonnie carefully studied the journal in her hands; this was among one of the best presents that someone could have given her. She nodded her head and grinned at the woman. "I promise."

"Good," Genevieve smiled. "And I know that naughty boy hasn't picked a suitable ring for you, so use mine until he does," she offered as she removed the diamond ring from her finger and placed it in Elonnie's hand.

"No, this is too much," Elonnie told her.

"Would you turn down a poor old woman?" Genevieve sadly frowned. She closed the ring in Elonnie's hand and kissed her forehead. "Just keep your promise, and give it back to me when you get the ring you deserve."

ONE HOUR LEFT until the wedding and Arlo found the company of her relatives to be enjoyable as he shot pool with them. It kept him distracted enough to purposefully ignore his own brothers who had found his strange behavior childish but amusing.

"Arlo Darcy, a word?" Gladstone called.

"Busy," Arlo replied, hitting the stick against the white ball and sending the red one rolling toward the hole.

Gladstone grabbed the ball before it rolled in and met eyes with his little brother. "Now, please," he commanded.

Arlo sighed in annoyance, finally handing Leon the pool stick and following after Gladstone. "This better be important," he told him. "I don't need you scrambling up my nerves any more than they already are."

"I have no intentions of scrambling anything, I was just going to give you your wedding present," he told him, handing him an envelope. "But seeing that your behavior has been rotten, perhaps I shouldn't."

Arlo carefully took the envelope from Gladstone's hand and opened it to find a check in the sum of ten thousand stire. He almost choked, staring up at his big brother. "Why, would—but I thought..."

"It's yours and your wife's; I can stop payment on it, should you decide to pull anything foolish like backing out. I'm giving it to you because you actually went through with this instead of trying to find a way out; and I know you're not going to regret it."

"Thank you, really, thank you," Arlo told him.

"And?" Gladstone crossed his arms.

"I apologize for avoiding you," Arlo replied.

"Apology accepted. Now do the same for Pritchard."

❧

To be honest, Elonnie paid little attention to the wedding, although she'd never admit it. She found herself too anxious to even hear the words coming from her paternal grandfather's mouth. She peeked around the room at everyone staring at her and, due to her nerves, she tried to imagine that they were only staring at Arlo. Arlo... He looked bored, but when she looked down at his leg, she saw it bouncing up and down—the fact that he was nervous meant something good, didn't it? Did it not mean that the event was somewhat important to him? She sat back and heaved a sigh too loud, causing him to turn to her with the same reprimanding stare she had been getting used to. "Sorry," she whispered. She looked down at his hand, and pondered grabbing hold of it; maybe that would calm the both of them down. But she also didn't want to be humiliated in front of everyone if he were to choose to pull away from her.

"Pay attention," he quietly ordered, noticing her eyes wandering around.

"May I hold your hand?" she whispered.

Arlo wished to tell her no, of course, but chose not to

make a scene; he sighed, opening up his hand for her to take and she did so with a big smile, holding tight to him.

Arlo felt a little sorry for her. Was she really excited about this? Because he didn't share the same feeling at all. He was only going through this because he was told to, really, and because it would prove beneficial for him in the future. His eyes traveled to the girl. It couldn't be all bad, could it? She looked lovely in her wedding gown, and she had managed to act calm the entire time. No crazy outbursts, no cartwheels in her dress; she even had managed to keep her shoes on her feet. Maybe, just maybe, as time went on, she would become more and more docile, like him. He half-smiled at the thought, which was quickly replaced by a nervous frown. Or would she become more outlandish after the marriage? The one thing the pair shared was the same view that marriage was permanent, so once he was locked in, what was to stop her from going wild? He felt her squeezing his hand.

"Pay attention," she mocked.

Arlo sat straight, focusing on her grandfather. He simply just wouldn't let her go wild; surely, he could contain her well. At times, she seemed to listen to him and at times it felt as if she wanted his approval, and so he just wouldn't give it to her if she acted a fool. She would be the perfect Kensington wife, like his mother. Quiet, calm, lovely, and obedient.

Dix

After what seemed like a minute to Elonnie, it was already time to leave the Wilhelm Manor and head home to the Ravenhill estate. Yes, home. That was to be her home now and as scary as it was, it was still exciting. She had always dreamed of the place and the secrets and adventures that it held. She leaned out the carriage window, waving goodbye to her family, careless that the action was unsafe. "Bye! Don't forget me! I'll still visit! Bye, Alex, I love you!"

"I love you too!" Alex called, throwing flowers in her direction.

"Miss Wilhelm, please," Arlo requested, tugging the girl back into the carriage. "You'll fall out and break your neck."

"Mrs. Kensington now," Elonnie corrected, removing the veil from her head.

"Mm," Arlo grumbled, looking out the window on his side.

"Oh, don't tell me you're already cross with me?" Elonnie sighed as her shoulders dropped. "What have I done?"

"Do you think my seeing to it that you don't kill yourself is a sign of being cross?" he questioned.

"Ugh, I can't stay in this dress another minute," she complained, turning her back to him. "Be a darling and untie me, will you?"

Arlo blinked his eyes in dismay. "E-Elonnie, you can't undress yourself in the carriage," he told her.

"Oh, darling, I have a suitable undergarment," she assured. "And it's much too hot to be in this dress any longer. Please?"

"No," he said firmly. "And there's no need for nick-names," he told her.

Elonnie lowered her eyes to the floor of the carriage; he seemed angry with her out of nowhere. It wasn't like his normal supercilious behavior, but something different. She prepared to ask him if he was cross with her, but chose to avoid the question, instead sitting back and fiddling with her hands, thinking of something else to say. "Oh, tell me about Ravenhill?" she said with excitement as she grabbed hold of his arm. "How long does it take to get from Therondia to there? And is there a place for me to dance?"

"It's only an estate with about one hundred rooms, including a ballroom; I'm sure it will be a struggle to find a place to dance," he retorted satirically.

"Arlie, you're being rude," she scowled.

"Do *not* call me Arlie," he requested, keeping his attention focused out the window.

Elonnie sighed, turning to the window on her side. He was obviously in a nasty mood, and of all days.... She decided she didn't want to further his uncalled-for attitude and kept quiet. "I hope you fix your attitude soon," she told him.

The silence was too much even for Arlo; he crossed his

left leg over his right and cleared his throat. "It will take thirty minutes or so," he told her, "to get from Therondia to Ravenhill."

"That's a decent ride. Do you think you can handle thirty minutes of silence, or do you prefer to talk?" she asked.

"Talking is fine, so long as it isn't anything foolish."

"And what is it you consider foolish?"

"I think you know what."

"That could lead to a serious problem, because I believe we have differing opinions on what's foolish and what's not," she stated. "Perhaps I don't want to hear about dreary politics and business talk."

"And I don't want to hear about fantasies and dragons and whatnot. But then again, you must admit that while you consider my hobbies boring, they aren't foolish. Yours are. At least mine are realistic."

"Must one always be realistic? It's good every now and then to be able to enjoy fantasies; the real world can be so dark at times."

"I guess everything is good, every now and then, but all the time? No."

"Then the same would go for being dreary," Elonnie defended. "You shouldn't be so boring all the time."

Arlo rolled his eyes before shifting his attention back out the window. "It's better than being childish all the time," he grumbled.

"At least I can be happy in unfortunate circumstances," Elonnie snapped, flipping her head to her window. She took a deep breath when she felt herself becoming hurt by his words and attitude, then began twisting the ring on her finger, reminding herself of Genevieve.

Arlo watched her from the corner of his eye and then

focused on the ring. "Where did you get that?" he asked, reaching for her hand.

Elonnie pulled her hand away from him. "Your grandmother gave it to me," she told him. "I mean Grandmother," she corrected, keenly analyzing the beautiful diamond. "She's my grandmother too now. Whether you like it or not."

"Why would Grandmother give you her ring?" he wondered aloud.

"Because the ring on a woman's finger is a symbol that she's married and unavailable."

"And what was the issue with the ring I gave you?" he asked.

"You mean that round piece of brass that's much too large for my finger? Nothing was wrong with it, Arlo, I just cannot fit it," she told him. "Perhaps if you had put a little thought into it, like I did for yours, it might have fit better," she concluded.

Arlo looked at the silver band around his finger and then at Elonnie, who was again staring out the window. Once more, silence plagued the vehicle. Even after spending some time with one another, they were still strangers, and that wasn't abnormal. One or two months is too short a time to get to know someone well.

Onze

The half hour felt like three hours, and Arlo felt a stress-lifting peace at seeing the estate in view. He could finally breathe. Next, he had to show the girl around and just hope that she wouldn't treat the age-old estate like a playground.

Elonnie gasped in awe at the beautiful plot of land. The place looked to be at least one hundred acres; she could see a forest of trees, lovely stone statues, flowery bushes, antique benches and more. She saw the main building, which wasn't too different from her home, and in the distance were what looked to be more homes. "Oh, Arlie," she gasped again, grabbing onto his leg. "How charming."

"Please don't call me Arlie," he requested and Elonnie frowned at him. When the carriage stopped, he could see she was ready to bolt out of the vehicle, so he swiftly grabbed hold of her wrist. "Wait," he told her.

"I can't wait," Elonnie cheered. "What's it like on the inside?"

"You'll see in just a few minutes, Miss Wilhelm, calm

yourself," he sighed, stepping out of the carriage and walking around to assist her out.

Instead of taking his hand to step down and out of the carriage, Elonnie leaped into his arms and the both of them almost tumbled over. "Mrs. Kensington," she corrected.

"Are you trying to break both our necks?" he hissed.

"Arlie," Elonnie gasped. "Are you calling me fat?"

Arlo didn't find the question to be worth an answer; he only offered her the same disappointed stare as he usually did and carried her inside the house.

Elonnie marveled at the estate, taking in every inch of it from the long cobblestone courtyard the sizable doors that led to the inside of the home. "Put me down, will you?" she playfully ordered, getting to her feet and hurrying inside the building, where she was greeted by a majestic staircase and entry hall. When she saw the entry hall, she breathed a gasp. She'd known he had to be downplaying the Ravenhill estate. It was just as she had imagined! A fantastical adventure filled with mystery and intrigue, just waiting to happen. The way it reminded her of her family manor only made it better; the balcony with its arched cutouts, the paintings on the walls, and the color of the golden sun gently beaming through the large windows on every side. "Oh, you have to show me around!" she squealed.

Arlo remained still at the entrance with his hands held together in front of him. "I can't keep up with you," he nitpicked.

She ran back toward him and took his hand. "Let's make haste! Please? I want to meet all the staff! And see all the rooms! And the ballroom! You said there was a ballroom!"

"Calm down," Arlo instructed.

Elonnie took a deep breath and contained herself before she nodded. She wrapped her arm around his, despite the fact that she knew he didn't want her to, and then looked at him. "Shall we?"

"Mm-hmm," Arlo replied. "While we walk, why don't we get a few things sorted out? For one, please refrain from calling me Arlie, I find it ugly and unnecessary. Second, every room in this house is over two hundred years old, so please, do not treat it like a playground...."

As the tour went on, Elonnie could barely enjoy the splendor of the estate, such as the mysterious hallways that were darkening as the sun set, the beauty and grace of the huge ballroom and its golden marble floor and hovering chandelier; the library with enough books to last a lifetime, and so on.... All she could focus on was Arlo's seemingly never-ending rule list. The kitchen is closed after eight-thirty and midnight snacks are dreadfully unhealthy so they're not allowed, the windows are never to be touched by human hands, no running in my house, and on and on.... They came to a white door with a bronze handle and Arlo ceased walking to face her.

"No frolicking around in the garden like you're eleven and none of those ballet jetés in the halls. I expect you to wear shoes when you desire to step outside and I expect you to only let your shoe-clad feet touch the grass, *not* your clothing," he said. Then he opened the door to reveal a bright bedroom with dark red carpet covering the floor, a large bed draped with white bed covers, and many a pillow. There were white walls and a fireplace on the wall at the far end of the room with two identical paintings of flowers on each side. On the right side of the room was a fancy vanity that looked far classier than the little one she had at home, with an oval-shaped mirror, surplus of little drawers, and poufy seat.

It was a very cozy and comfortable room, of that she was

sure, and after being bombarded with Arlo's instructions, she had grown a headache and was in need of a giant, fluffy bed like the one in the room. "This is where you'll be staying," her husband told her. "Rising time is around six-thirty, giving you enough time to get ready for breakfast, which will be ready in the dining room at seven-thirty, and then it's off to the Sunday service at nine. Any questions?"

Elonnie gulped, trying to process at least a little bit of what had just taken place. "Erm, aren't you staying with me?" she asked.

Arlo thought for a moment and then began to shake his head. "I don't see why that would be necessary," he replied.

"What?" Elonnie's face scrunched confusedly.

"I suppose I'll see you in the morning, then." He gave her a little smile. "Goodnight."

"Arlie!" she called.

"What did we discuss?"

"*We* didn't discuss anything; *you* rambled on about rule after rule for nearly an hour and now you're casting me off to the side as if I'm nothing to you?"

"Look, Miss Wilhelm, we're both exhausted, get some rest and we'll talk more tomorrow."

"Kensington!" she snapped.

"Right, of course," Arlo responded derisively. "Goodnight."

"Do I at least get a kiss goodnight?" she inquired.

"Is that what you want?" he asked.

"Yes, dear," she replied firmly and the annoyance in her voice almost made Arlo laugh.

Taking her face in his hands, he gave her forehead a small kiss and left the room. When he was gone, she took yet another deep breath, now just a tad bit more worried about the situation she had subjected herself to. "He's no

Prince Charming, that's for sure," she said to herself. She was startled at hearing a knock on the door and she stumbled a little as she ran over to it in her fluffy wedding dress.

She opened the door to be greeted by a slender woman who was a few inches taller than her. The sharp features of the woman were not at all frightening, although she gave off much of an intimidating aura. Her short, curly, grey hair and porcelain skin were a perfect mix, along with the long, classy, brown dress she wore. She was possibly in her mid-fifties. "Hullo," she smiled.

"Ma'am," she bowed respectfully. "The master sent me up with your belongings," she told her.

"Oh, thank you so much, Madam...?"

"Constance." She bowed again.

"Oh," Elonnie giggled, "no need for bows and the like," she assured her.

Constance waved in a few men and they carefully brought her trunks into the room and set them down where she wished them to go.

"Madam Constance," Elonnie called. "Thank you again," she told her when she faced her. "And do you know when he wakes up?" she asked.

"Six-fifteen. Not a minute after, not a minute before," Constance explained. "That's on Saturdays and Sundays; it's much earlier Monday through Friday."

"Thank you," Elonnie said.

Douze

The sound of the harsh falling rain was often an enjoyable sound to Arlo; but today it felt as if everything was getting on his nerves as he sat at the table, waiting impatiently for Elonnie to come down and take her place beside him. He huffed, looking down at his watch once more and then rolling his eyes. Seven-twenty-six. If she made them fall behind schedule, he was going to be in a bad mood for the entire day. "Constance!" he barked and the woman hurried to him. "Where is she?"

"Oh, not to worry, Master, she's—"

Elonnie entered the room dressed in her nightgown, humming a tune and carrying two plates. "Good morning, Arlie," she said, placing the plate before him. "I woke up just a little earlier than six-thirty, I hope you don't mind. But I wanted to get a head start on breakfast," she told him with great excitement. "It's a Whim Wiffle."

Arlo turned his nose up, looking down at the plate. The square shaped fluffy pastry was loaded with whipped sweet cream, diced strawberries, blueberries, and raspberries, then covered with nonpareil sprinkles and sifted confectioner's sugar. "What on earth would make you think I'd want to eat this sugary nonsense this early in the morning?" he asked.

Constance pursed her lips with a quick glower in Arlo's direction, already disappointed at how this was going to go. "Thank you for your hard work, Mrs. Elonnie," she told her, deciding to take her leave from the room.

Irritably, Arlo huffed, looking her up and down and wondering if he should tell her to go put on something suitable for walking around or just sit down. "Sit down," he decided.

Elonnie ignored the command. "You don't at least want to try it before you decide against it?" she asked.

"No, I do not. This is basically a dessert, Elonnie. And I've never desired to eat so much sugar," he complained, taking a stab at the Whim Whiffle with his fork and then pushing the plate away. "I told you, up at six-thirty, at the table before seven-thirty. I didn't tell you to go into the kitchen and start cooking, that's the point of the cook who is paid to do that. Not you."

Elonnie furrowed her brow. "Suppose I don't want to get up at six-thirty. Suppose I want to get up at six-fifteen?" She crossed her arms.

Arlo stood. "Excuse me?" he asked.

"You married me, you didn't adopt me," Elonnie reminded him. "I can get up when I want to get up. I tried to do something nice for you and you're throwing it back in my face like it's nothing but refuse."

Arlo shifted his eyes over to the pastry and then back to Elonnie. "If that's not refuse, I'm not sure what is," he chuckled.

"Oh, and what would you find delightful? Bland porridge or oatmeal and the like?" she asked just as another one of the servants entered the room and placed two bowls of porridge down on the table before them. The servant bowed and scurried out, somehow able to feel the tension in the room. "Mm-hmm," Elonnie rolled her eyes. "Eat your mush, Arlo. And I will enjoy my sugary nonsense," she told him, finally taking her seat. After a moment of quiet, she blinked her eyes over to him and pouted her lips. "Many fine suitors would give anything to have a wife who likes to cook for them," she stated.

"Those are the ones who are looking for a wife, Elonnie," he sighed, running his hand down his face.

"You could have said no," she reminded him.

"As you could have," he shrugged.

Elonnie gave her attention to her food and began cutting the pastry with her fork and knife. She wasn't going to fight with him; he could ruin his day with childish moping, but she wasn't going to ruin hers. Taking a bite of her breakfast, she smiled. "Just as good as Aunt Sonia's," she bragged.

"No doubt," he grumbled. Sitting up straight, he turned to her and again appraised the soft white nightgown she wore. "Why are you in your pajamas?" he asked. "I don't find it appropriate at all that you should be dressed in sleeping clothes and downstairs for all of the staff to see you."

"They're modest pajamas. And it's Sunday," she stated. "You knew already that I always dress in pajamas on Sundays and so you have no reason to be in shock."

"I told you last night that that was a no."

"No, you must have left it out of your five-hundred-and-sixty-page long novel of rules; that, or I zoned out while you were talking."

"Well, I'll tell you again today. No wearing pajamas for anything other than sleep."

Elonnie rolled her eyes and sat back, sinking into the chair. "Perhaps I should make a few rules of my own then," she started.

Arlo barked out a laugh, louder than she had heard him laugh before, startling her. "I'm curious to hear this," he told her. "What's rule number one, pray tell? One must dance in the Malachi Brook at the start of every winter?"

"What if I say yes?" She crossed her arms.

"Then you prove that you're utterly ridiculous," he shrugged. "We're at *my* home, Miss Wilhelm, therefore, my rules."

"We're at *our* home, Mr. Kensington," she defended. "Try to keep that in mind even if you don't want to."

"Finish eating so you can get dressed and we can go," he instructed.

"I'll take my time, thank you," she sassed.

"Then I'll go without you. You can take that up with the Lord," he told her, standing and starting out of the dining room.

"I will. And I'll ask Him to forgive you for your negative attitude too," she grumbled to herself.

❧

Elonnie was ready in time for the service; the short-sleeved, flowery lavender dress of cotton offered much comfort and an equal amount of style and it well matched the lavender ribbon that wrapped around the woven sun hat on her head. She stood on the last stair in the entry hall and watched for Arlo's reaction. "Do you like it?" she finally asked.

"If I say yes, you'll change, won't you?" he scoffed.

"Can you answer the question?" Elonnie entreated, stepping down to stand in front of him.

Arlo studied her, of course disappointed in the fact that she hadn't put her hair up. "The dress looks nice. Now are you quite ready?"

"Yes, Arlie, I'm ready," she replied.

THE PLACE of worship was dainty and small. Bright colors made up the room and, seeing as the rain had ceased and sun had begun to shine, the open windows served as a distraction for Elonnie, who kept turning to see the birds that would land on the window. She smiled, seeing a Goldfinch perched there, but frowned at feeling a soft nudge from Arlo. She sat up in her chair and focused on the man speaking; all had started to go well, she was interested in what he was saying and was able to keep her attention away from the window for a moment.

Arlo peeked over at her and almost grinned at seeing her in such a docile state. He returned his eyes forward and instantly grimaced at hearing a loud, snorted laugh come from his wife. "Elonnie," he hissed.

"Sorry," Elonnie replied.

After another brief silence, she laughed again. "What is the issue?" he asked, embarrassedly.

"You don't hear that man snoring?" she whispered.

Arlo's shoulders sank, now hearing the snoring coming from the sleeping man two rows ahead of them. "Enough," he told her.

She tried to calm herself and drown out the sound of the man's snores by focusing intently on the speaker and it worked until the sleeping man started hacking loud enough for the whole congregation to hear. Elonnie lost it. Tears streamed down her face as her body shook with laughter. "Is he okay?" she asked through her laughs.

"Miss Wilhelm, contain yourself," Arlo growled.

"I'm sorry, Arlie," she laughed.

"Let's go." Arlo stood up and tugged her elbow, signaling for her to do the same, then pulled her along as he walked out of the building.

When they were outside, Elonnie clutched onto his arm and held back giggles upon realizing he was headed back to the carriage. "Wait, I don't want to leave; please, I want to hear the rest of the talk," she begged.

"You're not going to make a scene. There are children in there who are better behaved than you are. You're not going to embarrass me anymore than you already have," he responded.

"Please, I'll stop laughing. It wasn't my fault."

"Are you done?" he placed his hands on his hips. "Have you got it all out of your system?"

Sucking her lips in, she refrained from laughing anymore and nodded her head in answer. He had a feeling she was lying, yet still finally decided to go back in, this time taking a seat in the far back.

Treize

F rom the diary of Elonnie Wilhelm Kensington:
    April 18ᵗʰ, 1795

This marks the third day of my new adventure, and the Ravenhill Estate is everything I dreamed it to be. Arlie, on the other hand, is not. Gorgeous as he is, he is just like the Nero tea he drinks—too strong, bland, and boring. I think the man would whitewash the fence and then watch with keen interest as the paint dries. Nevertheless, I intend to stick this out; after all, I said I would until death parts us. If I were to kill Arlie, I'd regret it; I know his grandmother would be awfully sad and I've already made a friend in her. She's already written to me, telling me that she will regularly write to me. Also, I do think that it would be Arlie who kills me if any killing were to take place, but I doubt it will... it's much too impractical for the man."

Elonnie closed her diary and looked out the window. She watched as Arlo sat in the garden, reading. Shakespeare's works, no doubt—she smiled just a little; he was a handsome brute, if only he weren't so stiff. She opened the window and leaned out of it. "Romeo!" she called, and immediately he looked up. "'Wherefore art thou, Romeo?'" she continued. She giggled, seeing the displeasure in his eyes. "I suppose you thought I didn't know Shakespeare," she bragged. "Well, I do. I once played Juliet in one of our plays."

Noticing her only covered by a chemise and a corset, Arlo's skin turned red with humiliation and disappointment before he shifted his eyes around the garden, seeing all the workers looking back and forth between them and at their work. He shut his book and stood. "Get out of the window, please," he said through clenched teeth.

"'Though she be but little, she is fierce!'" she continued her quotations as she combed through her hair. "A Midsummer Night's Dream."

"Miss Wilhelm, if I have to—"

"Oh, Arlie, must you be so stale? You'd never make it as a thespian," she shook her head, her comb now incidentally tangled at the ends of her hair.

"Splendid. Now, please go back into your room and shut the window. If I have to come up there and—" Arlo stopped when the comb flung out of Elonnie's hand and hit him in the head, causing a pain that he was sure to last for the rest of the day.

Elonnie gasped loudly, covering her mouth in shocked regret. Arlo didn't give much of a reaction, but from how far the tool fell she knew it had to hurt. That, and the rage she could see building up in his eyes. "Arlie, I—"

Arlo raised his index finger, in a sense telling her to 'be quiet' as he started back to the entry of the home.

"Darling, I wasn't—"

"Mm-mm," he shook his head.

"It was an accident," she promised.

"Constance!" Arlo called. "Laudanum!"

After he disappeared, Elonnie bit her thumbnail, looking around at the gardeners. "I should probably stay away from him until supper, huh?" she asked and received a nod from each of them. "It really was an accident," she assured them.

"We know," one of the women gave a sweet smile.

"She said she was little but fierce, didn't she!" one of the men laughed with his high-pitched, raspy voice, causing the others to break out in laughter. "Take your bows, Mrs. Kensington, he needed that," he added.

"Oh," Elonnie sheepishly giggled, covering her mouth. "Oh, don't let him hear you," she told the man. "Poor Arlie," she laughed.

❧

"GLISSADE, pas-de-chat, pas-de-bourrée, bourrée, bourrée, bourrée, coupé turn, pirouette and finish," Elonnie mumbled while she practiced her ballet in the ballroom. The ballroom was amongst her favorite rooms in the estate. The chandelier brought a golden glow to the room when the sun was at rest for the day and the marble glistened under the twinkling fires upon the grandiose light. The giant windows allowed a delicate view of the Malachi Brook, the quiet flowing body of water that trickled its way over into the ocean that led to Odsia, a neighboring country.

Under the stars, the water was even more beautiful; Elonnie had been in the ballroom for most of the day, so she was able to marvel at the views throughout the day and then the sunset that had taken place a few minutes ago. After the morning's incident, she chose not to get in the way of her mate in case he was still upset about it.

She stood in fourth position, ready to begin the first part of the choreography again..

"Lady Kensington," Constance called, entering the ballroom.

Elonnie jumped in a fright—boy, did Constance have a way of sneaking up on people. Unintentional, of course, but the gentleness of the woman's footsteps and elegance with which she walked could make her a perfect criminal if she so desired. "Yes, ma'am?" Elonnie asked.

"Mr. Kensington is waiting for you in the dining room," she alerted.

Elonnie grimaced. "Is he angry?" she asked.

"Isn't he always?" Constance grumbled. She forced a smile, looking down at the girl. "If you're speaking in reference to what happened earlier, then no, sweetheart," she shook her head.

"That's good," Elonnie breathed. "Thank you," she told her. She began toward the exit of the ballroom and Constance tapped her shoulder.

"He needs a good bonk on the head every now and then," she assured.

WHEN ELONNIE ENTERED the dining room, she saw him sitting at the table looking down at his watch—it was probably the third time he had done so and she was sure his patience with her was growing thin. "H-Hullo," she stammered, walking to the table.

Arlo turned to her and Elonnie realized that she hadn't changed out of her pastel blue ballet dress when she saw the dissatisfaction in his face. "Elonnie," he sighed.

83

"I know, I'm sorry. I forgot," she interjected. "But it is a pretty dress, you have to admit that."

Arlo stood up to pull her seat out for her, as he often tried to do. "It's too short," he told her as she sat down. "It's not meant for dining or daily activities. It's meant for dance practice and that's about it."

"Where is that law written?" she asked, her eyes following him as he took his seat.

"Common sense should make it so that it doesn't have to be written, right?"

"Must you speak in such a disparaging way?" Elonnie asked, a frown forming on her face.

"Was that disparaging too?" Arlo snickered. "I think it might just be my dialect, Miss Wilhelm."

Elonnie huffed, harshly sitting back in her chair. "I've agreed to take—" She ceased her complaint when the servants rushed in with their food and set the plates down on the table. Shepherd's Pie and garden salad. She turned her nose up at the main course and gave her attention back to Arlo. "I've agreed to take on your name out of respect for you. Please respect that," she ordered.

"Are you giving me orders now?" he asked.

"Yes, dear."

"There's no need for the nicknames," he assured her with the wave of his hand as he reached for the wine goblet before him.

"Then perhaps you should stop calling me Miss Wilhelm because it's nothing other than a nickname now," she firmly countered.

Choking on the wine due to his slight chuckles, he put the cup down. "It's quite odd when you've become riled up," he told her.

"And it's quite odd when you smile," she quipped. She

observed the dinner once more and then her eyes wandered around the room. "I don't like Shepherd's Pie, I hate most anything with mashed potatoes."

"If this is an act of rebellion against me, remember that I don't do the cooking here; the people you've become so fond of overnight do all the planning, straining, and sweating, so if you don't want to acknowledge their work to get back at me, then so be it. Sit there like a five-year-old as you always do and don't eat dinner. And don't come down here begging them to make you something else in the middle of the night when you wake up hungry," he instructed.

Elonnie took her bowl of salad and began eating it. "I said I don't enjoy Shepherd's Pie, that doesn't mean I don't appreciate a good salad," she told him.

Arlo observed her, looking her up and down as she ate the light salad. When she wasn't talking, it was easier to see what made her attractive—she finally had her hair up, although it was only because she had been dancing, it was still flatteringly twisted into a chignon. Of course to him, that wasn't what mattered. If he wanted to marry someone pretty he would have done so a while back. He jumped when Elonnie looked up and caught him staring in her direction, then returned his attention to the food in front of him.

"See something you like?" Elonnie smirked.

"Stop it," he told her.

"I suppose you have every right to stare if you wish, I am your wife, after all," she shrugged, now reaching for her goblet to sip her wine. She coughed, and refrained from spitting it back into the cup; forcing herself to swallow it, her face distorted in disgust. "I hate red wine," she complained.

"You seem to hate everything, Miss Wilhelm," he muttered.

Elonnie shook her head. *That wasn't true*; if anything, it was he who hated everything. Once again, she had no desire to argue with him; her goal was to know him better, and hopefully find the exciting side of him. "Darling, I was wondering if maybe we could go out riding tomorrow? Perhaps to Hammington Park."

"Go right ahead," he told her. "Just be back by four P.M., and no riding astride. Side saddle only."

"Arlie, I said we—you and I," she told him.

"I have things to do tomorrow, I apologize; but you're free to do as you wish so long as you stick to the rules. I should be back around five-thirty."

"Five-thirty?" she carped. "What time are you leaving?"

"Five-thirty," he replied. "Five-thirty A.M. to five-thirty P.M.."

"That's all day, Arlie. What on earth will you be doing?"

"I had a life before you came along, Miss; surely you don't expect me to just drop it all?"

"It's—it's customary for us to go away somewhere fun after our wedding, and while I enjoyed the Sunday worship, it's not exactly what I had in mind. I was thinking maybe we should go to Tamin; Carnivale season is coming up and I would just love to go to—"

"We're not going to one of those silly, outlandish, gaudy, Taminite festivals." He turned his nose up. "Eat your dinner."

Elonnie prepared to plead her case, but sighed, resting her hand in cheek and starting to eat her salad again.

"Elonnie," Arlo said. When she made eye contact with him, he nodded toward her elbow that rested on the table and she let out an exasperated sigh, sliding it off of the table and sitting back in her chair.

"You really are dreary," she let him know before she stood and snatched up the salad bowl. "Misérable reclus."

"Where do you think you're going?"

"To my room."

Quatorze

That night, mad as she was, Elonnie made her way down the long halls of the estate to Arlo's room. She took her time, though, not only was she still just a tad annoyed with him, but she loved the quiet state of the building at the late hour; the candle lights were dim and left many mysterious shadows on the wall and the warm burgundy carpet under her feet brought comfort to her soul.

She finally came to his door and readied to knock on it... but technically, it should have been her room too. She opened the door and barged into the room, startling the man who was sitting in the bed. He looked up from the book he was reading and raised an eyebrow. "Rule number twelve, I think it was: If the door is shut, knock," he reminded.

"You didn't kiss me goodnight," she stated.

"I realized that," he nodded. "You stormed off to bed early, do you recall?"

She walked closer to him and analyzed the book in his hands, *Clarissa* by Samuel Richardson; she pursed her lips and breathed a laugh. "Leave it to you to choose a long and depressing novel such as that one," she told him.

"Yes. Leave it to me. Goodnight."

Elonnie watched his eyes traveling over the words on the pages and then moved a little closer to his face, closing her eyes and slightly pouting out her lips. Arlo lifted his book up and pushed the cover against her lips. "You are cruel," Elonnie hissed.

Breathing a silent groan, Arlo cupped her face, squeezing her cheeks and giving her a kiss. "Goodnight," he told her.

"Goodnight," she said, flipping around and starting toward the door. Looking over her shoulder, she smiled half-way. "Can I stay here?" she asked.

"*Goodnight,*" he said more firmly and Elonnie sighed before she left the room. Arlo looked at the hand he used to cup her face...she had rather soft cheeks. He took one more look at the door before returning his concentration to his book.

❦

"APRIL 19TH, 1795:

I've been wed to this character of a woman for four days now and it seems as if I'll end up with an aching head for the rest of my life. She expects me to eat overly sugary breakfasts and desserts, to cater to her undying need for attention and to take pleasure in her endless jesting and fooling around.

That being said, I am not blind to the fact that she could make a good wife for a man, but I don't ever think she'll make a good wife for me. Nevertheless, nothing is impossible—she is still young and can be trained into what she should be. And so if I must be married to her, then I may as well mold her into what I would like for her to be." Arlo wrote in his journal the following morning.

He closed the book and placed it on the bedside table before he made his way down the hall to Elonnie's room to tell her goodbye for the day, just so that she couldn't complain that he hadn't later on. He knew she'd be sleeping, it was four-thirty AM, but that was on her. He gently opened the door and walked over to the bed, which, to his surprise, was empty. He sighed. Where was she and what on earth was she doing up at this hour?

Walking over to the bathroom, he knocked on the door and received no response. He contemplated if he should open the door and did just so, keeping his hand over his eyes just in case. "Elonnie?" he called.

Still no response.

Carefully removing his hand from his eyes, he saw that the bathroom was empty. He grabbed hold of the door knob when he almost slipped due to the floor being soaked with water. Clearly, she had already been in the tub. "Can't you dry up after yourself," he grumbled, storming out of the room and finally making his way back down the stairs. "Constance?" he called.

"Yes, Lord Kensington?" she asked, approaching him from the dining room.

"Miss Wilhelm isn't in her room," he stated.

"Miss Wilhelm?" a theatrically confused Constance asked.

Arlo rolled his eyes, placing his hands on his hips and

tapping his foot. "Mrs. Kensington," he corrected, hesitantly.

"Oh, of course!" Constance smiled. "No, she woke up early this morning to make breakfast for you and see you off before you left. She's down in the kitchen now. Shall I fetch her?"

"Please, before she finishes making some volcano of sugar that she expects me to eat."

Constance frowned at him. "You could have ended up with someone just like you, and I can tell you now, you would not have enjoyed it," she rebuked before she headed down to the kitchen.

"That would have been perfect if you'd asked me," Arlo mumbled to himself. Within minutes, Elonnie had entered the room, carrying two bowls. Arlo faced her and heaved a sigh of exasperation at seeing her in only her dressing gown. "Why are you—never mind. I told you to get up at six-thirty, did I not?"

"And then you said you were leaving at five-thirty and I wanted to see you off," she replied.

"I don't need you to see me off, Elonnie, I need you to follow the rules."

"With all due respect, you don't have a right to tell me when to get up in the morning. This isn't a prison? Or is it?"

"I can surely make it that way," he warned.

"Oh, don't you threaten me. Now come eat your food before it gets cold," she told him. She walked out of the entry hall toward the dining room and he followed. As she placed the bowls on the table, she glanced back at him. "Well, sit down," she said.

"No," he replied.

"Why not?" she asked.

"Because I don't have to listen to you."

"And yet you expect me to listen to you?"

"You know how the roles go in North Indigo," he crossed his arms. "You wanted to get married."

Elonnie took a deep breath before turning to face him. "I didn't, *Lord Kensington,* the arrangement wasn't under my control. I went along with it, yes, but so did you, and now I'm making the best of it," she replied. "As for the roles, my parents played them very well and they were partners, not master and servant. Now sit down and eat before this food goes to waste, that wouldn't be very advantageous, now would it?"

Arlo gave a most frightening glare and then humbled himself just a little to sit down at the table, but at the opposite side of where she had placed his bowl. He sat back and stared her in the eyes until she finally picked it up and moved it down to where he sat. Looking into the bowl, his lip curled; it looked like porridge, but it was orange, topped with a frothy cream and cinnamon. "What is this?" he groused.

"Pumpkin-spiced porridge," she replied, taking her seat.

"Why would I want—"

"Arlo, try it before you complain, *please,*" she breathed.

Shifting his glowering eyes over to her, he reached for a spoon and tasted the oddly-colored dish. His heart thumped with disappointment in himself when he realized that he actually enjoyed the taste of the food. He just hoped that it wasn't made obvious to the girl who began eating of hers.

"Well?" Elonnie asked.

"Better than a whim wiffle," he responded curtly.

Elonnie sat back, messing around with her side braid. "Does that mean that you like it?" she asked.

"Elonnie, I said it was—"

"Better than something that you didn't even try. It's a yes or no question, Arlie, just answer it."

"I suppose," he finally muttered in a bothered tone, throwing his hands up.

"Good, then," Elonnie said. She stirred her food around to ignore the quiet that set in and then she gave Arlo her attention. "You don't have to be mean, Arlie," she broke the silence. "Do you not understand that?

Arlo released a demeaning chuckle as he shook his head and sat against the chair. "Elonnie, I could tell you your hair looks nice braided like that and you'd take that to be mean," he scoffed.

"If you said it like that, yes I would," she replied. "If you meant it, I'm sure you could say it a lot more nicely."

"I don't understand why you do this," he groaned. "I didn't tell you to wake up and make food and see me off and all that; your feelings could have been spared had you just woke up at the time I told you to, do you not agree?"

Elonnie gave him an annoyed scowl, a face he hadn't seen before and that quite shocked him. It was almost like she would have tossed the remainder of her porridge into his lap in a second. "May I ask what you're doing today?" she inquired, clearly choosing to ignore the question he had asked.

"It's nothing that would interest you," he told her.

"How do you know that? You know nothing about me, remember?"

"I know enough about you," he stated. "And spending your day with a bunch of men like me is not something you'd enjoy."

She lowered her eyes. She didn't want an argument or to deal with anything that might stress her out for the day. "I think I'll go swimming in the brook," she said.

"No," he ordered.

"And why not?"

"Miss Wilhelm, you must conduct yourself as a lady," he reminded her. "You are nineteen years old, no longer a child; and you are not a wild Wilhelm bachelorette anymore. You're the wife of a noble now, act like it."

"You, noble," she derided.

The furrowing of his brow made it obvious the comment greatly offended him. "Excuse me?"

"'Miss Wilhelm, you're not a Wilhelm,'" she mocked. "It would seem I am—to you, anyway."

Arlo stood. "Have a good day today. No swimming in the brook. And put on something decent," he ordered before he stormed out of the dining room.

Quickly, Elonnie jumped to her feet and scurried to follow him. "Wait," she called.

Arlo froze. "What?"

She dropped her shoulders and stared at the floor. "Have a good day, Arlo," she sighed.

Quinze

"From the diary of Elonnie Wilhelm-Kensington,
April, 20th, 1795.

It's been nearly a week since I've been at the Ravenhill estate. How I wish I could read the mind of this dastardly man; it seems as if he is so cold at times, and yet the coldness feels like a defense to keep himself from at least befriending me. He is often in his study (working on something dreary, I'm sure), but I still don't understand why he can't share it with me. I can't help but wonder if he was this way as a little boy; if he locked out his brothers the way he locks me out and keeps to himself. I have a desire to ask Grandmother or even his brothers about it.

I do wonder if Arlie finds me at all desirable; growing up I was always told I was pretty, but I have yet to hear it from him. He does look at me, though—he doesn't know I notice it, but I do. They appear to be stares of admiration, yet I often wonder if he's doing it because he's judging me with his eyes as he does with his words. After all, he won't even let me in his room and it's a fight to get a goodnight kiss from him. I *hope he's just afraid to fall in love with me because of his pride..."*

Elonnie shut her diary and opened the notebook gifted to her by her grandmother-in-law. The day prior, she had begun writing a mystery story which was inspired by her surroundings in the Ravenhill estate to write. The building was mysterious and that was a fact. It was often quiet and seemingly empty as the workers did most of their work outside due to the lovely spring weather and her husband was always away or locked in his study. She began scribbling:

"The dark halls of Mr. Abernathy's estate were even darker after the murder of his wife. Who would have done such a thing to such a darling woman? Everyone there was a suspect, but everyone seemed to have a good excuse as to why they couldn't be the killer.

Lysander the inspector vowed to figure the murder out within forty-eight hours, and the killer knew this... as Lysander walked down the halls of the building around midnight that night, he had the strange feeling he was no longer alone, the wind spoke a gentle whistle that brushed through the curtains; but the creaking behind him couldn't have been due to the wind... no, not the wind... footsteps, quiet, careful footsteps. Then came the shadow on the wall causing the inspector to gasp, a knife! The shadow of a knife! In a quick moment—"

Elonnie's pen dragged across the paper as she jumped up in fear, feeling a hand on her shoulder. Turning around, she faced Constance and breathed a sigh of relief. "Oh, Miss Constance, you gave me a fright," she panted.

Constance giggled. "Perhaps the mystery stories are getting to your head," she winked. "Have you anymore for me to read?" she asked.

Elonnie smiled and nodded, handing her the book. "Tell me what you think, do you know who the killer is?"

Constance had her hand on her chin as her eyes traveled over the page; she nodded and Elonnie keenly watched her for her reactions. After she finished, she shut the book. "It's the butler," she said.

"Why do you say that?" Elonnie giggled.

"Isn't it always?" Constance asked.

"Why should the butler want to kill Mrs. Abernathy, though? They were good friends," Elonnie reminded her.

"Right," Constance nodded. "I suppose I need more clues; write faster, I'd like to know who did it," she encouraged.

Elonnie grinned, but soon her grin was stolen by a clouded expression. "Do you think he might be interested in reading it?" she asked, her eyes narrowing down to her twiddling fingers.

Constance offered a look a sympathy as she placed her hand over Elonnie's. "I think he would, just give it time," she encouraged.

Elonnie nodded then stood to gaze out the window. "If I were to go swimming after all, would he be dreadfully angry?" she asked.

Constance placed her hands on her lap and shrugged her shoulders. "Well, my dear, he'd have to find out that you went before he could get angry," she replied before sucking her lips in.

Elonnie grinned, rushing to her wardrobe and finding a suitable bathing gown. "Thank you," she told Constance.

※

THAT NIGHT, Elonnie prepared the tearoom as she awaited Arlo's return. The tearoom was what she expected it to be in this home; it wasn't boring in any way, but it was rather dark. Dark blue carpet graced the floor and the walls were just a few shades lighter than that; the drapes were light blue and covering the large bow window seeing as the sun had begun to set anyway. There was a fireplace similar to the ones that were throughout the estate and above it was a large golden mirror and two silhouette portraits of Arlo's parents on each side of it—she wondered for a moment about his father. He must have been just like Arlo. After taking a breath, she walked around the two chairs facing the fireplace and hoped it was dainty enough. It was past five-thirty and she hated the fact that she had been lied to, but at least she had gotten the chance to swim in the brook. Now she was even more satisfied that she had done so, and part of her wanted to tell him she had, just to anger him.

She opened a round pink and white striped box that had arrived that afternoon from Étienne. It contained two cups and matching saucers. One cup was plain black with a saucer just the same and the other was teal with red, blue, green, and yellow flowers decorated all over it and its saucer to match. Elonnie smiled, having an idea of what Étienne must have been thinking—she reached for the card inside the box and read it, translating it from French to English.

"Hello, my friend,

Since the wedding, I had been hoping to find the perfect gift for you and Mr. Kensington, and would you not agree that these tea sets match your personalities quite well? Please enjoy them, and I hope to see you very soon.

Your Friend,
Étienne."

"Oh, I wonder whose is whose?" She giggled, placing the cups upon the side tables that stood beside the chairs. It all looked picture perfect; the teacups, the cozy fire, and the pretty strawberry cupcakes with vanilla frosting that she placed the cups next to. She pursed her lips in irritation; by now, the water she had boiled for the tea was cold. Now she'd have to start it all over.

She put the Merry Berry tea into the cup gifted for her and the Nero tea bag into his. She wondered about the tea; she had often got on Arlo's case for complaining about things before trying them, but she had never tried the tea he liked because she insisted it would be too tasteless and bitter for her. It was just black tea, with a hint of cinnamon and a small trace of citrus; it couldn't hurt too bad to at least sip it one time.

The tearoom wasn't far from the front doors of the estate, so she was able to hear when they opened; strangely, she felt herself grow excited as she came to the conclusion that Arlo had returned. After her initial excitement came regret for her feelings; she shouldn't have anticipated his arrival the way she did, as he surely didn't feel any joy about seeing her. She straightened up, turning her back toward the entryway to the room and facing the fireplace. She wouldn't go running out to him, he could be the one to greet her first.

Elonnie bit her lip, hearing his footsteps getting closer to the room. Still, she wouldn't cave. He could come to her. She pulled at the cream gloves covering her hands and looked at herself in the mirror, admiring the mint green dress she wore, gifted to her by her sisters. She especially liked the shiny cream belt that wrapped around it.

Her hair wasn't up, but in two braided ponytails, still, she was sure he'd appreciate it. Her eyes met his through the mirror as he walked behind her and she gave him the slightest smile. Quickly, she removed it, shifting her eyes over to the clock on the wall, which indicated that it was seven o' three. "You said, five-thirty," she reminded him.

"Time flies when you're having fun," he responded.

"Ha—you? Having fun?" she laughed, turning to him.

"Just because it's a different fun than yours doesn't mean it isn't fun," he stated.

"Have you been working hard?" she asked.

"Is that supposed to be an insult?" he asked.

"Of course not!" she snapped. She fiddled with her ring under the glove and watched as his eyes traveled down her.

"Is it a special occasion?" he inquired.

"No," she replied. "Erm, I was wondering if—or, rather, I've set up tea for us," she told him, gesturing toward the table and chairs. "And, erm, Étienne sent us these teacups." She walked over to him and wrapped her arm around his, pulling him into the room. "I figured since we spent no time together earlier, it's only healthy that we do now. Also, I don't think we left things off in a safe place."

"Meaning?"

"Meaning you were mad with me and I was mad with you," she replied.

"Look, I appreciate the effort, but I'm tired and not in the mood for—"

Elonnie pushed him down into the chair and daintily strode over to sit in hers. "I wasn't asking, Arlie," she told him.

"You struck me!" Arlo complained, looking her up and down in disbelief.

"Oh, please," Elonnie tittered. "Nothing you wouldn't do to me." She reached for the teapot and poured water into each of their teacups before she turned her body to him. "So, I take it you like the dress?"

"I'm sorry?" Arlo asked.

"You asked if it was a special occasion when you saw my dress. Does that mean you like it?"

"It's acceptable," he replied.

"I see," she said, stirring honey and lemon into her tea. "Want anything in yours?"

Finally, Arlo reached for his cup. "No, thank you," he told her.

"Cupcake?" she offered.

Arlo turned his nose up in disgust, shaking his head.

"Why not?" she asked.

"You know I don't share your addiction to sweets," he stated.

Elonnie shrugged, taking a cupcake and biting it. "You're missing out," she bragged, her mouth full.

"This tea is cold," he said.

Elonnie tilted her head over to him with a puckered brow. "It was warm at five-thirty," she said.

He finished it anyway, then placed the cup on its saucer and the saucer back onto the table. Elonnie observed him as he now transferred his vision to the fireplace and seemed to relax just a tad. "Thank you," he told her and for a brief moment, she saw a soft smile directed at her from the man. In a second, it was washed away and he stood, clearing his throat. "This was...interesting. Goodnight."

Elonnie swiftly got to her feet and stood next to him.

"Nothing to talk about?" she asked. "How was your day? What did you do today?"

"Nothing exciting," he replied. "But enough to tire me out for the evening." He started out of the room and toward the staircase.

"Arlo Darcy Kensington!" Elonnie called.

Arlo turned back with a smirk on his face. "Oh, have I made you cross?" he asked, locking his hands behind his back.

"Yes," she nodded.

"How so?"

"Because you've been gone all day and you act as if you haven't; I set this up just for us to spend a fraction of time together and you don't seem to care."

"I said thank you, did I not?"

"Pbbt," Elonnie blew. "You aren't fair to me and you know that."

"I had the tea with you, Elonnie. I just said I was tired, you act as if I kicked you out of my home. What is this all about?"

"Everything, Arlo; I—I've been here nearly a week and you just act like I'm some visiting stranger. I find it highly inappropriate to...to be so far from you every night."

"Sue me for divorce, then; that's legal grounds, isn't it?" he chuckled, ready to exit the room again.

Elonnie reached for the remainder of her cupcake and tossed it at him. She covered her mouth in surprise when it struck him in the head, leaving the frosting stuck in his hair. "Elonnie, I have half a mind to do something to you that I never thought I would do to a woman," Arlo seethed.

When he turned back to her, she changed her face from the look of shock to one of resentment. "You have to face the music, I'm your wife; you could at least give me some small indication that you feel something for me."

Arlo raked his hand through his hair then shook off the frosting that latched onto his hand. "Miss Wilhelm, when were feelings ever a part of this arrangement?" he asked. "You see, you're the one responsible for all your pain, not me. We both went into this because we were told to, not because we love each other—you made up this picture-perfect marriage in your mind and you want me to fall in line with it so you can have your fairytale ending? No. Welcome to real life! Perhaps when you grow up just a little bit and begin acting the way a Kensington wife would be expected to act, then things will change!"

"Oh, is that your plan, Mr. Kensington? You expect me to sit here and be as boring as you are. Well, my dear, I'll have you know I'm not your shrew and I have no intentions of being tamed," she growled before flipping back toward the fireplace and folding her arms. "Go to bed, Arlo," she quietly instructed.

Seize

"**Lysander quickly turned to face his attacker, only to see it was nothing but the shadow of an empty suit of armor. He took a deep breath, finally relaxing himself—his mind was only playing a trick on him, and why shouldn't it? After all, there was a killer on his trail in this dark and massive building, and to add to his fears, the thunderstorm had just begun....**" Elonnie wrote. She closed the journal from Genevieve and continued walking down the dimly lit hallway— surely it was about midnight, but she couldn't sleep very well after the argument that took place earlier and writing seemed to be the only thing that could get her mind off of it; although, her writing didn't come out so well being that she walked as she wrote.

She stopped walking to look out the window and, fortunately for her, it was a starry night with a full moon to complement it. Sitting on the seat of the window, she happily took in the calm view and now wondered if she should run away—that would probably do them both a favor. Then Arlo would no longer have to put up with her and she'd no longer have to put up with Arlo. Or...she could do as he wanted and act the way a Kensington wife would be expected to act. She started to twist her ring around on her finger as she always did when she considered leaving, to remind her of Genevieve, her good friend. She would stay and she would stay true to herself no matter what.

She felt herself slowly dozing as she took in the sight of the quiet North Indigo night; just seeing the twinkling brook below her was enough to soothe her spirits and finally put her to sleep.

❦

WHEN THE SUN rose that morning, Elonnie blinked open her eyes and sat up in her bed. She used both hands to rub her eyes and looked around for a moment; of course she remembered falling asleep at the window, but she easily could have groggily made her way back to her room at some point that night. She yawned and looked at the clock in the corner. "Eight?" she groaned, ripping the covers off and jumping out of bed.

After she finished getting ready, she scurried down the stairs only to bump into Arlo in the entry hall. "Y-you?" she asked.

"What do you mean by that? It is my house, is it not?" he asked. "Which, if I may just remind you, running is not allowed in."

"I thought you'd be gone by now," Elonnie said.

"Well, normally I would be; only I understand how you

feel about leaving things off in a bad way, so I thought it would only be fair and mature to set things straight before I left."

"I think things are straight enough," Elonnie grimaced. "I hope you have a good day," she added. She offered a slight bow and turned toward the stairway to the kitchen.

"I should be back around three today," he told her. "I think it would be reasonable to go into town for a small tour, just so you can get to know the area should you desire to venture out on your own every now and then," he continued as he wheeled his hat around in his hands.

Elonnie turned to face him. "You mean, you and I?" she asked.

"I was thinking that. Some of the men from the worship hall were asking about you and I feel it's only fair to properly introduce you to the people around here. Unless, of course, you'd prefer otherwise; I could have Constance—"

"Erm, no, I would—I think I would like that, if we did it," she meekly accepted.

"Very well then. Three-thirty?"

"Yes. I'll be ready."

"Good," he said. He headed to the door, stopping in his tracks for just a moment before he began walking again.

Elonnie contemplated whether or not she should ask him for a goodbye kiss as she toyed around with the ballet slipper pendant on her necklace. "A-Arlo!" she called.

Arlo again ceased his walking to look back at her.

"I, erm, I think you know," Elonnie told him, keeping her eyes on the ground. She knew he knew what she was asking for, and this time he'd have to walk back to her to give it to her—she wasn't going to make the effort.

Arlo wasn't at all surprised, he had a feeling it was coming; realizing she remained where she stood, he strolled back to her and gave her head a kiss. "I'll see you in a small while," he awkwardly said. "Goodbye."

"Goodbye," Elonnie responded. After he was gone, she beamed. Could this have finally softened the enmity between them? She wouldn't allow herself to get too excited, as she knew Arlo was very up and down with his behavior and she wasn't even sure if he would be back when he said he would. Nevertheless, she would be ready, just as she had said she would be.

❧

ELONNIE HAD SPENT most of the day practicing her dance and writing her mystery story— she had no doubt that Constance would be eager to hear the continuation of the story. Now in her room, she made a wild mess of it, looking for the perfect outfit for the day's outing. As much as the girl desired to contain her excitement, she couldn't stop her heart from racing with anticipation at what the afternoon might bring; *would it be a romantic carriage ride through town, followed by a nice dinner after meeting his friends?* She lowered the purple dress that was now in her hands and her eyes clouded over with fear. *Or would his being around his friends compel him to humiliate her?* Shaking her head, she decided not to think that way; it would only stress her out.

She put the purple dress aside and chose a different one, one consisting of the colors white, lavender, and pink. The left and right sides of the dress were lavender, the center was white, and the belt was pink; it was a favorite of hers, not only because it was beautiful, but because it was comfortable.

Now it was two-forty-seven; she took a deep breath, just

hoping that Arlo would be back at three, just like he said he would, and yet she felt a rush of apprehension as she knew the time for him to return was coming upon her.

Elonnie put her dress on and unpinned her hair, letting her long ringlets fall down. She pinned one side of it back and topped it off with a flower pin that matched the lavender color of the dress. Her brown eyes widened with delight when she heard Arlo enter the home downstairs.

Just in time, she thought, preparing to run out of the room. She stopped herself in her tracks, realizing that she couldn't always look so desperate for his love and attention when it was clear he didn't want to give it to her. Straightening her face and her shoulders, she casually made her way down the stairs to the entry hall. "You said three," she told him, taking a peek at the clock. It read "two-fifty-five."

"You're irritated when I'm late and irritated when I'm early?" Arlo asked.

"I was just expecting you to be home at three, that's what you told me." She gave a careless shrug. "Anyhow, I'm ready when you are," she told him. Arlo considered the pretty dress for a moment and when Elonnie caught on to him, she gave a delicate twirl. "I don't know what catches your eye more, lavender or mint," she laughed sweetly. "Perhaps it's not the color, but the figure."

Arlo frowned, walking past her toward the staircase. "Give me just a moment and I'll be right with you," he said.

Elonnie nodded as he walked off. "Arlie, I'm most excited!" she blurted with a small bounce.

He looked over his shoulder, gave half a smile, and then continued up the stairs. When he had gone, Elonnie blew a curl out of her face and put her hands upon her waist—she had made herself look overly eager again and he remained indifferent. She walked into the tea room where she'd wait for him and took a seat.

❦

THE CARRIAGE RIDE wasn't too quiet since Elonnie sang and hummed for most of it as she sat across from Arlo; the man didn't seem to find her singing too irritating as he was engulfed in reading a newspaper, and she wasn't singing too loudly. He peeked his green eyes over the paper to look at her when he heard her singing the headline and arched his brow. "Must you?" he asked and she nodded. "Why?"

"Because I'm finding it a struggle to think of anything else I might sing," she replied, "so I'll make it up as I go."

Arlo raised the paper back up and continued reading and Elonnie continued singing. *Now* he was irritated. "Elonnie."

"Yes?" she sang.

"That's quite enough."

"If you wouldn't ignore me, I wouldn't have to find a way to entertain myself,'" she stated before switching over to his side of the carriage and laying her head on his shoulder.

"Miss, please, sit up," he requested.

"Mrs.," she corrected. Her eyes brightened, looking over his paper and seeing a recipe on it, right beside the news article of a murder. She forced herself under his arm and read the recipe. "Blueberry-raspberry muffins! Do you want those?" she asked.

"Do you have any idea how sweet that is?" Arlo asked. "And will you sit up?"

"No, I don't quite feel like sitting up," she shook her head. "You smell delightful, what is that?"

"Elonnie. You're misbehaving."

"I'm only just getting started, Mr. Kensington," she replied.

"I'll have the driver turn this carriage around if you don't sit up and act like a lady," he hissed.

"How about you allow me a place on your lap while you continue to read your paper and I'll mind my business as I shower you with passionate kisses?" she smirked.

"Elonnie Mary Wilhelm," he growled, abruptly shoving her up straight. "What has gotten into you?"

Elonnie was beside herself with laughter—Arlo's reactions were better than pure gold. His eyes were big and his cheeks blushed crimson with discomfort as he tried to keep his stern look of disapproval on his face.

"It's Kensington, and your bratty pout makes you more desirable—"

"Mr. Wickham!" Arlo called to the carriage driver. "Turn us around, we're—"

"No, no, please," Elonnie begged. "You've already told your friends we were coming."

"Sit back and act like a lady," he growled, putting a disciplinary finger in her face.

Elonnie gave a pout and a lowered brow as she sat back. "Tell me, darling, do I look like you?" she asked, a smile now creeping its way back on to her face. After the smile came the laughter and Arlo gave the most disappointed face as he sighed.

"Why are you being such a test?" he asked.

She twirled her hair around her finger and met eyes with him. "If you allow me the pleasure of lying my head on your shoulder, I will alter my behavior," she told him.

"No. You're going to behave because I told you to. Do I make myself clear?"

"No."

Arlo breathed deep, it was clear he was getting incensed; but the angrier he became, the funnier the situation was to Elonnie. She bit her lip, trying to contain her laughter, and he locked his hand around her wrist. "You are not going to make a fool of me, do you understand?" he snapped.

A little nervous now, Elonnie ceased her laughter before she pulled away from him. "Relax yourself," she told him.

"It is not I who needs to relax," Arlo countered. "Settle down, or we're turning back."

"Fine." She turned her nose up. She gave him a bothered glance before she slid away from him, as if she were punishing him, and peered out the window.

"Oh, how will I ever enjoy the rest of the ride now?" Arlo grumbled in a tone of sarcasm.

❧

WHEN THEY WERE in the town center, Elonnie breathed a swooned sigh at the lovely sights—though quiet, the center appeared busy, with many a shopkeeper and customer strolling about. She could see that they were in the middle of opening their outdoor carts and dining tables now that the weather was altering to warmth. "Let's have tea there!" she begged, pointing to a quaint boutique teahouse as she leaned halfway out the carriage window.

"We already have plans, Elonnie," he reminded her sternly before pulling her back into the carriage. "Would you delight in falling forward and cracking open your skull on the concrete?" he inquired.

"No. Would you delight in me doing so?" she asked.

"Ask me later," he replied just as the carriage came to a stop; of course, Elonnie was ready to jump out as she usually was. "Wait," Arlo instructed.

"For?" she asked.

"For me to come around and assist you out."

"So sweet of you, darling, but I'm quite capable of getting out on my own," she told him.

"Elonnie. Just once try not to make an argument out of something small. I'm just trying to be gentlemanly; is that not what you desire?" he asked.

"Fine. If it makes you feel better," she said, sitting back. "Go on, then."

Arlo stepped out of the carriage and made his way around to her side—she offered her outstretched hand to take his and stepped out with his assistance.

"Happy now?" she inquired, gently stroking his face. She wrapped her arm around his and he led the way along the brick road to a neat little coffeehouse, called "Elmshire's Brew." Elonnie liked the look of it, with its casement windows and brown brick architecture. "Lovely," she gasped.

Upon entering the building, he was instantly greeted by a group of seven men who were of mixed ages. About two of them looked to be close to Arlo's young age, while the rest of them were surely older than fifty. It didn't surprise Elonnie that he would prefer to spend his time with older people, nor did it bother her as she herself preferred the company of her elders.

"Is this the young man who swore against marriage?" one of them loudly laughed. A mix of blonde and grey colors covered his hair and his rounded beard. His beady blue eyes didn't look the least bit intimidating, nor did his short and stout figure, but the rough, loud voice and large cigar sticking out of his mouth did cause Elonnie to fall back behind her husband. "Let's see her, then," he said. "No need to be shy, we don't bite."

Arlo gave her a slight pull and turned back to her when he felt the resistance. "Elonnie, what's the matter?" he asked.

"I'll have you know, even I can get shy," she replied.

"Shy? I should say not," he scoffed. "The way you'll traverse the house in your nightgown or undergarments surely doesn't give off the impression of shy."

"That's my private space," she replied.

"Don't make a fool out of me, please," he commanded.

Elonnie took a deep breath, finally stepping forward and giving a respectful bow to the men. "Forgive me, good sirs, I'm quite timid," she told them.

"That's all right, we like timid," one of the others told her, definitely around the same age as her husband. His dark hair and light blue eyes appeared less friendly than the other man's.

"See," Arlo said to his friends as he took a seat along with Elonnie. "I told you she was beautiful," he said.

Elonnie turned her head to him, feeling mostly confused—she had to pry such words as that out of him and yet now it took little effort for him to tell his friends he appreciated how she looked.

"Yes, now we can see why you might have made such a choice in a bride," one of the others sneered as he adjusted his spectacles. He was a bit of an overweight man, with a second chin and a handlebar mustache—and clearly, he wasn't too pleased with Elonnie. All of the men seemed to be wearing the same suit, but Elonnie only thought that to be the case because they were all the same dark blue color.

"I'm sorry, what do you mean by that?" she spoke up, unsettled by his comment.

"Arlo is quite the sophisticated young man, it was rather odd to hear he had been married to a...showgirl," the man replied.

"I'm not a showgirl," she stated firmly.

"And what exactly would you call it?" he questioned.

"It would depend on which part of my work you're referring to," Elonnie replied. "If you're referring to my dancing, it would be ballerina or dancer," she told him. "My acting, thespian; my singing, vocalist."

"Overall it would fall into the category of showgirl," he scorned.

"And what are you? A lawyer?" Elonnie guessed with a condescending chuckle.

The men grumbled around the table amongst one another until the man she was speaking to straightened in his chair. "Yes," he nodded. "And?"

"And so, it's no surprise that you're ignorant when it comes to the exciting things of life. I'm a ballerina, meaning that I have more strength in my toe then you could ever dream of having, Mr. Second Chin, so I would suggest that—"

"Elonnie," Arlo growled. "I apologize on my wife's behalf, Mr. Elmsley," he told him.

"No need to apologize on my behalf, I'm not sorry."

"Arlo, surely you could have chosen a quiet wife," Mr. Elmsley complained.

"Well, I didn't choose her, my brothers did," Arlo quickly said.

"Oh, is that all you have to say?" Elonnie asked him. "See how fast one throws his wife beneath the carriage when the friends are around," she complained.

"I asked you not to make us look bad, how hard is that?" Arlo whispered.

"Perhaps you should take her outside and fix her, Arlo, otherwise she might fix you first," one of the others warned. Elonnie found his sharp nose unnerving, that along with his icy blue eyes and pale blonde hair that not only covered his hair but his chin.

"I can guarantee to you, Mister, that I will not be the one *fixed* by the end of this," she assured.

"Must you all be so rude?" the other younger man asked. Bright red hair and freckles surely didn't give him a villainous appearance. "Forgive them, Mrs. Kensington, they're not used to being around pretty women. You see, they only ever spend time with their wives and mothers," he joked.

Elonnie laughed aloud before embarrassedly covering her mouth—she didn't expect such a bold retort from the one with the kindest face. "And might I ask your name?" she inquired.

"Abington, Mister Gerald Abington."

"Well, I must say, Sir Abington, it is a pleasure—it's odd that a stranger should come to the defense of a woman faster than her own husband," Elonnie said with a sour smile. "But after all, he didn't choose me, his brothers did," she reiterated. "Right, *Arlie bear?*" The emphasis she added to the nickname made it clear she was out to embarrass him; and that's just what she did.

Arlo cringed in his chair as his friends laughed at the name and his skin turned red. "No nicknames, please," he quietly requested. He sat up and scooted his chair closer to the table. "Of course, I didn't bring Elonnie here to butt heads with all of you," he told them. "You wanted to meet her and she wanted to meet you."

Mr. Elmsley used his handkerchief to wipe his spectacles, keeping his pompous look upon his face. "Yes, letting a little theater girl ruin the evening would be quite unfortunate, now wouldn't it?"

"What is it you have against the girl? I find her rather charming," another man chimed in. His thick dark brows and chiseled face somehow managed to still look sociable and his soft dark hair and eyes only added to his easygoing, yet erudite look.

"I think that a woman of her age should learn to bite her tongue and sit back, Mr. Glasgow," Mr. Elmsley replied. "If you've spent little time in the real world, you haven't much say of what goes on in it."

"And at what age do you have a say, Mr. Elmsley?" Elonnie asked.

"When you've experienced life."

"And so, what does that mean for my *darling whim wiffle* of a husband?" she sassed and garnered another round of laughs for the pet name. "He's only two years my senior."

"Arlo knows the business side of life. He knows more than you could ever dream of knowing."

"Except happiness and creativity, clearly," Elonnie countered. "And if I might say, your argument is weak, because while you might know the business side of life, you know it because you were born into it and it was passed down to you; you may work hard now, but you did not work hard for your name. My parents and their siblings did and they continue making that name stronger as the years go by," she continued. "Also, you don't know the war side of life. There are men out there young enough to be your son who fought in wars and saw harsh things before actually getting the chance to settle down and live a safe life—but they wouldn't dare say you know nothing of life because you haven't experienced what they have," she told him. "The beauty of life is that we all have different experiences, Mr. Elmsley; perhaps you need the ballerina experience to loosen up a little. As does my charming, suddenly silent husband."

"Timid, indeed," Elmsley scoffed.

Slamming his hand on the table, Arlo's eyes narrowed on her and he pointed his finger at her. "Keep yourself composed, I will not tell you again," Arlo snapped.

Elonnie jumped, startled by the abrupt and humiliating tone. *How dare he?* Snappishly reprimanding her, again treating her as his little child, and in front of all these people. As badly as she desired to walk out of the establishment right there, she decided not to allow Arlo or Mr. Elmsley to chase her away. Later, she would get even with Arlo.

❧

STANDING OUTSIDE as they prepared to depart to their homes, Elonnie teetered left and right, waiting for Arlo to finish his conversation with the other men. She glanced over at Mr. Wickham and slightly backed away from the others, making her way over to the carriage. Jumping into the vehicle, she laughed, shutting the door. "He said you could take me home, he'll ride with his friends," she lied.

"Yes, Lady Kensington," Mr. Wickham nodded.

When the carriage pulled off, Elonnie stuck her hand out the window, waving at Arlo as it drove by him.

Arlo took a deep breath, skin flushing no matter how

hard he tried to keep his composure. "Treacherous brat," he grumbled.

Glasgow, who stood next to him, was beside himself with laughter. Throwing his arm around Arlo, he gave him a slight shake. "You married a fun one, Arlo. I can take you to your home."

Dix-sept

Constance gently combed Elonnie's hair as she related to her what took place in town. Though she had gotten her revenge, the way Arlo had spoken to her and allowed that man to speak to her still discouraged her. She didn't want the older woman to see her shed any tears over the matter and she didn't find the matter to be worthy of her tears. Perhaps it was time to stop giving Arlo chances to treat her the way he did and either humiliate him to the best of her ability when she received the chance, or be the perfect, quiet, calm wife. Once again she twisted her wedding ring from Genevieve around and she breathed heavily. "I suppose it's better I let the matter go, wouldn't you agree?" she sadly asked.

Constance placed her hands on her shoulders gently as she looked at her through the vanity mirror. "What do you think would make you the happiest?" she questioned.

"I think—"

"Elonnie Mary!" Arlo barked from the entry hall.

Elonnie rolled her eyes and stood, tightening her dressing gown and starting to the door. Upon taking hold of the knob, she froze. "I don't have to answer to him," she stated, returning to the vanity and sitting. "It sounds as if he's angry with me and why should I care about that? He'll always be angry with me."

"Don't you think you might want to go, just so that things don't get worse?" Constance asked.

"No," Elonnie replied. "Let him steam until his head should pop." Sheepishly, she looked up at the elder woman. "I also may have made the matter worse already," she admitted.

"What do you mean?"

Arlo swung the door open and stared at the girl, frustration filling his green eyes. "Did you not hear me call you?" he fumed.

"I heard you loud and clear, everyone did. My family in Therondia probably did," Elonnie playfully shrugged.

"Excuse us," he told Constance.

"Please don't do anything foolish," Constance quietly implored before exiting the room.

"Before you begin berating me for embarrassing you in front of your friends, did you by any chance ask them why they felt the need to insult me? Mr. Elmsley, that is?" Elonnie stood from her seat.

"They're not my concern, I'm not married to them. I tried to do something nice for you and you behaved indecently! And to leave me stranded out there?"

"Stranded? Arlo, don't be so dramatic. And yes, you're *not* married to them—therefore, they don't deserve your loyalty, respect, and protection before me!" she growled. "I don't care if you don't love me. If you desire a wife that respects you, then the least you can do is respect her in return."

"You've done nothing to earn my respect," Arlo told her.

"The feeling is mutual. Now get out," she ordered.

"Excuse me?" He took a step forward. "You cannot order me around in my own house."

"This is the room you gave to me, making it my property; I have a right to say who I want in it and who I want out," she snapped.

Arlo stepped closer to her, placing his hands on his hips and looking down at her. "Don't make me stand here all night," he warned.

"Arrogant, haughty, cruel, and overbearing," she insulted. "That's all you are, and for some reason it comes across to people as sophisticated and classy—but Arlo, my darling, you are far from that!" Swiftly he raised his backhand but Elonnie smirked. "Oh, do it," she teased. "Why not, after all? You've already proven to be ungentlemanly and cold."

Clenching his fist in an effort to remain calm, he lowered his hand. "Do you have any idea how esteemed a man like Mr. Elmsley is?" he asked.

"Do you have any idea how much I fail to care? He's not respectful and therefore he does not have my respect. You sat there, just like you did in Towne Hall, and thought nothing of the fact that that old pompous man was ill-mannered toward me! Like I told you earlier, if you want me to happily subject myself to you then please, allow me to see you as a protective head. Now I'm tired, Mr. Kensington, please leave the room, unless you'll finally be staying with me tonight." She crossed her arms. "But you wouldn't dare, for fear you might start falling in love. Funny how you find it so easy to compliment me to your friends but heaven forbid you do such a nice thing in private. I'm not a trophy, Arlo."

Gripping the knob, Arlo glanced back at her, an

annoyed look plastered across his face. "Far from a trophy, indeed. A punishment you are!" he hissed, opening the door and leaving the room.

NEEDLESS TO SAY, Elonnie couldn't sleep that night—so she decided to light a candle and stroll through the halls to make her way to the ballroom, her favorite room in the house. Even at such a late hour, she still took pleasure in dancing, although she didn't have the light of day on her side, the candles were enough and gave a gentle and delicate glow to the room. Dancing would relieve the disdain she was feeling for the man for the most part and it might tire her out enough to help her sleep.

She tied up the ribbons on her pointe shoes before opening a small box which contained a music box with the inscription: *"For the midnight dances..."* a wedding present from her brother-in-law, Pritchard. Elonnie polished the music box, wondering how on earth such an arrogant brat could have two sweet older brothers; no doubt Arlo was spoiled as a child, especially seeing as the age gap was quite distant between him and his brothers. When she opened it, it played a part of Mozart's *"Lacrimosa,"* one of the most beautiful and enchanting tunes.

Standing, she took a deep breath and waited for the tune to restart before she began dancing to it. Normally, the song would seem too dark for her taste, but Mozart had a way of making the dark just as elegant and charming as the light.

When she had concluded her dance, she continued walking around the dark halls of the estate; the deep slumber that had to be upon the rest of the household assured her that now the place was all hers and, while she adored the staff, that was satisfying. Everyone needs to enjoy some time alone. She walked along the hall and came across Arlo's study; from beneath the door, she could see a light on inside and she tapped her chin with her finger. Was he awake? She tried peeking through the keyhole, but it was much too small to make anything out—she considered knocking or walking in, but what if he was in there after all? Did she really want to see him?

Turning her back to the door, she heard footsteps in the room and hurried away from the door and down the stairs before he came out and found her there. When she got down to the entry hall, she covered her mouth, now laughing; the whole thing had begun to feel like a game now, as the rain and thunder had just started, casting a haunting air over the large building. She peeked around the corner of the staircase and she could hear that he was walking around, so she hid in the small closet inside the staircase, where she could hear if he were to come down the stairs or not.

After a few minutes, it became known to her that Arlo had surely headed to his room to go to sleep, so she made her way down to the kitchen to prep cupcakes—baking was a lot like dancing to her, soothing and distracting. She'd just make a simple pound cake, her grandma's recipe, but she'd turn it into cupcakes this time.

The rainstorm was calming as the drops trickled down the windows, and the batter was already smelling delightful.

"It's two o'clock in the morning," Arlo grumbled at the entrance to the kitchen with a small candle in his hand.

Elonnie screamed out, nearly dropping the cake batter out of her hands, but swiftly catching in and placing it safely onto the table. "What on earth did you do that for?" she breathed. "You gave me such an awful scare."

"That was not my intention," he told her. "I can't seem to sleep."

"Neither can I," she quietly replied.

"But I don't think now is the time for baking, Miss— Mrs.— Elonnie, it's far too late."

"Have I not been berated enough today?" she asked, rolling her eyes. She turned to her batter to add in the butter. As she mixed it in, she could hear him walking closer to her, which made her feel just a little apprehensive. Nevertheless, she continued mixing.

"May I inquire of what you're making?" he asked.

"Pound cake," she curtly replied.

"Then why do you have cupcake tins?"

"Because I'm making it into cupcakes," she said, her voice with a short tone. Tension filled the room and she tried her hardest to contain her emotions, but she was sure they were made evident to the man.

Arlo made no other response; he folded his arms and leaned against the table, watching her as she continued her work. "You're trembling," he stated.

"No, I'm not," she firmly lied, now mashing the eggs in.

"You understand that the scent of the cake will surely fill the house and awaken everyone, don't you?" he asked.

"Perhaps I don't care," she replied.

Arlo ran his hand through his hair and then walked around the table, letting his finger drag along the top of it—it was clear to Elonnie that he was holding something back from her as he filled the room with a disconcerting aura. It was odd of him to behave so awkwardly. "Elonnie," he started. "With regards to earlier..." He cleared his throat and placed his hands on the table.

Elonnie ceased her mashing and looked up at him with big eyes—now she had an idea why he was behaving strangely. "Yes?" she asked.

"I, erm, my goal was not exactly to hurt your feelings, nor has it ever been—it's not as if I'm trying to make you feel embarrassed," he stammered.

"Are you trying to apologize to me?" Elonnie asked, holding back a smile. How arrogant the man was—he couldn't even bring himself to say the words.

"I suppose, yes," he nodded. "But I need you to understand that you don't just speak to prominent people the way you spoke to Mr. Elmsley."

"He spoke to me that way first, Arlo, and just because my trade is fun and his is not doesn't mean he's any more prominent than I am," Elonnie stated.

"These men watched my brothers and I grow up; they taught us so much, for me to suddenly start lashing out at him the way you did, it would have been—"

"Arlo. Who made the first comment?" Elonnie asked. "I did not go in there with the intention of starting any fights, and before I could even get to know anyone, I was insulted. I didn't lash out at him."

"The second chin comment was a little much, no?"

"Was it as much as the showgirl comment?" Elonnie sassed.

Arlo sighed, raising his hands. "I didn't come down here to add more wood to the fire, I only wanted to...you know, say that."

"To say you were sorry? You won't die if you say the words, Arlo," Elonnie assured him.

His eyes shifted toward the window. "Yes, I'm sorry," he uttered.

"Apology accepted," she said, giving him a soft smile. "And I apologize for leaving you behind. And for what I said to Mr. Elmsley."

"Goodnight, then," he told her.

"Goodnight," she replied, then watched as he headed out of the kitchen. She noticed that he took a moment to glance back at her and she again started her baking preparation. She heard him quietly sigh and then continue walking. "Arlie," she called. "My goodnight kiss."

Arlo turned back, walking to the girl and kissing her temple.

And before he could leave, Elonnie showed the smirk of a braggart. "You know, Kate wins at the end," she said.

From the way his eyebrows crinkled, she knew it was taking him a moment to figure out the meaning of her saying. His face turned from confusion to a frown. "No. Petruchio does," he affirmed. "Kate becomes a golden young woman at the end because she learns to do as she's told and she does what her husband wants her to. He wins."

"She only does what he wants to spare his feelings," Elonnie smiled. "To let him think he had power."

"Yet he still gets what he desires."

"But she holds the power."

"You believe that, then," he told her, giving her a pat on the head.

"I will," she nodded with a simper, "and you'll see." Her face straightened as her eyes traveled upward, with attention given to the man's hand that stayed rested on her head. She faintly quivered as his hand gently stroked through her hair before he twirled a strand of it around his finger. She knew it was obvious that her breathing had intensified—affection? Was this genuine affection coming from him?

It was clear when Arlo realized what he was doing because he appeared to blink himself out of a reverie and take a step back. "Goodnight, Elonnie," he told her.

"B-bonsoir," Elonnie replied.

❧

"AND THAT'S why Mr. Abernathy killed his wife," Lysander explained as the once prominent and wealthy man was whisked away from his estate and taken to suffer the consequences of murder," Elonnie wrote. She tapped the pen against her mouth, trying to figure out if she loved the conclusion or not, then she closed the journal and kissed it.

Reaching for more ink and her diary, she rolled out her cramped shoulders just a little bit before preparing to write a new entry.

April 25ᵗʰ, 1795,

Today was not as eventful as I would have liked it to be; I did finish my mystery story, which I am proud to say I have, but other than that I only went into town for an hour to find something to make for dinner tonight. A few nights ago appeared to be somewhat eventful, as it seemed Arlie almost weakened to me. He even apologized to me in so many words for his behavior earlier that day. Perhaps I should have seen him today. I feel a slight pang of guilt for not doing so, but he can be so fickle, he probably had no desire to see me anyway."

Closing the diary, she stood and made her way downstairs to finish dinner—she was ordered not to cook, since they had paid someone to do that, but that didn't stop her.

She had been wanting to make something for dinner for quite some time now and today would be the day she did. Now, she wasn't all too fond of the traditional foods of North Indigo; it was the foods of Tamin that caused her mouth to water, and the spicy foods of a small country not too far from them called 'Grecia-Romaina.' This evening she had chosen to make a traditional Taminite dish; it was a rather simple pasta dish, with tomato sauce, sweet peppers, olives, capers, and chicken. It was far too modest for Arlo to complain about and definitely delicious enough for him to appreciate.

Setting the table with the assistance of Constance and three other servants, she was lost in her thoughts and she made it evident to the others by the way she kept ceasing her work and staring blankly ahead of her. "You've known Arlo ever since he was little, haven't you?" she finally asked Constance.

Constance gave a soft smile, nodding and putting down a napkin beside the place setting. "Yes," she told her.

"Was he ever in love?" Elonnie asked. "Like, I understand for a child to fall in love, that may be unlikely, but I feel that even as children we do develop a special fondness for an individual every now and then."

The servants tittered, placing the hors d'oeuvres upon the table.

"What is it?" Elonnie smiled at their giggles as she propped her hands onto her waist.

The petite one with the reedy blonde hair under her bonnet and big blue eyes looked up, covering her mouth. "For Lord Kensington, it was Miss Constance," she laughed.

"You?" Elonnie gasped, her eyes wide. "So Arlie would have preferred a much older gal, I take it," she snickered.

"Arlo was an interesting child." Constance shook her

head. "Far more spoiled than his brothers, no doubt. I think his parents were much too tired to discipline him in the same fashion they did his brothers by the time he was born."

"Arlie wasn't planned, I take it?" she quietly laughed.

"No, but still a treasure to his family," Constance replied. She smiled as if she had known an Arlo quite different from the one she knew now.

"Well, I'm delighted his parents didn't let him know he wasn't part of their plan over and over again," Elonnie dejectedly mumbled, readjusting the farce flowers in the vase upon the table. She took a step back to analyze the table and see to it that everything was in order. Proudly, she nodded her head at the picturesque dining arrangement—it was practical, yet colorful, something both of them could enjoy.

"Elonnie?" she heard a voice call from the entry hall.

"Arlo?" she gasped, glancing over to the clock on the wall. He was early. "Arlo, what are you doing here?" she asked, stepping out of the dining room and into the hall.

"It smells lovely in here," he said.

Elonnie perked up excitedly. "Thank you."

"Oh, you cooked?" he asked. Before she could answer, he brushed his question off. "Never mind that. I have a favor to ask you."

"And what is that?" Elonnie crossed her arms.

"Some of the gentlemen you met from the other day will be stopping over for the evening and so—"

"Well, it's a good thing I make large portions," Elonnie sighed. "How many others?"

"Elmsley, Glasgow, and Abington," he replied.

"Fortunately, the behavior of the latter two can combat the rudeness of the first," Elonnie grumbled. "Constance, could I bother you to retrieve three more settings?"

"Of course." Constance bowed before exiting the room.

"Actually," Arlo scratched his head. "Erm, I was rather hoping you might be able to entertain yourself...elsewhere? The ballroom, perhaps?"

Staring up at Arlo, any excitement that might have been left over in Elonnie's face had completely disappeared. Now, she was wearing a face of displeasure, almost anger. "I beg your pardon?" she asked, taking a step closer to him.

"Elonnie, we're supposed to be discussing something rather important and what would be viewed as boring to you; and I not only don't want to hear your complaining about how dreary we are, but I would also appreciate it if you didn't embarrass me," he explained.

Elonnie's face distorted into a scrunched pout as she lifted her hands like she was ready to grab him by the neck. "All right, Lord Kensington, I will stay out of your way. Enjoy the dinner I worked so hard on for you with your friends," she said. "Constance, darling! Only two more settings, I'll be having dinner on the ballroom floor," she called.

"Now, I didn't say that," Arlo frowned.

"Oh, why would you need to?" Elonnie scoffed. "I hope you enjoy yourself."

🙚❦🙘

As the time passed, Elonnie found herself rather bothered by the fact that Arlo's guests were still present. She, of course, had no issues with the friendly two of his friends—most of her frustration was at the pompous Elmsley and her boorish husband. After all, it was Arlo who had basically told her to go away as if she were his puppy, and just thinking of that caused her blood to boil.

She walked along the banister and readied to go downstairs for a drink, but decided against it as she recalled that she was practically banned from going down there. But did Arlo really have the right to tell her to hide on the upper floor until his friends decided to leave? She looked down at her clothing, a peach-colored ballet dress. Perhaps if Lord Kensington had allowed her to stay by his side for dinner then she would not have been an embarrassment to him, but he had chosen war instead.

Elonnie stepped down that staircase quiet as mouse and stood at the entrance of the dining room, where she faced Arlo and remained out of sight of the other three men. She grinned playfully as she waved at Arlo and swayed from side to side.

The baron's face turned pale and clouded over with fear when he saw her, prompting the others to turn around. Elonnie scurried to the side so that the others wouldn't see her and they turned back to Arlo, now concerned.

"Is everything all right?" Glasgow inquired.

"Hmm? Yes. Of course," he answered, sheepish.

"You looked as if you'd seen a ghost," Gerald laughed.

"Forgive me," Arlo requested through clenched teeth.

Elonnie peeked back into the dining room and smiled at Arlo, waving again before she started flipping her hair around. In response, Arlo slammed his hands on the table and she scattered away again.

"Mr. Kensington, are you sure you're all right?" Glasgow asked again.

Arlo forced himself to smile. "I am just swell," he lied. "That was an accident."

Elonnie covered her mouth and laughed silently, peeking in once more to see Arlo's frustration—he looked as if he might have struck her if he could only get to her, but that didn't instill any fear into the woman. Once more she stood at the entrance of the room and began to bourrée back and forth until Arlo heaved an antagonized sigh as he shot a glare in her direction.

"I think you might just be exhausted, Arlo," Gerald stated after seeing that Arlo's attention had been captivated once more. "We have been talking long and you're probably bored to death."

"It is late," Glasgow nodded, checking his pocket watch for the time. "I should get going, anyway; I would hate to keep the Missus waiting up for me. Give my regards to Lady Kensington."

"Oh, I will." Arlo again forced a grin.

As the others stood and headed into the entry hall, Elonnie hurried up the stairs and peered over until they left. She watched Arlo, standing at the door for a brief amount of time before he spun to meet eyes with her. She tittered, seeing the skin of his face turn scarlet. "If I were you, I'd find a place to hide," Arlo growled.

Elonnie laughed, clapping her hands. "Oh, I do love hide and seek," she replied.

"Elonnie. Mary." He slowly made his way to the staircase and then began to climb up the stairs.

"You're not really cross with me, are you? Perhaps you should have considered how I might feel about you brushing me off in the manner that you did."

"I'm giving you ample time to get away, is that not kind of me?" he asked.

"I'm waiting until you're just a little closer; I adore the thrill," Elonnie responded coquettishly.

When he made it to the first landing, she yelped, then took off running into her room where she shut the door and locked it behind her. Out of breath from running and laughing, she leaned against the door and tried to peep through the keyhole to see if he was near. It was quiet, and that was a good sign, although she found the moment fairly fun.

She moved away from the door and began changing into her pajamas, but jumped at the sound to the door unlocking. Her eyes grew big when Arlo opened the door and she stumbled back. "What an invasion of privacy!" she snapped, trying to hold in laughter. "That's cheating, it's against the rules!"

"Rules of what?" he questioned.

"The entire game, Arlo!" She backed up against the wall and leered at him. "Out," she ordered with a giggle.

He grabbed her by the arms, yanking her closer to him, and though he was stronger in comparison, she still fought to free herself. "Listen closely," Arlo hissed.

"Let go!" Elonnie demanded, no longer finding the situation amusing.

"Stop fighting me," he ordered. "This should be the last time I have to tell you that everything is not a game!"

"Don't you raise your voice to me!"

"That's how we deal with children, Elonnie; we raise our voices to them and hope they can get it through their heads how they're supposed to act!"

"Perhaps we're both children, darling; after all, you're standing here throwing a temper tantrum as we speak." Sliding out of his grip, she moved away from him, seeing his flushed cheeks; it wasn't uncommon for him to get upset with her, but now he looked more than just upset—he was angry. "Leave," she said, once again backing herself up against the wall. "Goodnight."

"I will not set foot out of this room until you apologize for your stupidity."

"Don't you dare start insulting my intelligence, Arlo Darcy!"

"You do a fine job insulting your own intelligence, Elonnie, when you act like a foolish little girl and do everything you can to make me infuriated!"

Elonnie took a deep breath and swallowed; he was getting louder and closer and now she regretted her earlier behavior. "Perhaps I—"

"Silence!" he barked.

"Don't you tell me—"

Elonnie jumped when Arlo struck the vase of flowers off from the fireplace. Though the vase wasn't aimed at her, she ducked, covering her head. "I *will* tell you, Elonnie; someone has to! You play too much and *I'm tired of it!*" he bellowed.

"Keep your temper!" Elonnie entreated, keeping herself turned away from him.

Grabbing a hold of her, he faced her towards him. "Why on earth would Gladstone think it was fair to stick me with a nineteen-year-old baby? If you don't want me to treat you as a little child then I would suggest you start acting like a woman! *Do I make myself clear?*"

Elonnie kept silent, shivering in his grip and keeping her large, fear-stricken eyes on him. She had never seen a man like this before, so angry and hostile. She wanted nothing more than for him to leave the room immediately. Keeping her startled gaze on his eyes, she nodded.

Now realizing how far he had gone, Arlo's stern glare softened. He turned his attention to the broken vase. For a moment a look of regret flashed across his face, feeling the girl trembling in his grasp. "Good, then," he quietly said.

Elonnie yanked her arms away, finally giving way to her

tears. She sat on the floor and lowered her head into her hand. "Leave," she requested.

Unsure of how to react, Arlo looked down at her. Elonnie had never cried before. Did he really frighten her that much? "Elonnie...don't be so sensitive," he told her.

She stood up and walked over to sit at the vanity. Taking a tissue, she began drying her eyes as she sniffled. "Can you please leave?" she asked again.

Arlo readied to exit the room, but felt compelled to walk closer to where she sat. "I wasn't trying to make you cry," he said.

"You did. Goodnight."

"Goodnight," he sighed.

❧

SITTING out on the balcony as the full moon glistened over the area, Elonnie relaxed. Though dark, she could hear the trickling of the Malachi Brook in the distance, which offered a calming atmosphere after the argument she and Arlo had earlier that evening. From inside, she heard her door open, followed by the sound of her husband's voice quietly calling for her. She readied to answer, but instead thought that if she didn't, he might think she had run away. Let him panic for a moment, if he would even care.

"Elonnie, it's late and it's cold out here," Arlo said, peeking out at her.

She sighed—he'd found her. "I'm aware," she replied.

"It's, erm, it's quite all right to be sensitive," he told her.

Turning her head to him, she gave a confused look. "Pardon?"

"I mean I didn't mean to tell you that earlier. I didn't mean to tell you not to be sensitive. I just heard it often and so...anyway, I suppose that would only apply to us men, so having only brothers, I'm not so used to handling women and their feelings."

"That does not apply to men, either, Arlo," Elonnie said, now understanding what he was trying to say.

Arlo looked at the chair across from hers and nodded at it. "May I?" he asked.

Elonnie nodded and he sat down. "You're not dressed for bed," she said.

"No, I wasn't quite finished with work," he replied.

"It's good to stop working every now and then. Maybe that would allow you to have fun every once in a while."

"Maybe," Arlo shrugged. "But one must not be so lax."

"And one must not be so severe."

When things got quiet, the sound of the brook kept things from being awkward. Arlo looked at Elonnie, who stared up at the star-filled sky, then watched as she wrapped her arms around herself when the wind blew. He stood, removed his jacket, and placed it around her before resting his hands on her shoulders. "I'll try not to do that again, Elonnie," he promised. "I never had any desire to make you —or anyone, for that matter—cry like that." He kissed her cheek and returned inside the house.

Elonnie couldn't hold back a smile as she snuggled into the warm jacket and returned her attention to the sky.

Dix-huit

May 15th, 1795,

I cannot believe it's been a month since I've been married to Arlie. I feel like the routine is just that—a routine. I've tried to keep things exciting for myself, but it can be hard when all you're expected to do is wake up, stay out of the way, wait for Arlo to return, eat, and go to sleep. Arlie has yet to make himself understandable; he remains quiet and to himself, unless of course he's displeased with me, which is often. I warned him once before that I had no intentions of conforming to the standards he wishes upon me, but I still do try to make him happy; I live with him and so if he's happy, I'm happy, and as much as he'd never admit to it, if I'm happy, he's happy. I'm still so curious about him, especially when I see how he reacts to me in a soft manner, although he tries to wash it away when he does. I caught him once again staring at me, and slowly a smile crept onto his face; he was pleased with what he saw and I know it, though Arlie would die before he would confess to it. Still, he keeps his distance from me, only offering the occasional goodnight *or goodbye kiss if I request it. I think I should try to give him a hug and see how he reacts.*

Anyway, I've planned something special for tonight. All I can hope is that he doesn't throw a tantrum about it—I think the fact that we've been married for a month and we're both still alive is worth celebrating."

Elonnie bared an excited grin as she shut her diary and hurried downstairs to finish the preparation in the library. Taking it all in, she breathed deep; she had set the area up like a campsite, with many floor pillows and blankets in the center of the floor and over the chairs to make a fort. She frowned. This was something she loved to do with Alex, Bella, and Maddie...she missed those kids with all her heart, and her nerves rattled at the thought of Arlo hating the entire setup. She chuckled at the letters she'd receive from Alex and Maddie, of course the grammar and handwriting were far from perfect, but the thought of them thinking of her was enough to keep her going. She took a quick peek out of the window after a loud crash of thunder and frowned—she was never comfortable with people being out during such ugly storms, and Arlo wasn't back yet.

When he did arrive, Elonnie sprinted out of the library to greet him in the entry hall—part of her felt a morsel of uneasiness as she was never sure of where they stood. When she caught sight of him, she gasped; he was drenched, his clothes dripping from the sheets of rain outside, and his scowl was worse than usual, if that was even possible. Seeing how mad he looked, she took a step back, trying to think of the right thing to say. "Erm...good evening."

Arlo looked at her and, to her surprise, his face relaxed, almost as if he was relieved to see her. "Good evening," he quietly replied. "It smells rather lovely in here," he admitted.

"Like what?" she asked, grinning.

"Fruity, like a delicately sweet fragrance?"

She showed a look of pride as she bobbed up and down; walking over to the candle on the shelf, she took hold of it and brought it closer to him. "Pearberry," she explained. "Do you remember the other day when you were frustrated with me for getting wax all over the place? Well, it's because I made this with my own hands, for the special occasion," she bragged, showing him the small candle.

Taking it from her, he smelled it once more and gave a shrug of approval at the scent. "What is a pearberry?" he asked, muddled.

"The scent of this candle," she said, pointing to it.

Arlo sighed, deciding to ignore the nonsense. "What is the special occasion?"

"Do you not know what today is?"

"May fifteenth," he answered.

"Mm-hmm," she nodded. "And that means?" Elonnie asked in a singsong voice as she coyly swayed from side to side with her hands behind her back.

"It should not be raining so aggressively," he gritted, raking back his sopping hair.

Elonnie found his answer amusing; walking over to him, she wrapped her arm around his and led him further into the home. "True," she nodded. "But it's also our anniversary," she said.

"That's not possible," he replied. "It hasn't been a year."

"No, but it's been a month," Elonnie replied. "A whole month."

"That's not an anniversary," he told her.

"I know, Arlie, but I still find it worth celebrating. And so, I intend for us to celebrate it!"

"How so? Dancing in the rain?" Arlo rolled his eyes.

Elonnie's eyes sparkled, ceasing her walking and stepping in front of him. "Arlie, would you?" she gasped.

"Of course not! Does it look like I was happy to be out there?" he complained.

Elonnie breathed a sigh, again wrapping her arm around his. "That wasn't what I had in mind," she told him. "I've made a cake. Your favorite, Grandma's pound cake."

"All due respect to your Grandma, but that is not my favorite cake," he said.

"Then why does it disappear so fast if I'm not eating it, nor are the servants?" she asked.

Arlo sheepishly bit his lip, shifting his eyes to the other side of the room. He freed his arm from hers and stepped away. "I'm drenched, there's no need for you to be also," he told her.

"I was hoping we might be able to have dance in the ballroom...just you and I?"

"I regret to inform you I'm not one for dancing," Arlo responded.

"I thought not," Elonnie said glumly. She returned her gaze to him and gestured towards the stairs. "Please, get into something dry so I can show you the surprise in the library," she instructed.

"What did you do to the library?" he sulked.

"Go dry off before you catch a chill."

"I hope you haven't caused any—" He stepped closer to her, seeing the brass ring he had given her sharing space with the ballet pendant on the necklace around her neck. Half a smile spread his lips. "Look at that," he whispered.

"At what?" Elonnie asked, looking down.

"Nothing," Arlo said. "I'll be right back down."

❧

As THE COUPLE stood at the entrance of the library, Arlo closed his eyes in discontentment while his shoulders dropped; the blankets stretched from one chair to the other, and there must have been about thirty blankets in the room —and beneath them were all the pillows and cushions. "Elonnie," he groaned.

Seeing his displeasure, Elonnie lowered her head; she knew it was hit or miss, but she had rather hoped it would have been something other than what she expected. "It's a fort, Arlo. Have you never had one?" she asked.

"I didn't ask what it was, I know what it is; I've had plenty of forts before, all when I was a *child*," he murmured. "Gladstone and Pritchard made them for me," he stated, his tone altering. Silently, he leaned against a blanket-clad couch. "Always during thunderstorms like this one, when Papa was away. I was frightened he wouldn't come back and they did it to calm me down, while Grandmother would make steamed chocolate...her special recipe." His cheeks dimpled.

Elonnie froze before she swallowed, fearing any sudden movement might murder the soft moment. Arlo was smiling. She watched as his hand gently brushed the blanket over the couch he leaned against, and she mistakenly released a small chirp, feeling her excitement bubbling through.

Arlo turned to look at her, his smile faded. "But that was when I was a kid," he said. "This is child's play, Elonnie. We're past this."

"Just put a little chink in your armor for tonight, Arlo—try to have fun," she begged. "Or at least try to relax."

"Elonnie—"

"When was the last time I asked you for anything?" she questioned in a whimper. "I never do, Arlie, you know that."

Arlo grimaced at the idea, but eventually his scowl softened. "Very well. Just this once," he said.

With that, Elonnie let out a squeal, dashing to him and locking him in an embrace. "Thank you," she told him. She kept him in the hug, just to see how long it would be before he'd remove her or tell her to get off. "Arlie?" she quietly said.

"Hmm?"

"You're awfully soft and cuddly," she giggled.

"Oh, come off it," he scoffed with a pinched expression. He clasped onto her arms and prepared to pry her off of him, but she tightened her grip around his waist.

"Hold on," she encouraged. "Can I ask you a question?"

"I won't necessarily answer, but go on."

"What happened to Mr. Kensington?" she carefully inquired. Silence whispered through the room before she looked up at him to be greeted by a displeased expression.

"I don't think it's your place to ask me that question, Elonnie," he cautioned.

"Forgive me, then, but I would like to know something about him if you don't mind sharing it with me."

"I do mind," he added.

"Why do you fear talking about—"

"I do mind," he decisively repeated.

"All right, then," Elonnie sighed. "I won't push the issue," she promised. "Just please, if you wouldn't mind, I would really appreciate a smile, less tension, and no arguments."

Arlo turned to look at the pillow fort on the library floor and Elonnie could see how hard he was trying to hold back a smile—she could often tell when he was thinking hard on something. He returned his attention to her and then shocked her with an unrequested kiss on the head. Of course, she did everything in her power not to show that she was indeed thrilled, but instead stepped back, giving him a teensy smile. "Get comfortable," she instructed before heading to the kitchen to retrieve the cake.

LYING BESIDE HIM THAT NIGHT, she knew she wanted the answer to her burning questions. And although it was probably close to midnight, she knew for a fact he was awake as he kept tossing and turning, most likely uncomfortable due to her presence. "Arlie, why do you hate me?" she asked.

"What a foolish notion," he replied.

"It's not foolish, nor a notion. It's obvious from the way you speak to me and ignore me and treat me—"

"Did I not just agree to sleep on a library floor for you?"

"I appreciated the act, dear, but it is not necessarily proof of love—or rather, proof of approval, since I know where you stand on the love issue."

Arlo sighed. "You wouldn't understand," he told her.

"Why not?" she asked. "Just tell me."

"I don't hate you," he stated. "I just don't feel we're compatible."

"Why not?"

"We're not."

"Why?"

He sucked his teeth, scoffing. "Because you're a little too childish for my taste."

"How?"

"Right now, you're asking too many questions," he replied. "As a child would."

Elonnie laughed. "I'm trying to annoy you this time, that's all," she told him. "I think you need to stop being so stiff. Or...you could always strangle me where I lay, like Mr. Abernathy did to his wife."

His eyes widened in fear, turning his head to his wife. "Who is Mr. Abernathy?" he asked.

"A fictional work of mine," she yawned, cuddling up to him as she shut her eyes.

"Fictional work?" he asked.

"Mm-hmm. It's a mystery novel; I've been working on it since I arrived at Ravenhill, it's the most perfect setting," she explained with a tiredness in her voice.

"A mystery," he contemplated aloud. "A mystery," he repeated and Elonnie could feel him quietly chuckling. "I think you've spoiled the ending for me, darling," he told her.

Elonnie's eyes popped open. *Darling? Did he mean to say that?* She decided to keep quiet about it, closing her eyes and allowing herself to begin drifting off to sleep.

She knew that Arlo had realized he let the term of endearment slip when she could feel his heart start racing; but there was no going back now. He had already said it. "Erm, why does he kill her?" he asked. "You already told me the culprit, may as well share the motive."

"Because...he needed her..." Elonnie mumbled, falling asleep.

Arlo frowned. Well, he could always find out tomorrow. He prepared to turn over, but looked down at his wife, lying so comfortably on his shoulder. Choosing not to move and wake her, he gently rested his head upon hers, falling asleep.

THE NEXT DAY while sitting at the table, the two continuously exchanged glances at one another. The silence wasn't as awkward as it used to be, but still, each of them was trying to figure out a way to make conversation.

"Erm, you never told me why Mr. Abernathy killed his wife," Arlo finally said.

Elonnie giggled, almost spitting her juice out. She placed her cup down and leaned just a little closer to him. "Her inheritance," she whispered.

"Inheritance," Arlo repeated, sitting back in his chair.

"After her death he was set to inherit 95,000 stire. He'd be set for life. Along with that, they didn't get along like they used to," she explained.

"I see," Arlo nodded. "And do you believe it's possible to fall out of love?"

Elonnie pondered the question for a moment and then shook her head. "No. That's why it's fiction."

Arlo chuckled. *What a naïve girl.* "You know, if I were to die, you'd inherit almost as much as Mr. Abernathy," he told her.

"Ah, perhaps I should strangle you in your sleep," she grinned. She again reached for her cup to take a drink. "It isn't at all possible; you'd be much too strong for me. You could just flip over and strangle me instead. I'd have to do things cleverly...poison, perhaps."

Arlo snorted out a loud laugh, louder than Elonnie had ever heard before, and there were the dimples and the big eyes. "You're not getting ideas, are you? I'm sure I've given you many reasons to *want* to dispose of me, but I humbly beg that you don't."

"I wouldn't; it's much too cruel, and I love your—I love

Grandmother and she'd be awful sad if I were to kill 'the baby,'" she teased.

Arlo blushed, looking forward as his pupils shrank. "Oh, so she's told you about that nickname." He pulled at his collar.

"It's the price of being born last," she shrugged. "I've been branded with it as well. You're not alone."

"It's nice to not be alone," Arlo smiled. His eyes lingered on her for quite some time before she looked up and smiled back at him.

"You know, you're dreadfully handsome when you smile," she told him with caution.

"Really?" he asked and she nodded. "Thank you. I've never heard that before."

"No?" she asked and he shook his head. She snickered, covering her mouth. "They'd have to see it to be able to tell you," she told him. She took a deep breath before she carefully reached to put her hand over his. "It could be good for you to smile more," she encouraged.

"There aren't too many reasons to do so," he grumbled.

"That just depends on how content you are," she advised. "This is why I say it's better to see things like children do," she continued. "A box to you and me is just a piece of refuse in need of discarding, but give Bella a box and she's happy for a long time."

"We're not children."

"But we can learn from them."

After taking a few more moments to study her features, Arlo removed his hand from under hers, stood, gave a slight bow, and readied to exit the dining room. "I'll probably be gone until late tonight, there's no reason for you to wait up for me," he told her.

Elonnie's face clouded over—he had realized he was

softening to her and raised his guard up again. She wanted to plead with him to stay or return sooner, but seeing as progress was already being made, she felt scared she might burn all of it to ashes. "Very well, then," she softly said, resting her cheek in her hand and stirring a spoon around in her tea.

"MAY 16*TH*, 1795,

I have a bad feeling we'll be spinning in circles, Arlie and I; it's almost as if every time he starts to warm up to me, he frightens himself back into his state of being a recluse. I guess I should be overall thankful that he's only quiet and not harsh, but I just wish I could get him to open up and soften. I'm terribly afraid that I might just be starting to grow romantically fond of the man. While I believe that should be a good thing, I can see he doesn't feel the same way about me. Perhaps I could just try to get him to befriend me and then I can focus on romantic attraction."

Elonnie leaped out of her seat and peered out the window; the sun shined over the garden and there was no need for her to remain inside for the entirety of the day. She walked down the lengthy hallway and stopped at the entrance to Arlo's study. Part of her wanted to go in, but she always had the feeling that she wasn't allowed in there; he had never forbidden her from going in, but the way he'd only creep the door open and peek out when she would knock made it pretty obvious that she was not invited there. *How mysterious....* Biting on the knuckle of her index finger, she finally decided to take a peek inside.

She opened the door and snuck in—it was just as any regular study. Made mostly of wood, there were wooden panels for walls and two bookcases built into the wall at the back of the room. There was a roll-top desk in the center with its top open and many a scattered paper upon it. It was a cozy room, a place where it seemed easy to get a lot of work done, as it was far quieter than the rest of the house. There was only one window, which let in a minute amount of lighting, as it was covered by burgundy drapes. But all around the room were covered easels, as if the room was once the studio of an artist. She was curious about what was under the coverings, but her attention was drawn to the desk.

Elonnie walked over to the desk and reached for one of the papers—a letter, to be exact—reading:

"*Dear Father,*

I am once again trying to write this letter and it remains impossible. I want to apologize to you in so many ways, but then I'd have to realize that I've made a grave error and—"

Hearing the door creak, Elonnie gasped, popping her head up and seeing Constance in the doorway. "Child, what do you think you're doing?" she asked, her blue eyes big and worried.

"Oh, erm, I was curious about the study and I—" Elonnie ceased in her speech at seeing Constance shaking her head.

"Lord Kensington wants no one in the study, not even his wife," she warned before waving her hand. "Come now, I won't say a word."

Elonnie felt paralyzed with fear as her mind now decided to come to conclusions. She peeked down at the letter in her hands then back up at Constance.

"Come along," Constance said.

Elonnie dropped the letter back onto the desk and scurried out of the room. "I wasn't trying to pry," she assured. "I just assumed that since he never told me not to go in there, and since he said I was welcomed to go anywhere in the house, that—"

"No need to worry." Constance gave her an encouraging smile. "The secret is safe with me. And now you know."

Following a few steps behind Constance, Elonnie's eyes narrowed on the carpet; she kept quiet before looking up at the older woman. "Does Arlie talk much about Mr. Kensington—his father, that is?" she asked.

"No," Constance sighed.

"If I might ask, when did he pass away?"

"The twenty-fifth of this month will make it five years ago," Constance said, clearly saddened by the thought of Mr. Kensington's passing.

"I hope this isn't an ugly sort of question, but did Arlie get along with him well?" she asked, biting her lip in fear of how Constance might respond to such an inquiry.

Constance stopped walking, tilting her head to the side as she turned to face her with a confused look. "Of course," she replied. "It's rare for a son to not get along with his father, wouldn't you agree?"

"Yes," Elonnie nodded, forcing a smile. "I'm sorry for asking such a silly question," she told her. "Thank you for watching out for me," she added, and then proceeded to head to her room.

❧

MAY 20TH, 1795,

It seems as if Arlo might know I went into his study, yet he hasn't said a word about it. I feel that he would surely grow cross if he were to find out, which causes me to doubt that he does know. But still, he's once again reverted to his standoffish state, only ever saying anything to me if I initiate the conversation, and the occasional goodbye or goodnight kiss when requested.

I can't help but wonder about his letter to his father. Why was he sorry and what grave error could he have possibly made? It couldn't be time to think like Inspector Lysander, could it? Or am I being ridiculous?

Other than that, the keen analyses have continued and I can't understand why he concentrates so much on me, sometimes even having the boldness to not look away when I catch him. But I suppose I should be flattered, as this could be his way of telling me he appreciates my appearance."

Unsure of what else to write, Elonnie brushed the feathers of her pen along her cheek before finally putting it and her diary away. She reached for her mail and cheeped joyfully at seeing a letter from Genevieve. It read,

"DEAREST ELONNIE,

I am thrilled to hear that the baby hasn't been giving you the hardest of times. Below is the recipe you requested:

One cup of boiled milk.

Two tablespoons of melted chocolate.

A pinch of cinnamon.

The scrapings of one vanilla bean pod.

I trust that this will come out just as good as mine, if not better, and I'm extremely excited to read this mystery you've told me about.

Your friend and grandmother,

Genevieve."

Excitedly, Elonnie dashed into the kitchen, where she was welcomed by the working staff. She was prepared to try her hand at the recipe before Arlo's return. Her excitement died out a little as she thought of him. Today he hadn't told her much of anything, he'd just left, not even giving her an idea of when he might be back. However, she wouldn't dwell on the negative things. Surely the chocolate drink from his childhood would soften him, no matter what mood he might be in.

Dix-neuf

Elonnie paced back and forth in the music room, walking around the black grand piano in the center and reading a letter from her family as she bit on her thumbnail. Closing the letter, she looked around the room, which happened to now be filled with the golden glow of the sunset's light. It poured through the giant windows that made up the walls of the area and twinkled across the marble floor—she resented the fact that not much time was spent in the music room.

Sitting on the piano bench and staring over to the giant harp in the right corner of the room; she wondered if Arlo had ever even played one of these instruments or whether or not they were just there for show, like she felt she was. She opened the letter again and reread it; a new ballet was being put on by the family, and she felt as if she hadn't performed in ages. Of course she wanted to accept the originating role, and she believed that Arlo wouldn't care; it would be starting in Warencia, a country south of them, and she'd be staying there for a few months and then she'd return. He barely saw her anyway and often reminded her that this was only a practical arrangement, not one from love, so why would he say no?

Hearing his arrival, she ran out of the music room, through the library, and into the entry hall where he was now standing. She wouldn't just jump into asking him—first, she'd get him comfortable, have the lovely pearberry candle burning, and then she would offer him the steamed chocolate and that would sweeten him up to say yes.

"Good evening, darling," she curtsied.

"Evening," he replied, not offering much insight on his mood through his facial expressions. He reached into his jacket pocket, retrieving a small box and handing it out to her. "I, well, a little girl was selling these little hazelnut chocolates and I figured you may—seeing as you love sugar so much—I thought you might like them," he told her.

Elonnie grinned, her heart warming at the idea that he'd been thinking of her. "Thank you!" she said with delight, taking the box and licking her lips at the tiny chocolates inside. "I will like them. Erm, please, sit and get comfortable; I've made something special for you," she told him.

"Special?" he asked.

"Yes," Elonnie nodded.

"Consumable?" he inquired.

"Why, of course," a confused Elonnie giggled.

"Hmm," Arlo said, "judging by our conversation a few days ago, something makes me wary about what food or drink you might offer me."

"Oh, Arlie, don't be silly," Elonnie giggled. "If you wouldn't mind, I'd like for you to take a seat in the tearoom with me," she continued, offering an elbow.

"What's the issue? You're acting quite different," Arlo recognized.

"No issue, my dear," Elonnie shook her head as she

walked him to the tearoom. She had him sit and then took the seat beside him before pouring the comforting drink into his cup.

Instantly, he recognized the aroma and he blinked his twinkling eyes. "Did you—"

Elonnie grinned, nodding her head. "I do hope you like it," she breathed. "I got the recipe from Grandmother, do try it!"

Arlo swallowed. There was no way this would taste like his grandmother's; and knowing Elonnie, she had probably added four cups of sugar to the mixture. "W-what's in it?" he cautiously asked.

Elonnie laughed. "I just followed the recipe, Arlie," she assured.

Arlo peeked into the cup and then sipped it. It wasn't nasty, but it still wasn't his grandmother's; perhaps that was only because she wasn't his grandmother. "Thank you," he told her.

"Well, do you like it?" she nervously chuckled.

"Yes," he nodded.

Elonnie jumped, startled that she had received a simple 'yes' for possibly the first time. "I'm glad to hear that," she beamed. "Erm, Arlo, can I ask you something?"

"Oh boy," Arlo sighed, sitting back in the chair and crossing his legs.

"Actually, read this," she told him, handing him the letter from her family.

For a moment, Arlo kept his eyes on her, then read the letter—Elonnie focused attentively on his reactions to see if she could gauge what he might say. "What are you showing me?" he asked, green eyes moving up from the letter and over to her.

"Did you read it?"

"Yes. Are you asking if you can go to Warencia for a few months?" he asked.

Elonnie gulped. "Mm-hmm," she nodded.

"How is that appropriate?"

"I beg your pardon?" She scowled.

"Would it be appropriate for me to leave you for a few months despite the fact that we're married?" he inquired.

"You leave me every day, sometimes without a word or even a hint of where you might be going, and you're talking about inappropriate?" She stood up. "Arlo, since I've been here I haven't ever been treated as a wife. Just a girl who lives with you—you treat me no differently from the staff, only you ordered that I don't do any work around here! It feels as if I haven't performed in ages, and I would really like to."

"Elonnie, I just gave you a gift," he reminded her. "And you say I just treat you like someone who lives here?"

"Oh, Arlo, surely you don't believe that that's what makes one feel like a marriage mate," she groaned.

"Look," he said, standing up and looking down at her. "You showed me this to ask me and I'm telling you no. Is that clear?"

"No, that's not fair at all," Elonnie replied.

"You asked me and I gave you an answer," he reiterated. "If your plan was to disregard that or argue, then why did you ask in the first place?"

"Because I wanted to show you the proper respect," she replied.

"All right, then the matter is settled. No."

Elonnie took a deep breath, turning her back to him. "If that's the case, can you please stop neglecting me?" she asked, facing him again.

"Neglect?" Arlo chuckled. "You are not neglected, Elonnie."

"If I wasn't here, you'd be going about your business the way you are now—how is a few months apart inappropriate? It's literally what life is now, only you're the one who's doing something they like, while I'm here doing nothing!"

"You can go out; I've shown you the city, that's on you. Other than that, you already know how I feel about all the silly shows your family puts on. I don't want—"

"Silly shows?" she squealed, annoyed. "Arlo Darcy Kensington, how dare you?"

Arlo lifted the card up to read it, "'Premise: a faerie princess meets a dark-hearted rogue and through magic and dance she shows him the bright side of life.' What kind of nonsense is that? What is a faerie princess?" He pointed his finger at her, taking a step closer. "Your name is *Kensington* now. Meaning what you do reflects back to me." Tossing the card down on the side table, his eyes locked in on hers. "Other than that, who plays the rogue?" he interrogated. "Not me and, quite frankly, I don't want some other man's hands on *my* wife."

"Maybe he could teach you a thing or two," Elonnie sassed, shifting her eyes over to the fireplace.

Clearly affronted at the comment, Arlo grabbed her by the arms and pulled her closer to him. "What will it take for you to watch your mouth?" he hissed.

"Oh, this is the closest we've ever been," Elonnie continued in her cheeky tone. "Now unhand me!" She pulled away and stepped back. "Who are you to tell me I can't go? Suppose I decide to leave when you're gone one day? You wouldn't have the slightest clue, and when you finally realize I'm missing, *if you do,* you wouldn't even care!"

"I'm far too exhausted to put up with your disrespect," he complained.

"Aren't you always," Elonnie growled.

He handed her the cup of the drink she made. "Next time, try dark chocolate instead of milk if you want it to taste like Grandmother's," he insulted.

"You are just plain ill-mannered and rude," she snapped, slamming the cup down onto the side table. "I won't try to do anything nice for you anymore. I hope you're happy with yourself; you truly are spoiled rotten, trop relou! I won't go, I'll stay here and just be absolutely miserable, since that's what you want!"

"You're choosing to be miserable, please don't accuse me of being the issue. No one told you to stay here and bake and scribble nonsense into your notebook all day; these are all choices you've made on your own," Arlo huffed. "Go out, go make some friends in the area or something. You act as if you don't have a massive home with an entire ballroom for you to dance in, or a library with thousands of books! Let's not forget that the whole reason you agreed to this was because you'd get to come to Ravenhill—and now, after a short while, you're tired of it?"

"That's not the point, Arlo. Do you really have to be so clueless?"

"Then what is the point? You want to work? Then try to find meaningful work, nothing childish and outlandish, please. Once again, you asked me for permission to go to Warencia and I am not giving it to you; now stop acting like a child and play your role right!"

"I was just trying to do us both a favor by getting out of your way," Elonnie whimpered and stormed out of the tearoom.

"Elonnie!" Arlo called and the girl ignored him. He sat

down again and sighed, running his hand through his hair and sitting back.

Constance approached and stood at the entrance of the room. "Now what have you done?" she asked.

Arlo responded with a groan.

"I see," Constance nodded. She took the seat beside him and faced him. "Arlo, why did you react like that?" she asked.

"I don't think it's right that a wife should leave her husband for months," he replied.

"Is that it? Is that all?" she asked, leaning her head to the side.

"Gladstone and Pritchard would be steaming if they found out that we were separated—and what about all my friends? Surely, I'd be the talk of the town if they were to find out my wife left me," he rambled.

"So, this is more about your pride than it is about Elonnie's feelings?" Constance questioned, crossing her leg.

"And if it is?" he asked.

"Or,"—She stood and paced the room, stopping in front of the fireplace to look at the portrait of his parents. —"do you not like the idea of coming home and she's not here?" She peeked back at him.

"Well, it would be inappropriate," he repeated, crossing his arms defiantly.

"Inappropriate for you to miss her so much?" Constance laughed.

"Steady on." Arlo stood. "This is about practicality and you know that, Miss Constance."

"All right, if you insist," Constance shrugged. "But you should understand that you may well lose her soon, and not just for a few months, if you refuse to humble yourself already." She left the baron in the room alone and once more he took his seat.

Arlo reached for the cup with the steamed chocolate and ran his finger around the rim of it—perhaps he could have handled that matter much differently; after all, it seemed she had gone out of her way to do something nice for him. And even though it was milk chocolate and not dark chocolate, it was the thought that counted. He looked out the windows and saw the ember glow of evening approaching. Maybe he could try his hand at doing something nice for her.

❧

THAT NIGHT as Elonnie sat at her vanity detangling her hair in preparation for bed, she heard a knock at the door. "Come in," she called. She couldn't avoid the mixed feelings stirring through her when she saw her husband standing there. Oddly, she felt slightly pleased to see him, but at the same time, fearful. Now what did she do wrong? Coupled with those feelings was anger; the way he had spoken to her earlier was unacceptable. "Yes?" she quietly said.

Arlo walked closer to her and placed a flat, medium box on the vanity. "I, erm, earlier I suppose I was a tad too aggressive. And, I, uh, well, I stepped out for a moment and when I saw this I thought you might like it," he told her.

Elonnie looked at the box and then at him. "What is it?" she inquired.

"You'll have to open it," he said.

Elonnie obeyed, opening the box to see a lovely blue dress with long sleeves and white and yellow floral decorations. Her jaw dropped; with grateful eyes she looked up at him, jumping from her seat and taking it out of the box to hold it up against her. "Oh, Arlo!" she gasped. "Look how gorgeous!" She spun towards the mirror, and her face scrunched with delight. "Help me try it on!" she requested, removing her dressing gown.

Initially, he panicked, ready to turn away, but he quickly remembered that they were bound in wedlock.

She donned the blue day dress and was very delighted at how it fit. "I love it," she breathed. She did her best not to show just how excited she was, otherwise he might regret having given her the gift. "M-May I give you a kiss?" she asked.

Arlo shifted his eyes down, contemplating the request. "Yes," he said.

Elonnie raised to the balls of her feet to give him a soft and quick kiss. "Thank you for this, darling," she said. She visibly saddened as she looked down and turned away. "Arlo, I don't want things to be like this," she said. "I can't express how much I appreciate this gift, but I don't want you to think it's all right for you to speak to me so harshly, so long as you make up for it with a present."

"Of course not," Arlo replied. "Elonnie, I know that was wrong, I just don't know how to fix it. It's not that I was trying to hurt your feelings or anything, I only—"

"Tell me you're sorry," Elonnie requested, "and mean it."

"Did I not make it clear that I was when I—"

"Say it."

"I am sorry," he uttered.

Elonnie stood there quietly; she knew it was a struggle for him to humble himself, still, he needed to do it. "I forgive you," she told him. "And I feel I should apologize as well."

"No need, you've done nothing wrong." Arlo smiled as he headed to the door. "I'll let you go to sleep," he told her after opening the door. He shut it back and his eyes traveled over to her—he had no plan to divorce her; he needed to accept that she would be around for quite a while. 'Til death do they part' was what he had promised. "Elonnie?" he asked.

"Yes?"

He took a deep breath, looking as if he was having an internal battle in his head. Finally, he took her face in his hands and kissed her lips—a kiss like he had never given her before...one might mistake it for true love, if not careful. Elonnie's brown eyes shimmered when he let her go.

"I...a hidden talent you have there," she laughed. "Be a little more generous with those."

"You...would you—I would like for you to stay with me tonight. Perhaps you should stay with me from now on... considering," he said.

"Is that what you really want?" she chirped.

"Yes," he nodded. "Yes, I do," he stated, offering his hand.

Elonnie smiled shyly and prepared to accept his hand. Slowly, her smile faded and she retreated her hand. Did she anger him so much that he was considering strangling her in bed like Mr. Abernathy?

"Is something wrong?" Arlo asked.

Realizing how silly it was, Elonnie chuckled and finally took his hand. "Nothing," she said.

Vingt

When Elonnie awakened, she blinked open her eyes and set them on Arlo. Shocked to see him still home even though it was most likely after six, her eyes grew big. He hadn't really noticed her; he seemed far too busy scribbling something in a leather-bound journal. Elonnie raised onto her elbows and tried to see what he was doing, but he swiftly shut the book and she jumped. "What are you doing?" she asked.

"When did you wake up?" Arlo asked.

"Just a moment ago," she replied, resting her head on his lap. "Can I see what you were writing?" she requested. She smiled at feeling his fingers gently twisting around in her hair.

"No. You can get up and get dressed, we're going somewhere."

Excitedly, she leaped out of bed and fixed her eyes on him. "Going somewhere? Where?" she asked.

"You'll see," he replied.

Elonnie squealed, getting the feeling that this would be the best day ever—she hurried to the washroom door and as she prepared to open it, Arlo called her. "Yes?" she turned to him.

"Are you really miserable here?" he asked.

Elonnie looked down as she held her hands together; the tone in his voice sounded like genuine concern and the look on his face appeared gloomy, as if her answer truly mattered to him. "Of course not," she shook her head. "I love Ravenhill, but that's not the only reason I accepted this arrangement," she assured.

The answer pleased Arlo, and that was made evident by the smile he gave, showing his dimples, though he tried to make it a little less obvious. "Very well," he nodded, and Elonnie headed into the washroom.

❦

ON SUCH A SUNNY morning as this one, it felt strange for Elonnie to see very few people strolling about. But the city was more of a business city, and so on a weekday, surely everyone was working. And even though it was always nice to see many people out enjoying the beautiful spring days, Elonnie appreciated the feeling of it just being her and Arlo. Carefully, she slid closer to him and he quickly peeked over at her before returning his attention to the road. "Yes?" he asked, noticing the look on her face.

"Arlie, would you shy away from me again if I told you...?" she started before turning away from him.

"If you told me what?" he probed, bracing for whatever might come out of her mouth.

"If I told you I was growing fonder of you?"

Arlo's hands tightened around the reins and he appeared to lock his teeth together— Elonnie couldn't tell if he was cringing at the idea of her falling in love with him or if he were fighting with all his strength to keep from grinning. She hoped it was the latter, but he did a great job at keeping himself unreadable. Clearing his throat, he adjusted himself to sit straighter and kept his eyes on the road. "That's not all bad," he told her. "After all, it's better that we get along, isn't it?"

Elonnie smiled, sitting back. "Yes, it is," she replied.

As the carriage arrived at the location, Elonnie tried to hide the fact that she wasn't entirely pleased with the choice. The large white building gave off the aura that it wasn't much of an exciting place on the inside, with its giant pedestals and lack of decoration. "The Museum of Art and History?" her voice cracked.

"I think you'll enjoy it; you haven't even given it a chance, Elonnie," Arlo sighed.

"I'm not against art, but I'm not one with a mind for history," Elonnie laughed.

"Except pirates," Arlo stated.

"Except pirates," Elonnie agreed. She started out of the carriage, but again sat back, deciding that she would wait for Arlo to come around and assist her out.

They walked into the establishment; it's not that it wasn't a beautiful place, but it was quiet. Too quiet. Even with at least ten other couples in the room, it was almost as if one was forbidden to speak in such an area. The only sounds were the footsteps that gently walked across the gold marble floor.

All the white walls made it feel like only the pure belonged, but the bland colors that around the building were surely to heighten the attention on the art. There was canvas after canvas and statue after statue, hand-carved and hand-painted. Elonnie knew much work was put into each design and so she had no desire to complain about the artworks, although they did seem quite simple. She turned to the canvas that had nothing aside from a black splotch casted on it. She turned her nose up, not with disdain, but with perplexity—maybe this painting meant something deep, or perhaps it meant nothing at all. "'1701, Arnie Langford, The Black Day,'" she read the card beside the painting.

"It's a story of a mother losing her only son in death. It's something that no one should feel and that not many can understand," Arlo explained.

Elonnie looked at the card that only had the name of the piece, the year it was painted, and the artist's name listed on it. Then she turned to Arlo. "How do you know that?" she asked.

"That's my interpretation of it," he told her. "That's the beauty of art museums and paintings, you have to interpret it yourself."

"And you truly think that's what it means?" Elonnie held back a giggle. Her face straightened. "That's not to say I think little of your interpretation, I just wish you wouldn't interpret it so sadly." Elonnie bit her lip and turned to the painting. "I think it's different," she told him. "I think it's a rain cloud, and he's preparing to make a rainbow. Despite the fact that some may think a black day means something bad, it means something good, because you can only see rainbows after dark days," she concluded.

"Of course you read it that way," Arlo sighed. He turned away from The Black Day and set his sights on another artwork, one made from clay, sculpted into the shape of a head. The mouth was wide open as if it screamed and the eyes were missing, with red paint smeared down to the cheeks. "What about this one?" he asked. There was no way she could make this one into a charming fairytale.

"Hmm," Elonnie thought. "He's singing," she stated. "He may not have the gift of sight, so he takes advantage of his gift of speech to sing songs of joy."

"His eyes were ripped from their sockets, it looks like. I don't think he's singing."

"I know he is. They cannot defeat him, as hard as they try. He can still see the light in things, which happens to be represented by the red, even when blind."

"Elonnie Mary, where on earth would you get an idea like that?" Arlo laughed, a little too loud, resulting in quick glares from the others around them. "This is called *Weeping Red,* it's not positive."

"Anything can be if you make it," Elonnie affirmed confidently as she turned away from him. Her eyes sparkled at seeing a painting of a sunset over a horizon. She gasped in awe before snatching his hand and rushing over to it. "*Sunset,*" she read in a dreamy tone. She looked up at Arlo. "What do you think this one means?"

"It means that everything must come to its end," Arlo replied.

Elonnie's lips formed a pout. "Oh, must you be so dreary?" she asked. "No, it simply shows how the world is connected by that wonderful golden sphere of energy, and once it's traded places with the moon, it's simply watching over another part of the world," she explained.

Arlo smiled down at her, although she didn't see him—it was one of *those* smiles, the ones when you're unaware that you're doing it. Coming to his senses, he pointed to a painting on the other side of the room and guided her to it. "What about her?" he asked.

Elonnie's head tilted to the side as she analyzed the painting of a girl curled into a corner of a room, with golden tears in her eyes and her arms wrapped around her knees. "Hmm," she said.

Arlo smirked—she couldn't make the best of this one and she knew it. He wasn't sure if he wanted to stump her, or if he wanted to see if she could really make everything positive.

After a moment of considering the artwork, Elonnie blinked her eyes. "She's heartbroken because someone she keeps trying to please is displeased with her," she quietly said. "But the tears she cries are tears of gold; this is a sign that the good within her is going to cause her to have a happily ever after."

Arlo's face softened, looking at the painting once more. She was still able to find a good outlook for the sad-looking circumstance, but was she speaking of her own situation? "I don't think anyone is displeased with her," he said. "Who would be displeased with someone who cries gold?"

"Many," Elonnie replied.

"I think she's selfish."

"What?" Elonnie gasped.

"She's selfish and money-loving, and so she's been cursed to cry gold and be lonely for the rest of her life and wallow in her selfishness."

"She is not selfish, Arlo!"

"Shhh," Arlo instructed after they received more glares. "Why does she mean so much to you?" he prodded.

"Because she's a victim, trying to make the best of her situation, and you're calling her selfish," Elonnie replied.

The girl had taken it personally. She did see herself as the girl in the painting. Did she really think that he was displeased with her, as hard as she tried to please him? He looked at the painting again and then at Elonnie. Well, it wasn't as if he hadn't always criticized every little thing she did, and it wasn't like he didn't leave for hours without her and then expect her to make the best of that. "I changed my interpretation," he told her.

"You can't do that," Elonnie replied.

"Where is that law written?" he inquired before turning back to the drawing. "I think she has much commendation and sweet things to offer. But she doesn't know how to, you see; she would like to tell someone plainly that she thinks they look especially beautiful today, and that she does, in fact, enjoy the pleasure of their company. But she doesn't know how to do that, because something is frightening her away from doing so," he said.

Elonnie looked up at him. "What is frightening her?" she asked.

"She's unsure," he sullenly replied. They both returned their gazes to the painting of the crying woman, and then Arlo pulled Elonnie away towards the exit. "I think that's enough for today, wouldn't you agree?" he said. "I'm sure I've bored you long enough."

Vingt-un

"*M*ay 25th, 1795.

I think it's possible that Arlie might just be falling in love with me; although, I still get the sense that he's fighting with himself not to. Sometimes he finds himself softening too much and then he raises his guard again and starts to act stoic and dreary. As for the stares, I noticed that the way he looks at me is the same way he studied the art in the museum the other day. He's trying to read me, but I don't understand why he doesn't just ask what he desires to know, surely, I would tell him. Perhaps he's trying to learn something about me that I, myself, am unaware of. Maybe I should study him just the same...after all, he has been strange as of the 20th, like something is bothering him, and this time I don't believe it's me."

Lying on the floor of her former room, Elonnie looked up from her diary and rested her cheek in her hand; she readied to write again, but the door creaking open caught her by surprise. She gasped, turning to see Arlo standing in the doorway. "Oh, hi," she smiled, turning back and closing her diary.

"Hi," Arlo replied. "I was, erm, I was looking all over for you," he told her—she could hear his voice almost trembling.

"Is everything all right?" she asked, now shuffling a deck of cards.

Arlo walked into the room, standing over her before lying down on her back. Elonnie's eyebrow raised at his strange behavior. She tried not to laugh, as she wasn't sure what was going on with him at the moment. "Everything is...as it often is," he told her.

"What does that mean?"

Arlo gulped, laying his head on her shoulder and wrapping his arms around her. "It isn't horrid, but it isn't great either."

"Arlie, what's the matter?" Elonnie asked, concern in her tone. Arlo kissed her shoulder. Then she felt him messing around with her springy hair. "Arlo, tell me what's wrong," she said, feeling at her hair. "What is that? What did you put in my hair?" she giggled.

"A hairbow," he said.

"A hairbow?" she squealed. "Let me see it!"

He removed the blue satin bow from her hair and put it on the floor in front of them. "I just saw it when I was out and it made me think of...well, in some ways I thought perhaps it might be something you would like," he shrugged.

Elonnie's eyes sparkled, staring at the gift. "Oh, Arlie, how thoughtful," she whispered.

"You like it, then?" he asked.

"Of course I do," she replied.

"Good," Arlo said, putting it back in her hair and lying his head back down.

"But something is really bothering you," she said. "Tell

me what it is and I won't say a word to anyone else. It's all right to be vulnerable, Arlo."

"I'm not vulnerable, I'm only exhausted," he defended.

Elonnie sighed, giving thought to her reply. "Did something happen today?"

"No."

"Do you need anything, darling?"

Arlo sighed. "Just peace," he replied.

Elonnie prepared to say something, but she returned her attention to her cards, baring a tiny smile. *Did he really go to her to find peace?* She reached her hand back and gave his head a gentle rub. "Then I'll keep silent," she said, now beginning to arrange her card game. She glanced ahead at the crackling fireplace and couldn't help but wonder why Arlo was so down—then she remembered. May 25th was Mr. Kensington's death anniversary. Her eyes glistened a little as she was about to question him on it, but instead, she left it alone. If Arlo wanted to talk about it, he would have, and his taking comfort in her presence was enough. "Are you comfortable?" she asked.

"Mm-hmm. Am I heavy?"

"Dreadfully," Elonnie giggled.

Arlo groaned as he rolled off of her; he propped himself up on his elbows and watched as she placed the cards down one by one.

"Would you care to join me?" she asked.

"What is it?"

"Day and Night," she explained, "you have to match each card to its opposite."

"For example?"

"Day and night," she said with a laugh, pointing to the cards picturing the daytime and the nighttime. "Winter and summer, fire and water, and so on. Whoever gets the most matches wins the game. It can just as easily be played alone if it doesn't seem your type of game," she said. She looked at Arlo—whose dark green eyes were fixed intently on her while his hand now gently rubbed her back—then shyly bit her lip, turning her attention back to the game.

"I actually would like to play," he quietly said.

Facing him a second time, her eyes brightened. "Really?"

"That is, if you don't mind?"

"Arlie, I would love it if you did. Since it's two of us, we have to roll the die to see how many chances we get," she said as she cheerily reached for the white and black die. "It will be one, two, three, or four turns; then you flip two cards around to see if it matches. Quite simple."

Arlo used his finger to move a dangling curl behind her ear before sliding closer to her. "Ladies first," he told her.

Elonnie rolled the die. "Two chances," she beamed. She flipped a card that had the illustration of a baby on it. "All right, what do you think I should look for to match?"

"Gravestones," Arlo replied.

"Arlie..." Elonnie frowned.

"Life and death, no?" he asked. "That's a genuine question."

"No, Arlo. I need to find the old man. Young and old."

"Oh."

"Lord Dreary," she teased. Her eyes met his and she offered him a smile. "But what would day be without night?"

"Lonely, broken, and disheartened...night without day, anyway," he said, a sadness in his eyes as they traveled over the cards.

Elonnie blinked, wondering if he was referring to himself as night and her as day. She caressed his face with her hand and then flipped another card. "Oh, darn," she sighed at having turned over the sea card. "Well, I have one more chance." Flipping another card, she found the inside card. She pouted her lips and turned it back over. "Your turn," she told him.

Arlo's cheeks slightly dimpled while his eyes lingered on her. "I appreciate your face," he told her.

"Pardon?" Elonnie laughed.

"Your face. I appreciate it."

"Oh, Arlie, the way you say things," Elonnie sighed. "For what it's worth, I find you just as attractive," she told him.

He reached for the die and then kissed her cheek.

Vingt-deux

Joyfully, Elonnie ran out of the home and raced towards the arriving guest. Reaching Genevieve, she threw her arms around the woman and locked her arm around hers. "It's always such a pleasure to see you, Grandmother," she beamed. "And I have so much more to tell you."

"The excitement in your face gives me the impression that perhaps my grandson isn't behaving as headstrong as he so often does," Genevieve said.

"Arlie and I have become more than friends, that's for certain," Elonnie replied. She clutched tighter to Genevieve's arm. "I only hope that doesn't wear off, as is the habit with him. He'll warm up to me, and let his guard down, and then once he realizes it, again he enters his state of detached behavior."

"Oh, that boy," Genevieve sighed.

"But I mustn't bring you down with such bleak talk," Elonnie told her. "Because even though he seems to grow distant at times, it never compares to how we started out, and for that I'm grateful. Though he's awfully cryptic with his compliments, he gives them out more than he did previously."

"Arlo has never been the best at sharing his feelings—I'm sure you've come to know a little more about Mr. Kensington?" Genevieve asked.

"Well, not really," Elonnie replied. "He's more of a topic Arlo tries to stay away from."

A gentle pat on the hand assured Elonnie that Genevieve understood her feelings. "Mr. Kensington was an interesting man. He was everything that a head should be; very good to my daughter as well as their children, and even myself," she told her. "But he could have been a little warmer, and I believe he was becoming just a little warmer right before his passing," she said. She and Elonnie took a seat in the courtyard. "Feelings were something he felt best kept within, though; not that he didn't love his family, he did, and showed them that in many ways. Only...I think we all could use a little more work when it comes to expressing our love for one another."

"I agree," Elonnie breathed. More of it began to make sense now. Arlo was generous when it came to gifts; it was almost as if that was his way of showing feelings. While that wasn't all bad, it would be nice to hear simple sayings like: I'm sorry, I was thinking about you, and of course, I love you.

"When you meet his other grandparents, then I think you'll understand him more, and more about his father," Genevieve told her. The look in her blue eyes made it evident that this wasn't something she'd want to look forward to.

Vingt-trois

From the hallway window, Constance watched as Elonnie practiced her ballet by the Malachi Brook. She giggled at the fact that the young lady just couldn't resist spending time in or near the water, and then she jumped, hearing that the master had entered the estate. He was earlier than usual. The woman lifted the skirt of her dress and hurried down the stairs to greet him in the entry hall. "Lord Kensington, whatever are you doing home?" she asked.

"I know it's early, but I have guests with me. Where's my wife?" he asked.

"Guests?" Constance inquired.

Just then, two more entered the building; one was a woman with a pompous look on her face, and although she was fairly smaller than Constance herself, with how high she held her head, she looked as if she was looking down on her. The man had the same superior look as his wife, his more of the puckered brow they'd often see on Arlo. Both of them, although well into their seventies, managed to keep themselves looking healthy and strong.

Their clothing was the finest in all of North Indigo, similar to that of royalty, wearing simple but elegant cream colors and black accents. Their bright white hair shined radiantly upon their heads and the woman's blue eyes complemented it, as did the man's green eyes.

Constance gulped. His grandparents were here, most likely to meet Elonnie, and Elonnie was exactly where she shouldn't have been.

"Constance?" Arlo repeated, his voice slightly cracking. It was almost bizarre to see him shook up. "My wife?"

"She's, erm, well, I haven't seen her recently," she lied. She knew how Mr. and Mrs. Kensington would react to finding Elonnie in a brook dancing ballet.

"Odd," Arlo said quietly. He gently placed his hand upon Constance's shoulder and nodded over to his grandparents. "Keep them company for me, will you?" he requested and then started up the stairs.

"Wait! Lord Kensington, why don't I go find her?" Constance suggested.

"No, that won't be necessary," Arlo assured.

Mrs. Kensington cleared her throat, grabbing Constance's attention; she pursed her lips, examining the woman, and took a step forward. "A pleasure as always, Miss Constance," she said.

"Likewise, Madam Kensington," Constance curtsied.

❦

"ELONNIE!" Arlo continued searching the home, but she was nowhere to be found, and he was sure that his grandparents were already getting impatient. He now realized that she had to be in the ballroom, practicing her ballet.

Hurrying down the hall to the ballroom, he walked into

the spacious area—to his surprise, she wasn't in there either. "Elonnie?" he mumbled defeatedly. He prepared to leave the ballroom until he saw what he could see out the window, a figure dancing in the Malachi Brook. Now? When his overly uptight grandparents were here? She was doing this now? His shoulders dropped. "Elonnie, why do you do this to me?" he grumbled.

As he returned down the stairs, Constance could see in his face that he had found Elonnie. He forced a smile, reaching the final step, and turned to Mr. and Mrs. Kensington. "Might I request that you and Grandfather wait in the tearoom for Lady Kensington and I?" he said, taking his grandmother's hand and then kissing it. "I'll be right with you. And this is kind of a surprise for Elonnie, otherwise, I trust she would have been ready."

"Hmm," Mrs. Kensington groaned. She wrapped her arm around the arm of her husband and they followed Constance to the tearoom.

◦◦◦

ELONNIE RESTARTED her routine for the second time and as she whipped into a pirouette, she saw Arlo go by and almost fell out of the turn. "Arlie!" she warbled.

"Elonnie, why are you doing this?" Arlo sighed.

"I thought you wouldn't be home until later," she panicked. "I usually—"

"What do you mean by that?" Arlo interjected. "And you usually what? Disobey my orders? Because I told you not to swim in the brook!" he snapped.

"I'm not swimming. I was practicing my dance. I didn't even get into the water," she lied.

"Why, then, are you soaking wet?" he asked. "Never

mind, there's not much time to discuss this," he told her. "Come inside and dry off," he ordered, pulling her out of the water and into the home. He was clutching tightly to a soaking Elonnie as he snuck past the tearoom and up the stairs. He could breathe once they were at the entrance to the bedroom. He pushed her inside and followed, shutting the door behind them. "Do you have anything simple and sophisticated?" he asked.

"Most of my dresses are," an offended Elonnie replied, placing her hands on her hips as Arlo rummaged through her wardrobe. "Arlie? Why are you acting like this?"

He grabbed hold of a cream dress of cotton, with a semi-sweetheart top, a lace belt around the waist, and long sleeves. It was perfect—classic and pretty. "This one is lovely," he said, grabbing her arm and pulling off the wet dress she wore.

"Arlie!" she squeaked.

"Elonnie, hurry."

"You're being a rake," she teased, falling limp into his arms.

"Stop. Playing," he ordered through a clenched jaw and she straightened up.

"There's no need to take that tone with me," she told him, pointing a finger in his face. "I know how to put a dress on, thank you very much," she added, snatching the dress from him.

After she finished getting dressed, Arlo appraised her to make sure she was up to par with his grandparent's standards. The dress was gorgeous and refined, her hair was up in a chignon, and her jewelry was modest, but sparkling enough. He nodded his approval and then stepped closer to her. "If I can request just one favor?" he started.

"All right, but you will owe me a favor in return," she warned.

"Refrain from acting like yourself tonight."

Elonnie's eyes widened and her mouth opened in a gasp as she took a step back. "Arlo Darcy! If you expect—"

"Elonnie, I mean no harm. My grandparents are not used to someone with a background like yours, that's all. They expected all of us to marry calm wives from quiet families and business-type families."

"I am from a quiet and business-type family," Elonnie frowned.

"I know, but not the sort of business deemed respectable by their standards."

"Ha!" Elonnie scoffed. "Well then, I have no desire to meet such awful people."

"Elonnie, please. If you don't come downstairs and if you should ruin this evening...I'll—I'll punish you," he threatened.

"Oooh, how?" Elonnie flirted.

Arlo ran his hand down his face and sighed heavily. "Why are you doing this?" he groaned. "I'm begging you to behave yourself tonight. I don't ask you for anything, you know that. Now I ask you, please behave yourself, just for tonight."

"You ask me for a lot of things, Mr. Kensington," she told him. "However, I will try to do as you please. But as I stated before, you will return the favor."

"All right, then, that's fair, so long as it isn't too eccentric," he replied. "And no, I will not get you a puppy," he added and Elonnie pouted. He offered his arm out to her and she accepted it.

When they made their way to the entry of the tearoom,

Elonnie knew all the eyes were on her; she tried her best to keep her nerves from heightening, but the cold stares coming from the elder Kensingtons was more than just intimidating. "Madam, sir." She gave a slight curtsy. "Arlie has told me so much about you," she lied.

"Arlie?" Mr. Kensington arched his eyebrow.

"Arlo. My apologies," Elonnie replied.

Mrs. Kensington stood from her seat and walked over to study the girl even further. "Elegant neck; pretty, full lips. Slim waist, almost too slim."

Elonnie self-consciously looked down at herself and then swiftly lifted her head when the older woman cleared her throat, almost ordering her to straighten up again.

"Nice hair, though I'm sure that it tangles easily," Mrs. Kensington continued. She reached for the ballet shoes pendant on the necklace around Elonnie's neck. "Arlo tells me you're a dancer," she said.

"Yes, madam," Elonnie cautiously responded.

"Strong legs," she said. "I trust they are not masculine."

"No, they're lovely," Arlo blurted, resulting in everyone's eyes now being directed on him. He swallowed, straightening up and allowing his grandmother to continue her appraisal.

"Is she obedient?" She looked at Arlo.

"Erm—"

"What kind of question is that?" Elonnie frowned.

"She speaks when not prompted to," Mrs. Kensington judged.

"She is...obedient," Arlo lied.

"Are you respectful?" the woman asked Elonnie.

"When someone is worthy of respect," Elonnie retorted.

"Whatever does that mean?" Mrs. Kensington gasped.

"She means yes," Arlo interjected, placing his hands on Elonnie's arms in a tightened grip. "She was just curious to see how you'd react."

Constance entered the room. "Dinner is ready," she said.

ELONNIE WISHED dinner would have gone much smoother, but it seemed that with every utterance from the elderly couple's mouths, things became worse. They lacked the respect that they desired from others and surely felt that they were far more important than her and her family. The entire dinner, they spent picking apart everything she did— how she sat, ate, spoke and so on. They were even bold enough to tell her they chose to not be present at the wedding due to the fact that they didn't want to be associated with a family so 'whimsical.' What worsened the matter was that the way they said things was not in a tone that sounded callous, but rather calm and collected, no doubt to remain appearing loftier than her.

And what did her husband do? Nothing. He only sat there, clearly disconcerted by the treatment of his wife by mostly his grandmother, but not quite disconcerted enough to make the old lady shut up.

"I don't think a married woman needs to spend her time writing fiction novels and the like. And I don't think you need to worry anymore about your family's company, as you are no longer a Wilhelm, but a Kensington. And I think it is time you cease biting on that lip, or else it should lose its beauty. If Arlo can't have a perfect wife, he deserves a pretty one," Mrs. Kensington commanded.

Elonnie stopped biting her lip and pushed her food

away—her appetite was long gone by now. "No one has a perfect wife," she boldly stated. "As no one has a perfect husband. One day, I shall have as many wrinkles as you do, Mrs. Kensington. And then what should Arlo do?"

Arlo's eyes widened, naturally surprised that the girl was bold enough to stand up to his grandmother, but fearful of what the older woman might do to her.

"Is that a way to speak to a woman more than twice your age, young lady?" Mr. Kensington asked.

"I stated a fact, Mr. Kensington. No one is perfect, and the features I have now are surely to fade with age. So, what should Arlo do now? Divorce me? On what grounds? How bad that would look upon your Kensington name," Elonnie defended.

"You said she was respectful," Mrs. Kensington complained, now becoming more hostile than before. "And she's far from it! You should learn to hold your tongue and know your place, little girl, before it gets you into trouble. If I had it my way, your family never would have been able to sink their claws into one of my grandsons as they have been trying to for the longest time! Especially after you all caused that horrible attack on my son's legacy, nearly destroying everything he had worked for. Or was that part of the trap?"

"My family has not shown any interest in arrangements with your family," Elonnie affirmed. "That's just something you like to tell yourself to feel better at night. Mrs. Kensington, the world is far too big to revolve around you or your offspring!" She regretted each time she had lashed out against the woman, as she had broken her promise to behave, but she couldn't allow herself to sit there and get bullied by these two when she had done nothing deserving of such an attack.

"Take that girl and toss her over your knee one of these

days," Mrs. Kensington ordered her grandson. "Teach her respect as her parents failed to."

Fuming, Elonnie clutched the armrests of her chair. "How dare—"

"That's about enough of this," Arlo finally cut in.

"Well, I wondered when you would finally step up and control this young and reckless *child*," Mrs. Kensington snapped.

Quietly, Arlo swallowed. "I was not referring to Elonnie, Grandmother," he said.

Elonnie's eyes widened in surprise, but she remained quiet in her seat so as not to be disappointed.

"The entire carriage ride here, you spewed insult after insult about my wife and her family, and when you arrived you continued to do the same thing. You disliked her before you even met her and decided you were going to attack her when you saw her—and this entire evening, you have been nothing but cold and discourteous without even trying to be open-minded and kind," Arlo told them, keeping a calm and reverential tone. "I asked Elonnie to show you the proper respect and she did until it started to hurt her feelings and you lashed out at her family. So, no, I'm not going to 'take her over my knee.' I'm just going to inform her that I regret the fact that I didn't step in sooner."

"Arlo Darcy Kensington!" his grandmother growled. "How dare you speak to me in such a way? You allow a showgirl to show me no respect and behave in the same manner? What would your father say? He never would agree to this union, even you know that!"

"Even if he didn't, he would never disrespect my wife," Arlo replied. "Please leave," he requested.

After a moment of sitting with their mouths hanging

open, his grandparents stood, keeping their composure. "This could well backfire on you, young man," his grandfather warned.

"I don't doubt that," Arlo replied. "Thank you for coming."

Even after the older couple had left the premises, Elonnie remained speechless in her seat, staring at Arlo like he was possibly the most beautiful thing she had ever seen. *Did he really take her side over his own grandparents?* Her lips curved into a smile. "Thank you, Arlo," she breathed.

Arlo fiddled with the ring on his finger. "It wasn't a fair fight, as it was two against one, and so it only made sense for me to intercede," he told her.

Elonnie grinned and threw herself into his lap, wrapping her arms around him. "Tell the truth," she told him.

"Elonnie, don't make a scene," Arlo requested.

"I'm not making a scene, just say that you care about me."

"I never said I didn't," Arlo replied. "Aren't you going to finish your dinner?"

"No," she shook her head. "I'm going to stay here, cradled safely in your arms, until you say you almost love me," she replied, kissing his temple, then his cheek, and then his lips.

"It wouldn't be very honorable of me to sit here and let them maltreat you unnecessarily. You told me this before."

"Must everything be about honor with you? Just admit you did something sweet for me because your heart is growing warm," she demanded.

"I'm glad you're satisfied with me, Elonnie. Now, please, stand," he requested curtly.

"No," Elonnie shook her head, laying her head down

upon his shoulder and closing her eyes. "You'll have to carry me," she told him.

"You're impossible," Arlo sighed, standing and carrying her in his arms.

"On the contrary, Mr. Kensington, I think it's you who's impossible," Elonnie replied.

Vingt-quatre

Being awakened from her sleep by the sound of scribbling, she opened her eyes and watched Arlo, focused intently on his leather-bound journal. He looked at her and she could see in his eyes that she had startled him. He shut the book and placed it on the nightstand to his right. "Good morning," he said.

Elonnie sat up and leaned forward, trying to peer around her husband to see the journal. "What is that? Your secrets?" she smirked.

"Whatever it is, it's none of your concern," Arlo replied, tapping her nose with his finger.

Elonnie climbed out of the bed and donned her dressing gown. She smiled a coy smile at Arlo before she walked into the washroom. When she came back out, she freed her hair from the braid it was in and began styling it. "Is your morning all planned out already?" she asked.

"Yes."

"And do I have a role in it?"

Arlo sat quietly for a moment and then looked around the room. "If you'd like to, it's nothing you'd find enjoyable,

I can tell you that now. I have something to go over with Mr. Elmsley," he warned.

Elonnie turned her nose up, lowering her brush as her shoulders dropped. "Well, I hope you know that if he offends me, he will be offended in return," she warned.

"Then perhaps it's better if you don't come along."

Elonnie turned to him. "Are you saying you won't defend me the way you did last night?" she asked.

"I'm saying why not avoid a confrontation all together?"

"Because, believe it or not, I quite enjoy your company, Arlo Darcy Kensington." Elonnie pursed her lips, turning to the mirror.

Arlo took a careful step closer to her. "Do you really?" he asked, his tone soft and sincere.

Slightly taken aback by his sincerity, Elonnie turned back to him. "Yes," she nodded. "Do you have a problem with that?"

"No." Arlo reached for the brush in her hand and took it, starting to brush his own hair. "You should really use your own," he told her. "I'm tired of finding your hair in mine."

"Your brush is softer. Though my hair is textured, the fragility of it is far greater than yours. Also, we are one flesh, that means your brush is mine," she said with firm conviction.

"That's not what it means," Arlo replied. "Stop using my brush and hurry and get dressed if you'll be accompanying me today."

❦

As Elonnie sat closer to Arlo than she normally did, she was feeling mostly gleeful, as she didn't feel the usual tenseness coming from the baron. She twirled the misty blue parasol around in her hand and then looked down at her matching dress; he hadn't noticed it and though he didn't often say much about her dresses, he didn't seem to look at this one as much. "Do you like my dress?" she asked.

"Yes, I do," he nodded.

"Good." Sliding closer to him, she twirled his hair around her finger. "Can I receive an honest answer to the question I'm about to ask?"

"That's a disconcerting opening question," Arlo nervously chuckled.

"Arlie, I see you staring at me, and often; and it's only been getting worse lately. Will you tell me why?"

Arlo sighed, sounding annoyed. "And if I didn't then you would say, 'Arlie why is it that you find me so undesirable?' If you have a problem with my looking at you, I will stop."

"I never said I had a problem, I only ask because it's peculiar the way you do it—and I must say, I do feel rather attractive when you do," she bragged coyishly as she sat back.

"I'm glad I can accommodate your constant need for attention," he retorted.

"Arlo Darcy!" she snapped, lips forming a pout as she crossed her arms.

Arlo could no longer hold back his smirk as he loosened his grip on the reins–he was growing relatively fond of getting on her nerves. "It's all jests, my dear."

"I don't like the way you call me dear," she told him.

"Sweet, melancholy morning, Elonnie Mary. What do you want from me?" Arlo murmured.

"Perhaps, stick with darling, or even call me princess," she sweetly said.

"Not likely," he shook his head. "That is unless, of course, your parents would like to run for the monarchy?"

"Ugh," Elonnie rolled her eyes.

"But 'darling,' we can work on that," he promised.

⚘

WHEN THEY FINALLY ARRIVED AT the bank, Elonnie knew this was going to be far from exciting. The cold stone architecture of the building was similar to that of a gravestone, with a giant door, squared and colored black. She wasn't entirely sure what they were going to do or how long they'd be, but she figured that if she just kept quiet and clung to Arlo, it would be over soon.

They went inside the building, welcomed by marbled cream tiles and stone pillar after stone pillar. The area was clean and organized, so different from how she had last seen it after her dancing fiasco nearly ruined it. The bankers were chatting with each other, surely about to take a small break from the work, and the row of tellers to their left were busy caring for the wealthy customers before them. The place had many people inside, yet due to its spacious nature, it didn't feel crowded in the least. Far ahead on the right, Elonnie could see an elderly man peering over at her, as if he had recognized her from somewhere. Her brown eyes widened and she buried her face into Arlo's arm. No doubt, the man recognized her from the last time she was in the bank.

"What do you think you're doing?" he asked.

"Perhaps I should wait outside," she nervously said.

"No. Just keep still, Elonnie; stay with me," he requested.

"Oh, darling, you don't understand," she insisted, removing his hand from her arm.

"Mr. Kensington," a fellow approached. "And wife."

Elonnie turned her focus away from Arlo and to the approaching gent; seeing him, she grinned, though her eyes continued shifting around the bank. "Mr. Glasgow," she greeted. "What a pleasure to see you again."

"Likewise, it's nice that Mr. Kensington has finally decided to let his better half out of the house," he joked, offering a gentlemanly kiss on her hand.

"Aw, how charming," Elonnie giggled. "Yes, I've been freed from my prison, ever since I've found favor with my Arlie," she played.

Arlo cleared his throat awkwardly and fiddled around with the cufflinks on the wrists of his shirt. "I don't believe it was mentioned before, but Mr. Glasgow here is an investor."

"Oh?" Elonnie looked back and forth between the two men. "And are you hoping to get him to invest in something?"

"I should say so."

Her eyes filled with excitement as she gripped Arlo's hand. "What is it? A theater? A shelter for the dogs?"

"A railroad," Arlo explained, "from here to Warencia or Odsia."

"Well, I don't consider that to be dreary," Elonnie mused. Her eyes again wandered to the old man eyeing her suspiciously. Turning back to Arlo, she saw Mr. Elmsley approaching and frowned. "I'll let you gentlemen discuss this matter—surely, my input isn't needed," she told them. After a curtsy, she left them and proceeded towards the exit of the bank.

DEEP IN CONVERSATION, Arlo, Mr. Glasgow, and Mr. Elmsley slowly paced the bank. "The one issue is the approval from the countries," Glasgow stated. "The odds of Warencia allowing a railroad from here to there are unlikely, as they have yet to be trusting of our country."

"My family has always been good friends with the Lockridges of Odsia," Arlo stated. "I'm sure they'd marvel at the idea. I haven't told Elonnie yet, but the eldest son, Prince Dorian, is engaged to the princess of Tamin, and they've invited us to their engagement ball. I think the girl might lose her head if she should find out she's invited to a royal ball," he chuckled.

Glasgow smiled. Arlo was giving a much different reaction to his wife than he had weeks ago at the coffee shop. "For the railroad to Odsia, you'll have my backing," he nodded. "So long as you get the approval from the royal family."

As Arlo prepared to shake Mr. Glasgow's hand, the sound of someone running through the bank stopped him. He turned around only to see Elonnie hurrying towards him. He sighed disappointedly, seeing that all eyes were now focused on her.

"I see she still hasn't been put into her place," Mr. Elmsley grumbled. "That kind of behavior may go over well in Therondia, but in Ravenhill, it doesn't."

Arlo sighed, taking another look at Elonnie; all attention was on her now. "Elonnie!" he called, his voice echoing through the expansive room. Losing her balance because of the slippery marble, she slid right into Arlo, who was able to remain sturdy enough to keep them both upright. "I shouldn't have to tell you not to run inside an establishment such as this one," he groaned. "Or shall we have yet another disaster?"

"Sorry, darling," she said, a sheepish glance meeting his eyes before she gave a sour smile, turning to the older gent beside her husband. "Mr. Elmsley, what a pleasure to see you again," she lied.

"I have a spare leash if you should need it," Mr. Elmsley suggested to Arlo.

"Oh, what a gentleman," she said, sarcastically.

"With all due respect, Mr. Elmsley, I wish you wouldn't say such things about my wife," Arlo said quietly.

"I beg your pardon?" Mr. Elmsley wheezed.

"I mean no disrespect to you, but to compare the woman I married to a dog is something that would never even cross my mind if we were talking about Mrs. Elmsley."

Elonnie refrained from showing a victorious and brag-gadocios grin as she wrapped her arms around Arlo's waist. He gave a subtle nudge, as the bank was not the place for such a display of affection, and she unwillingly released him.

"I'll see to it that Elonnie shows you the proper respect, as she should," Arlo continued with a warning glance in her direction. "But is it so much to ask that you offer her the respect she deserves?"

Shooting a disgusted look in the direction of the girl, Mr. Elmsley gave a shrug. "I suppose," he forced.

"Thank you," Arlo smiled. "I wish you well until we see one another again," he told Mr. Elmsley as he held his arm out for Elonnie to take. "Good day, Mr. Elmsley."

"Good day, Mr. Elmsley." Elonnie forced a smile.

"Good day."

As they departed the bank, Elonnie looked up at Arlo, grinning from ear to ear, as if she had gained a victory over him. "I think you're falling for me, Arlo Kensington," she boasted.

"Elonnie, whether I like it or not, you're my wife and, as a respectable gentleman, it's important for me to—"

"Oh, blah, blah, blah," she said with a laugh. "I'll let you believe that."

"Elonnie?" he looked down at her.

"Yes?"

"Thank you for not doing something that would have ended in the bank being set aflame," he said.

"Do you really find me that wild?" she asked.

"I find you highly unpredictable and that's threatening enough," he replied. "And let's not pretend something like it hasn't happened."

Elonnie tilted her head. "Well then, you're welcome," she said. "May I steer us home?"

Arlo bit his lip, looking at the carriage just a few steps away. "I don't see why not," he answered.

Vingt-cinq

"Elonnie, what are you *doing?!*" Arlo yelled as the carriage zoomed through the city. Side shop after side shop was crushed by the racing horses, as were the planters upon the sidewalks. The pedestrians leaped out of the way of the oncoming vehicle as it swept over a garden, leaving it in shambles, followed by a beautiful gazebo.

"I wanted to see how fast they could go! I can't stop them! We're gonna die!" Elonnie screamed.

"Pull the reins! Calm down and pull the reins—*you're going to hit the cat!*"

Seeing the black-and-white cat in the way of the horses, Elonnie screamed out and covered her eyes, accidentally letting the reins go.

"Have you *gone mad?*" Arlo bellowed. His eyes grew big as the carriage bumbled over the cat and he managed to grab a hold of the reins, pulling back as hard as he could to finally get the beasts to come to a halt. He took nearly five minutes to regain his composure before turning his large eyes over to Elonnie.

"I'm sorry, darling," she said sheepishly.

"Do not 'darling' me," he growled in a cautionary whisper. Gaining the courage to look behind them, he could see the mess that had been made and he could feel himself just dying at the thought of trying to fix things. "I am in so much trouble..." he weakly said. "My brothers are going to murder me."

"It was an accident," Elonnie stated. "Your brothers are sweethearts, they'll go easy on you," she encouraged, reaching for his hand.

"On *me?* On *us!* This is *your* mess. What happened to one flesh? And now it's 'They'll go easy on you?' No, dear, this is your mess; the only reason I'm worried is because my brothers think you sinless."

"We can find a way to fix this, we don't even have to tell them," she said.

"You ruined half of the city, Elonnie; you destroyed several gardens and you killed someone's cat!" he snapped.

"Please don't yell," she requested. "I'm sorry."

"You're telling the owner the cat is dead."

"Oh, don't make me, Arlo, please! I'm so sorry! I wasn't trying to make such a horrible mess, I promise! My family can pay for it, there's no need to worry about—"

"Can they bring back the cat?"

"No."

"You will tell whoever's pet that was the news. And I will be smart enough next time to remember who I'm dealing with before I allow you to do anything!"

"Arlo, I really am sorry, I hope you don't think I'm playing," she told him.

ELONNIE SPENT most of the evening in the ballroom, practicing her ballet; she felt that by how quiet Arlo had been, he wasn't thrilled to be in her company after the morning's escapade. She decided that she'd punish herself in her own way for her earlier error and spend most of her time on 'petit allegro.'

Most of her hoped that it would only be a moment until Constance entered the ballroom to let her know that Lord Kensington was requesting her presence, but she doubted that would happen, and if it did, it would be to berate her. Things had started out so well that morning—if only she hadn't lost control of the horses. Elonnie sat on the ground and removed her pointe shoes before giving her aching feet a small rub. She grimaced at the sight of red staining the big toe area of her tights, although it was nothing new.

Standing, she limped her way to the door, where she was greeted by Arlo. She gasped and stumbled back just a little. "Mr. Kensington," she addressed.

"Aside from the cat issue, my brothers found the whole thing rather amusing," he told her.

"Did they?" Elonnie gasped, gripping the pendant on her necklace. "I suppose that's good news."

"In some ways, yes," he nodded. "No doubt if it were me, I would have been beheaded, so...." He frowned, before a sizable smile grew on his face, flashing those dimples that Elonnie appreciated seeing. "Thank you," he said.

"Thank me?" she asked, confused.

"I've never seen Pritchard laugh so hard," he told her. "Honestly, on the floor—he was on the floor, Elonnie. Literally. He's always so quiet and can hardly break a smile even when he's ecstatic, but you broke him. They said it was so unlike me, they never thought anything like it would happen."

Elonnie giggled. "I do wish I could have seen that," she admitted.

Arlo stepped closer to her and leaned beside her ear. "He even laughed about the cat," he whispered. "Seeing as it was a stray."

Elonnie gasped, clutching her chest and then covering her mouth. "Oh, but still, the poor thing!"

"Perhaps Pritchard is the dark-hearted one of us," he chuckled. His eyes studied her for a moment and then narrowed on the bloodstain on her tights, shifting his features into a frown. "Are you injured?" he asked.

"Oh, erm, no, I—" Elonnie started. "Slightly, it's not uncommon, though; but it can be a struggle to get around when it happens," she said.

"I see. Well, if you're finished with your ballet, I was hoping you might want to—to, erm...just, sit and, you know, like we did not too long ago, by the fireplace in the tearoom," he stammered. "You see, I have news to share with you and, erm, I don't see why it shouldn't be done under...more comfortable circumstances."

Elonnie swallowed a laugh, having never seen him so discombobulated before. "I would love to," she told him. "It, erm, it might take me a while to get from here to the room to change, with this issue." She looked down at her foot. "Perhaps you could carry me?"

Arlo arched his eyebrow, pursing his lips. "All right, Lady Kensington, but don't think this will be a common occurrence," he told her before sweeping her off of the ground. "You know, you're light as a feather," he told her as he carried her down the hall.

"Thank you," she uttered sweetly. The evening was commencing, and it was always a beautiful sight to Elonnie as the golden glow of the sun began to kiss the hallways of the intriguing and grandiose estate. She peered at the giant windows, which welcomed the light in, and then returned her attention to her partner. Elonnie gulped, observing the golden glow clashing with the green of his eyes and she bit on her bottom lip. "Arlo, I think I love you," she said.

He nearly dropped her, shocked at how abruptly she blurted the words out. He tried to manage a sentence, but all he could get out was: "That's nice of you."

Elonnie tilted her head in confusion. Initially she was baffled, almost hurt, by the response, but seeing the nonplussed glint in his eyes, she giggled. "I didn't mean to give you a fright," she told him. "I just thought you should know."

He placed her down at the entrance of the room and peeked down the hallway. "I, uh, I'll be downstairs whenever you're ready," he said.

"Is that really all you have to say, Arlie?" Elonnie pouted.

"Erm, I think that it's rather good that we should be good friends, you know, and so affection is not all bad at all. Of course, we want this to work for the sake of the community and whatnot, and therefore the sharing of affection isn't horrid—it's as it should be," Arlo rambled.

"What on earth are you talking about?" Elonnie asked, visibly lost.

"I'm talking about *that*."

"That?"

"We'll discuss this another time, Elonnie," he told her. "I hope you'll still join me." He turned away and headed down the hall to the staircase, where he peeked back at her, but quickly returned his attention to the stairs at seeing her looking at him.

After he walked down, Elonnie groaned. He was so

strange at times, but could she really be upset? A month or two ago, he would have just told her that she was crazy for feeling that way; that it was infatuation and this was just a business arrangement. But instead, he fumbled his words almost as a fool would; telling her that her feelings were as they should be, from what she understood. Was that his way of trying to tell her he felt the same way? Elonnie fiddled with the necklace around her neck, finally closing the bedroom door and ambling to the wardrobe, where she reached for the dress he had brought her. She sat on the bed and reached for her diary that was under her pillow, followed by the pen on the nightstand. Before dipping it into the ink, she tapped it against her lips as she thought.

"*June 10th, 1795:*

I cannot help but wonder what Mr. Kensington, the patriarch that is, was like. Arlo has been behaving in the strangest manner and I can't help but wonder if that's what his father was like. I'd be ungrateful to say I thought it was bad—after all, he hasn't been cold like he was when I first met him. I wonder if that means he's actually starting to fall in love with me... I can only hope so, because I think I might be falling for him."

She closed the diary and placed it on her nightstand, now looking over to his side of the bed and seeing that top-secret leather-bound journal. Excitement rushed through her body and she checked the door to make sure no one was coming, then rolled over the bed to grab hold of it. It was like a victory, having the book in her possession, as she felt that this would probably be a vital key in unearthing anything she desired to know about the man.

She knew she had to be swift; she couldn't keep him waiting, or he might return to check on her. She opened the book to the first page and waited a moment before turning any further. Did she want Arlo to look through her diary when she wasn't present? Or would that feel like a rude intrusion of privacy? She sighed, ready to put the journal back, just as the door to the room clicked open.

"What are you doing?" Arlo asked. "You're not even dressed, I thought you were...." His eyes fixed upon the journal she held and he leaped beside her, grabbing her wrist to wrestle it out of her hands. "What do you think you're doing?!" he snapped.

"I didn't open it! You're hurting my arm!" she told him with a laugh, pulling away.

"If it hurts, why are you laughing?" he asked.

"I'm a fool for pain, darling, you know that," she toyed, now keeping the journal in a tighter grip, just for the sake of the game.

"Elonnie Mary Kensington, let it go," he ordered.

"That's the second time today you referred to me as 'Kensington,'" she beamed. "What do you have in here, anyway? Plans for my mysterious demise?"

"Yes! Now give it back to me!" he demanded.

"You'll have to kiss me first," she told him.

"I always kiss you. Give it to me, Elonnie, now."

"You're such a liar," she laughed.

"You need to learn how to stop playing around," he hissed.

"Now I'm really worried about what's in this journal," she breathed through her laughs. "Could it be another woman?" she gasped, teasingly.

"Give me the journal, Elonnie."

"I wasn't even going to open it, but now that you've made a scene, it's become my life's goal to read it," she continued.

Arlo sat up, taking her diary and watching as the playfulness dissolved from her face. "No, Arlo, give it back!" she begged, jumping off of the bed and snatching at it.

He raised his hand so that she couldn't reach it and smiled. "Journal," he commanded.

Elonnie frowned, handing him the book. And with that, he offered her back her diary. "Dreary," she complained, pouting.

"You've tired me out, I'm going to bed now. I hope you know you've ruined this evening," he said, walking past her and climbing into the bed. "I'm too old for your games."

Elonnie turned to him and looked down at him. "You're only twenty-one," she reminded him.

"That's old enough."

"I know you're trying to punish me," she laughed. "I know you're not really going to bed because you're still in your day clothes, and nothing makes you more uncomfortable than to be in your day clothes in bed. I've noticed it."

He turned to her with a puckered brow and lifted to his elbows. "Fine then, I just won't share the news with you about the royal engagement party," he said.

Her eyes twinkled as they grew big. "Royal engagement party?" she squealed.

"A prince and a princess," he nodded. "I'd disclose the details, but I'm much too tired now—I'll just get dressed for bed and go to sleep."

Elonnie smirked, folding her arms as she watched him roll out of the bed to walk to the wardrobe. "You're only joshing," she said. "You're making it all up to make me beg you to tell me, just so you can laugh in my face."

"Have I ever lied to you before?" he asked.

"Possibly," she shrugged. "You aren't completely honest with me," she stated, glancing at the journal.

"As you are not with me," he retorted.

"Aw, please, Arlie! Tell me, please?" she begged.

"The princess of Tamin is engaged to Prince Dorian Lockridge of Odsia, they've invited us to their engagement ball," he finally explained.

"Ah!" Elonnie screamed with delight, falling onto the bed. "Arlie! I could die! If I do, take my corpse to the party! When is it? Where is it—Tamin, Odsia? What's the theme?! Do I really get to go to a princess' engagement ball? Do we get to go to the wedding too?!"

"If you don't make a flamboyant scene, they may want to invite us," he replied.

"I won't, I promise!" she assured him. "Oh, aren't you just the best!"

"Me? This has nothing to do with me," he chuckled.

"Well, they're not inviting us because of me," she stated. "It's because of you, my soft, lovely Arlie bear."

"No, don't call me that," he requested.

"Okay, my big, fluffy Arlie bear," she replied.

Vingt-six

Arlo began to grow tired, having spent most of his day sitting in his brother's office, focusing on his own new work ventures. He looked at his older brother, who was working just as hard, now flipping through account logs. Gladstone looked over at Arlo and smiled. "What are you working on?" he asked.

"Nothing," Arlo replied, covering his work.

"Nothing seems rather tiresome," Gladstone chuckled, without a doubt noticing the dark circles under his little brother's eyes.

"I take pride in being industrious," Arlo told him.

"I won't take that away from you, you are indeed a busy body." Gladstone returned his attention to his work before he prudently glimpsed over at Arlo, who also began working again. "How is Elonnie?" he asked.

Arlo kept his eyes on his work, although his thoughts wandered to his spouse. His face loosened from the tense focus and softened into a smile—suddenly, he felt comfort. His body relaxed as some (though not all) of his stress dissolved; he knew that in a little while, he'd return home to

Elonnie, who would be gleefully waiting for him, to tell him something puerile or show him something peculiar. He washed the thoughts away along with any sign of a softened state before he peeked over at Gladstone, making sure he hadn't caught on to his emotions.

"She's well," he finally responded, sitting up in his chair.

"Good," his brother replied. "I hope the two of you are getting along well," he continued.

"Yes," Arlo shrugged. "Neither of us are deceased after all."

JULY 5, 1795,

There's something strange about Arlo. He's acting like a suspect in a murder novel; hiding in his study for hours upon hours and keeping it locked when he's not around. I thought we had grown closer, but perhaps we haven't. Perhaps he'd like me to believe we have so that when my guard is down, he can dispose of me and possess my inheritance, like Mr. Abernathy.

He stares at me more now, but it's changing. He's studying me. Keenly studying me, as if he wishes to sell me piece by piece to an underground doctor of some sort. Just the other day, he entered my room as I sat at my vanity and gently rested his chin upon my shoulder as he looked into the mirror with me. He said nothing, he did nothing; I kissed his cheek and then he left...."

After writing in her diary, Elonnie strolled down the halls of the quiet estate, making her way to the stairs that led to the attic. She had given the staff the day off, as she wanted a moment to enjoy the building alone—she did miss

Constance's company, as well as the company of her husband, but she didn't want to join him in the city today. She just wanted to enjoy the charm of the Ravenhill estate for a moment. Along with that, she had to finish preparing for their departure to Tamin the following day.

She knew Arlo would be home soon, and she did her best to explore every crevice of the property before he returned. She had never been to the attic before, and peering up the wooden stairs which led to it caused her to wonder if she really wanted to go up there alone. It was surely dark and cold and possibly frightening. She reached for the handrail, but her attention swayed towards the door to the left of her...the study. The enigmatic study.

She was about to return to her venture in the attic, reasoning that Arlo had his secrets and she had hers. She knew Constance had told her that she wasn't allowed in there, but things were different now; she and Arlo were close and, surely, he wouldn't mind if she went in every once in a while. After all, what secrets could a boring study hold?

She was delighted to find that the bronze skeleton key to the room had been forgotten in the keyhole—it was almost as if he had wanted her to go in—then she opened the door. It was much brighter than when she last saw it, as now the one window was no longer covered by the drapes. She smiled; it looked so quaint and cozy now, just because of a little sunlight.

Her eyes gazing around the room, she noticed that the easels which she hadn't given much attention to before were uncovered—not only uncovered, but with paintings on them. There were intricate paintings of colorful flowers, birds, landscapes, and more. Her lips parted in pleasant surprise as she realized that the only one who could have been responsible for such works of art was Arlo. Her hand gently stroked a painting of a mother and her young son as she stared in wonderment and let out a quiet and gleeful laugh.

"Arlie, why would you keep this a secret?" she whispered, pacing the room and studying each piece. She focused in on one and gasped loudly with enchantment. Ballet shoes, a dreamy painting of the pink pointe shoe clad feet of a ballerina, with a background of lavender watercolors and one rose before the feet. *How beautiful*.

Next, was a portrait of a girl.

Not just any girl—it was her. How he managed to capture every little detail in this portrait was beyond her, from the curl pattern of her hair, to the mole in the upper corner of her left cheek.

The painting beside it was her again, a portrait from a different angle, and the next, a full body drawing in the pink, white, and lavender dress. She knew that was his favorite dress on her, and that was made more evident when she saw three other artworks of her wearing it. Including one where she lay in a field of daisies, entitled: *"Her Favorite."*

While she found what he was doing a little alarming, she couldn't say that she hated it. She could tell how he felt about art when they had gone to the gallery some time ago, though she didn't know she had been living with such a skilled artist for the past few months. Clearly, she was worthy of such keen attention from the man and he found her interesting and attractive enough to paint over and over again.

But why didn't he tell me, or ask me before he made them? Now she could understand why he would sometimes be locked in on her.

Her attention captivated by the works, she hadn't heard when Arlo returned, nor when he had come up the stairs. She only heard her name called in a low and aggravated growl: "Elonnie Mary."

Elonnie gasped, spinning around to face Arlo, who stood at the entrance of the room. "Arlie?!" she said, quavering.

"Why on earth are you in here? Did I not tell you the study was off limits?"

"You never said that, you just—"

"I made it awfully clear!"

"Why are you upset about this? And why haven't you let me in here? You never told me you were such an amazing artist, Arlo. Why not?" she asked.

"Get out," he ordered.

"No. Surely you have more hidden talents that I would like to know about. You can't shut me out of the creative part of your life when you know it would interest me!"

"This is an invasion of privacy. How dare you?!" he snapped.

"And this isn't?" Elonnie asked, pointing to the paintings. "If you wanted to paint me, all you had to do was ask! But you didn't; you thought it was all right if you just went on ahead without my permission and kept it a secret! I am not at fault here!"

"Get out," he repeated, more sternly.

"Don't you have an audacity, fluage étrange," Elonnie complained, tossing the skeleton key onto the floor and finally storming out of the room.

MARCHING BACK and forth outside of the carriage in front of the home, Arlo took another glance at his pocket watch. "Is there a reason she's taking so long? At this rate, the ship will be long gone before we reach the harbor," he complained.

Just then, Elonnie exited the home and walked towards the carriage; she was donned in a bland white, draping garb that resembled one of the window curtains and her face was covered by a black lace mask.

Arlo sighed, annoyedly. "Is this some sort of protest?" he inquired.

"Mm-hmm," she nodded.

He opened the carriage door, allowing her to climb in, and she did so, saying nothing else, just keeping her face towards the window on her side. It was bright and early and she wasn't eager to go on a twenty-minute carriage ride to the port, but she was eager to attend the engagement ball, and even eager to ride on a ship. There was still very much tension over what had happened the previous day and while at times she thought she should be flattered that she inspired an artistic streak in Arlo, she knew he should have asked—or at least told her about his paintings of her. At the same time, she wanted to apologize for invading his private space, yet, held back due to her own pride. Maybe what bothered her the most was the fact that he kept all his exciting attributes hidden away from her, knowing full well she'd love to know of them.

Elonnie decided that she wouldn't help him anymore— if the way she looked was what inspired him, then she'd hide it.

AFTER THEY HAD BOARDED the boat, it was about ten minutes into the ride when Arlo looked over at her and she remained silent. She was stubbornly keeping her focus wherever he wasn't. "Part of me does wish that I could have seen at least one play with you as the lead," Arlo broke the silence. "With how dramatic you are, surely it would have made humorous entertainment."

"Hmph," Elonnie replied. "Tyran pourri."

"You may look quite foolish with that mask on," he warned. "Someone may think you have ill intentions for the passengers aboard."

"I have ill intentions for one of the passengers aboard," she grumbled.

"Don't threaten me, Elonnie," he told her. "Maybe stop overreacting about all this; if you hadn't been where I told you not to go, this wouldn't have happened."

Elonnie turned to him for the first time that day. "I'm the only one to blame?" she asked. "You're really going to try to persuade me to believe that I've done something wrong?"

"You were given access to everywhere but one private space, Elonnie."

That was true, she knew that. "I think it better for me not to argue with you, otherwise I might become too frustrated and strike you," she told him.

"If you really must, then do so swiftly. Once we're on Odsian waters and then in Tamin, it's outlawed to violently put your hands on your spouse—so if you do so, you may have to spend a few months imprisoned, Lady Kensington," he retorted.

"I will not strike you. I would never do that."

Vingt-sept

After what felt like a month of sailing, the couple arrived in Tamin; while it was only a trip of seven days' time, the tension between the two made it feel like forever. But arriving in the glimmering country caused Elonnie's feelings to spiral out of control in a positive way.

Tamin was nothing like North Indigo. The Tuscan architectures that were kissed with embellishments of fruits carved into the stone were enough to make one believe they were living in a fairytale. The markets were much larger than they were in her country, and it was a place one might consider to be gaudy. She wondered how Arlo would survive in a place such as this—a place with dancers in the street, small parties on almost every corner, and even a mini-theater just up ahead where a woman sang opera before an audience. "I'll forgive you, if you allow us to take up residence here," she gasped, her eyes roaming over the area once more.

"Never," Arlo replied. "A pretty country, yes, but I already have a headache from all the commotion."

"Oh, the palace is probably a dream," she beamed. A

look of insecurity flashed across her face as many eyes began to wander to her.

"It's the drape ensemble and the mask," Arlo told her, looking at the clothing she wore today. It was another outfit that appeared to be made from the carpets of their home, fitting like a dome over the girl. "Would you care to escape the public? I'm positive that you're also in need of rest after nearly retching on the boat. I didn't take you for one to get queasy at sea—unless, of course, it's Arlo Darcy the second?"

"I should hope not; I would rather not do the world such a disservice," she countered and Arlo frowned angrily, unmistakably offended at the comment. "Now, now, we're on the grounds of Tamin. Don't do something illegal," she teased.

❧

SITTING at the vanity in the lavish chateau the following evening, Elonnie took another glimpse around the room. Even after being there overnight, it was still hard to take in—everything in Tamin was so extravagant, even the most modest areas. The ceilings were painted with designs of angelic beings in the sky, with golden designs at each of the four corners; the walls were golden marble and sparkling. There was a soft white carpet beneath her feet, and the bed in the middle of the room was large enough for maybe four or five people. As she combed through her hair, she wondered how the prince of Odsia had ended up with the princess of this country. No doubt they were just like she and Arlo, one reserved and one spirited.

She looked up at the ceiling again and pondered whether or not Arlo could paint such a design. He most likely could, but she didn't want to think of it now. She looked up in the mirror of the vanity and made eye contact with Arlo, who sat in the chair in the corner behind her. "Stop staring at me," she ordered.

"Will you be wearing another hideous garb tonight at the ball?" he asked with a smirk.

Elonnie ignored him, returning her attention to her hair. She knew she wasn't going to risk looking ridiculous at the celebration, and she didn't want Arlo to feel any sense of arrogance because of that. "You're forbidden from looking at me for the entirety of the night," she finally said. "Homme insensé."

"Elonnie, this needs to be fixed," he insisted. "We're not going into a public crowd so divided like this."

"Apologize to me, then," she said, turning to him.

"You first."

Elonnie scoffed, turning back to the mirror. "No. You first."

"Very well then, I regret that you went where you weren't supposed to be and found something you weren't happy with," he said. "Your turn."

"I regret that you've been creepily sketching and painting me for who knows how long and keeping it a secret from me and that I had to find out on my own and not from you telling me," she said.

"It's not creepy. You're my wife."

Glancing back at him, she stuck her tongue out and once more returned her attention to the mirror. She reached for her necklace and put it back on before standing and grabbing her gown out of the wardrobe. It was a silk peach gown, with short sleeves and white lace trims, and she had white gloves to match.

"You take an awfully long time to get ready. We're going to be late," Arlo stated.

"I'll take longer should you keep complaining," she warned, walking behind the room divider. Arlo sat back in his chair, reaching for the journal that was on the small table beside him and opening it to begin drawing.

Hearing the sound of the scribbles on the paper, Elonnie peeked out from behind the divider. "What are you doing?" she asked, alarmed.

"Nothing," Arlo replied. "Finish getting dressed, please. Show some respect for the couple who has invited you to their ball."

"Please don't order me around," she requested.

"I should have left you in North Indigo; I could have come up with some excuse," Arlo said.

Walking out from behind the divider fully dressed, Elonnie gave an annoyed look as she donned her gloves. Arlo smiled, turning his journal around to show her the rough sketches he had made of her making that exact face, spitting her tongue out and pouting. She quickly tried to reach for the journal, but he was too swift in pulling it back.

"You're being mighty insufferable, Arlo Kensington."

Vingt-huit

Elonnie had been to many a ball in her lifetime, but none of them compared to this one—a royal engagement ball. She knew she would be talking about this for ages. There were masked men standing at nearly nine feet as they balanced on stilts; jugglers, women decked out in the finest of their finery, and even a well-known singer. Elonnie wished it was her nana, but she knew her family would be preparing for their new tour. She was drawn to the right side of the ballroom from the entrance; it was easy to recognize this was the bride's family, as they were all Taminites—bright-eyed and bushy-tailed, simmering with excitement and engaged in rowdy conversation.

She turned her head to the left and saw the groom's side, the Odsians; it was almost like looking at a party of Arlos. It's not that she found them boring or disinteresting, but they were so different from the bride's family. She was excited to meet the couple, hoping they were fonder of each other than she and Arlo were when they had started out.

"I was invited by the groom," Arlo informed her. "We'll have to sit on their side."

Elonnie took one more longing glance at the Taminites, but chose to quietly follow Arlo. It wasn't her place to make a scene at someone's special event, and she'd never wish to do such a thing.

"Miss, you dropped this," a man said from behind her.

Elonnie turned to face him. He was a dark-haired Taminite with honey-nut eyes and shaded facial hair. Elonnie looked down at his hand; it was empty. "Dropped something?" she laughed.

He looked down at his hand and acted as if he were shocked before reaching behind her and giving the illusion of pulling a bright jewel out of the air. "Here it is," he smiled.

Elonnie gasped, clapping her hands. "Just like magic!" she squealed.

Arlo turned back. His features clouded over, casting a frown upon his face at seeing her being offered an expensive jewel by some man. "Can I help you?" he asked, taking his place beside his wife.

"Forgive me, I didn't know the lady was spoken for," the man said.

"Yes, forgive him." A woman approached; she shared the same honey-nut brown eyes as the man, and her head was crowned with radiant red hair, a few shades lighter than the dark red lipstick painted on her lips.

Elonnie soaked in the woman's sparkling golden gown that elegantly flowed behind her wherever she walked and immediately concluded that this was indeed the bride, the princess.

"My younger brother takes pleasure in playing coy whenever the chance is given him," she explained. "And forgive me," she said, then bowed. "I'm Elandra Lorenza—

soon to be Lockridge—and this is my younger brother, Kassian."

"At your service," Kassian smiled, taking Elonnie's hand and offering a kiss upon it.

"Charmed." Arlo frowned at Kassian, then gave his attention to the princess and smiled. "It's a pleasure, Your Highness," he said with a bow. "My wife has been eager to make your acquaintance." He looked at Elonnie, who was still frozen at being in the presence of royalty. He gulped, embarrassed. "Clearly she's taken in by the splendor of your wonderful abode."

"Oh, I don't doubt it," Elandra laughed, taking a quick gander at the palace. "It truly is a treasure to my family, and has been for so many years."

"It's wonderful," Arlo told her. He shot a discreet look of disapproval down at his wife and gently nudged her. "Isn't it splendid, dear?" he asked.

"I've been eager to make your acquaintance!" Elonnie finally blurted.

"I trust she'll catch up with us quite soon," Arlo chuckled, nervously.

"Oh, she needn't feel pressured around me," Elandra encouraged, stepping over to Elonnie and placing a friendly arm around her. "Tell me your name."

Elonnie froze up again.

"Elonnie," Arlo interjected.

"Elonnie," Elandra smiled. "Elonnie as in 'Wilhelm?'" she asked.

Elonnie gulped. "Yes, it's splendid," she nodded, looking around at the palace.

Red with humiliation, Arlo covered his face with his hand. *Did she really need to act this way in front of the princess of the country?* "Elonnie, wake up," he commanded.

"Yes," Elonnie said. "I mean, erm, what was the question?" she asked Elandra.

Elandra giggled. "Isn't she adorable? I was inquiring about whether or not you were the Elonnie Wilhelm, the dancer?"

"Oh, yes, Your Majesty."

"Highness," Arlo corrected.

"Highness," Elonnie echoed.

Elandra's eyes sparkled before she grabbed hold of her hand. "Dorian, darling!" she called, waving her fiancé over to where they stood. The young man ceased his conversation with another man, who looked to be his brother, and made his way to his fiancée.

"Arlo Kensington," he greeted with a hug. "It's a pleasure to see you again."

Elonnie watched as Dorian wrapped his arm around the princess' waist, giving her a soft smile—she could see that this was true love, just like a fairytale. And they were a lovely couple. Dorian's black hair and green eyes matching well with Elandra's red and brown. She smiled, losing the tension in her body.

"Elonnie here is one of the Whimsical Wilhelms of Therondia, North Indigo," Elandra said excitedly. "I understand it wasn't in the plans, but if she doesn't dance for us, I don't know what I'll do. That is, of course, if you're willing?" she asked.

Elonnie laughed nervously. "If you truly wish it," she said. "I haven't my hard ballet shoes," she stated. "But perhaps I could try something new?"

Arlo swallowed. *Something new?* She was going to embarrass him, somehow. Surely, she was looking for a way to get back at him for their earlier fight, and this would be her way of doing it.

"I love new," Elandra smiled, pulling Elonnie along to announce the performance to the crowd.

As they walked off, Dorian beamed, watching his intended, and then turned his attention to Arlo. "You didn't say the missus was one of the Therondia Wilhelms," he stated.

"I try to keep that a secret," Arlo grumbled to himself. "She is something," he spoke up. "It seems we ended up in the same predicament."

"It does appear that way," Dorian laughed, taking another look at his fiancée. His smile grew bigger. "I wouldn't have it any other way," he said. "I thought that marrying Her Highness was going to be the worst thing I could possibly imagine. However, now I realize she's perfect. She's optimistic, patient, kind, and generous and I can't wait to spend the rest of my life with her."

Arlo gave half a grin, hearing his friend mush over his bride-to-be. Then he looked at Elonnie who began her dance. It was a beautiful dance in the style of ballet, only with more freedom and with airy, flowing movements. His smile grew deeper as he watched her dancing—he had never really seen her perform before. He had only seen her practice a few steps every now and then, but seeing it all pieced together was something special. It was art. He wished he could have seen her do it more often; perchance, she would let him watch her at times. He frowned. *She won't, not after the painting issue.*

After Elonnie concluded her dance, the crowd applauded her, even Arlo. Grinning from ear to ear, he walked closer to her. He'd swallow his pride and tell her, he'd tell her he loved it, every minute of it.

Before he could step any closer, she was surrounded by a crowd, mostly the Taminites—showering her with praise and adoration. Initially, he was pleased with it; she was gifted and he wished he had seen that before. And seeing how the princess of Tamin was satisfied with her performance, he knew Elonnie would be over the moon for the rest of the trip. He was sure that she'd come running over to him in a moment, gushing over what just took place and asking if he enjoyed it.

His pleasant disposition dissolved, however, when she didn't come running to him. After the crowd subsided, the dancing began as the orchestra strummed up a charming waltz, and there she was, now dancing with one of the guests.

"I should probably dance with my fiancée," Dorian grinned. "We'll talk more after," he assured, leaving Arlo by himself.

Arlo figured he would take a seat. After this dance, Elonnie would ask him to dance with her. They hadn't danced with each other once ever since they had been married, as it wasn't the practice to have a wedding dance in North Indigo. He checked the time; the night was only just beginning. Looking back up at his wife, he smiled a tad at seeing how joyful she was.

As the song concluded, he perked up, waiting for her to ask him for the next one...and she didn't. She began dancing with one of the other Taminite men. He sat back. *Perhaps the next.*

Most of the guests occupied the dance-floor, with very few sitting at their tables conversing. After each song, Arlo looked over to see whether or not Elonnie intended to make her way back to their table, but with every new song, she began to dance with a new partner. Now he was getting irritated, seeing this as an attack against him. She wasn't doing it for fun, but to make him look bad and humiliate him. Why else would she make such a frivolous scene, dancing with every man present besides him?

Grasping the champagne flute on his table, he gulped it down without taking a breath, followed by the one left for Elonnie. A child of about three years of age approached him and pointed to the glass, requesting it. "I think you're a little too small," Arlo told him, annoyed by his presence.

Again, the boy pointed to the glass, focusing his big blue eyes on it.

"No." Arlo turned his nose up at the child and then looked back out at all the dancing couples; his skin reddened at his wife being so contently occupied as he crossed his arms and legs. Turning back to the table, the flute was gone and now in the hands of the little boy. "You're a sneaky little brat, aren't you?" Arlo grumbled.

"Marcellus!" Elandra snapped, hurrying over to snatch the glass away from the child. "No. Very bad," she reprimanded. Her face softened as she gave her attention to Arlo. "He's very curious at times," she warned, picking the boy up. "You're much too young for this, little one," she told him before giving the child a kiss on the cheek.

"Hmm?" the child said, once again requesting the glass as he pointed to it.

"No," she repeated, leading to a wretched tantrum, which she ignored. "Why aren't you dancing?" she inquired of Arlo. "Are you not enjoying yourself?"

"Oh, it isn't that, Your Highness; I'm having a splendid time," he lied. "As is my wife...clearly," he added, more sourly.

"Well, I hope that you'll join the majority on the dance

floor soon," Elandra smiled, taking Marcellus back to her brother-in-law.

Sitting alone again, Arlo turned his head to see Elonnie now dancing with Kassian, that flirtatious prince. That was the final straw. He stood from his chair and walked out onto the floor where he stood before his spouse. "If you've finished throwing yourself at every man here who you can get your hands on, I think it's time to go," he snapped, just loud enough for most to hear.

"Excuse me?" Elonnie shivered.

"I'm exhausted and ready to leave," he curtly stated. "If you don't mind, I expect you to join me."

Mortified, Elonnie looked back at everyone awkwardly staring at them. Before she lowered her head and stepped closer to Arlo. "I don't know what you think you're doing, but I'm not going to get into an argument with you. Not here," she whispered.

"Let's go," he ordered.

Elonnie tried to study his face to see what the issue might have been, but aside from the blatant disappointment that was directed at her, she couldn't read much else. She followed behind him quietly, waiting until they were away from the crowd to say anything else.

Vingt-neuf

After changing into her nightgown, Elonnie walked from behind the divider and looked over at Arlo, who sat quietly on the bed, reading. "Will you remain in your silent tantrum, or are you going to tell me what your problem is?" she finally asked, breaking a silence that had lasted for the entire ride from the palace to the château.

Arlo said nothing in reply.

"Arlo. If you're upset with me, then say what it is I did. Don't behave like a child. Was it not you who swore against childish behavior?" she continued as she packed away the last of her things and laid out her traveling clothes for the following day. "Will you really subject me to this? If you're not going to explain why you're angry, then you've lost the right to be angry."

Arlo turned the page in the book and continued reading.

"Are you going to ignore me for a seven-day trip?" she inquired. She rolled her eyes, losing patience when she was ignored once more, and climbed into the bed. "You are the worst," she said. Blinking, she looked at the book in his hands and scoffed. "Othello? Will you smother me, is that it?" she asked.

Arlo shut the book, blew out the candle on his nightstand, and laid down as he pulled the covers over himself.

"Goodnight, Arlo," Elonnie said, her voice cold, like she might have struck him over the head in a minute. "Morveux gâté," she grumbled.

JULY 21, 1795:

I have no doubt that Lady Kensington considers me to be the villain in her story at this point in time, yet I know for a fact that I am not. I know well what her intentions were last night at the engagement ball when she offered herself to practically every man she could that wasn't me.

She has most likely caught on to how I feel about her and so now she intends to use it against me in the cruelest ways possible. I should have never allowed myself to become vulnerable to this woman. If she can happily disregard me with little regret, then I will see to it that she does regret it.

Arlo looked down at Elonnie who was still fast asleep, then he shifted his focus back to his journal, now sketching a picture under his entry. Looking back and forth from his journal to Elonnie's face, he felt his cheeks growing red with resentment, despite continuing his illustration of her. He grimaced when she started to turn her head to face the other side of the room. Then he gently slid his finger under her temple to turn her face back in his direction and completed his sketch.

Elonnie opened her eyes and Arlo closed his journal before climbing out of bed and putting the very last of his belongings into his trunk. Sitting up, Elonnie looked at him and smiled, to which he responded with a frown.

"Are we still mortal enemies?" she questioned. "Am I still Desmonda and you Othello? Do not forget that Desmonda was the victim, Arlo."

"I'm sure you'd like to believe that you are," he retorted. "Please hurry to prepare to depart. I shan't leave you here, although you may well like that."

Elonnie readied to respond fiercely, yet decided she'd get ready for their departure instead. "Very well, Lord Kensington," she snapped.

Trente

A s the pair entered their home, Arlo immediately headed off in the opposite direction of his wife, leaving her frustrated in the entry hall of the estate.

"Arlo. Don't do this," she said. "Do you really think this is fair? Are you not the one who was so against me to begin with because you found me too childish?" she asked. "Your behavior is far beyond childish. Not speaking to me, nor providing me with an explanation as to why you're behaving in this manner."

"Elonnie, enough," Arlo told her.

"If that's the way you feel, then I will gladly go home," she warned.

Arlo now faced her. "You are home," he reminded her, now moving towards her. He grabbed hold of the ring on the chain around her neck and held it up as far as he could. "Remember? Don't forget that!" he hissed.

"Arlo, don't you make me forget it," she said.

"I beg your pardon?"

"You have no right to be upset with me, and if you do, I deserve to know why you are! I don't know how long you intend to keep this nonsense up, but I guarantee that I am not putting up with it."

"Elonnie, everything you did was solely to make me this way, don't pretend that it wasn't."

"Arlo, I don't know what's wrong, nor do I know what heinous crime I've committed that's turned you so fiercely against me. But I want to, Arlo, I really do," she pleaded. "Is this about going into your study? You're right in that I shouldn't have done it, I realized that. It was a private area and I trespassed, but I don't think this punishment is fair."

"You don't know? That's a terrible shame if you're being honest," Arlo said quietly. He turned away from her to exit the room, but she grabbed hold of his arm.

"Arlo, please don't do this," she told him. "The only way for us to fix this is by you telling me how I've wronged you."

"We're both exhausted and I'm in no mood to discuss this," he replied.

"Then don't expect it to get solved and *do not* expect me to just stand here and submit to this childish behavior."

"And what exactly do you intend to do? Leave?" he asked.

"Yes," she said. "I'll go back home."

"After making yourself look like a tramp then that would surely only spoil your reputation even further," he retorted. "You might want to consider keeping that in mind, Mrs. Kensington!" With that, he stormed off.

"Arlie," Elonnie whimpered. "You said you wouldn't make this happen again," she reminded him, as tears flowed down her cheeks.

After taking a quick look back at her, he chose to continue walking away.

"JULY 30TH, 1795:

I have yet to learn of what wrong I've done, but all I know is that Arlo has reverted to his cold and off behavior without giving me the explanation I deserve. I doubt my performance at the ball bothered him because I trust he would have pulled me from the floor before I even finished.

He's been able to keep this arrogant, immature disposition going on for over a week; saying only short sentences, leaving without giving any indication as to when he'll be back, and even sleeping in the guest room—my first room— every now and then. Any more of this and I shall be forced to return to Therondia."

Hearing Arlo open and close the door to the study, Elonnie closed her diary, and stood to exit the room. Hurrying down the stairs, she could see Arlo headed to the front door. "Arlo!" she called.

Stopping at the door, he slightly looked over his shoulder. "What is it?" he asked.

"If you walk out that door without explaining anything to me, I won't be here when you get back—that's a warning," she cautioned.

Arlo smirked disparagingly before shaking his head and walking out the door. He knew when Elonnie was bluffing. "I quiver with fear. Get your head out of that fiction, Elonnie," he called back.

Elonnie balled her fists as he walked out, breathing heavily as she tried her best to keep her tears from falling down her face—but she eventually succumbed. Racing back up the stairs, she ran into her room to pack her trunk. If he was going to be cruel, she had no intention of sticking around for it. Let him laugh in her face as if her threats were empty—he would soon find out that they were, in fact, valid.

꧁꧂

"DEAREST GENEVIEVE,

With all due respect to you and your family, I regret to inform you that I will be spending some time back home with my family. Arlo has turned on me, and with no explanation. When he is ready to tell me what I've done to anger him, I will happily return.

I can only hope that this in no way affects our relationship and I don't have ill will against your grandson, but I know I cannot continue like this without understanding why. He refuses to open up and explain what it is I've done to offend him.

In time, I hope to see you soon.

Your friend,

Elonnie," Genevieve read aloud.

"What is the meaning of all this?" Gladstone complained, rereading the letter a second time. "What did that impudent child do? I'm going over there now and I'll surely give Arlo Darcy the beating he always deserved yet never received as a child."

"Gladstone, don't," Elise stood. "We haven't heard both sides of the story, nor do we know the entirety of it. Quite frankly, it's not our business. It's between the two of them," she stated.

"Are you suggesting it was possibly the girl's fault? This is Arlo we're speaking of," Pritchard chimed in.

"I'm not blaming Elonnie, I'm only saying that it's important that we try not to get involved. Elonnie disclosed to us what she wanted to and she didn't ask us to get involved," Elise replied.

Genevieve sighed, standing up from her chair and walking over to the fireplace where Pritchard stood. "I doubt there's any need to discipline him. I think he's going to learn his lesson the hardest way," she softly said.

❧

"SHE WHAT?!" Arlo exclaimed, pacing back and forth in the entry hall before Constance.

"Left, left, left!" Constance exasperatedly repeated. "She went home to Therondia because she was tired of the undeserved mistreatment."

"Undeserved? Mistreatment?" Arlo complained. "I have not once mistreated that young lady and you know it! After what she did to me, I should have been the one who left."

"You did, didn't you?" Constance crossed her arms. "What is it she did to you?"

"Oh, where do I start?" Arlo growled. "First, she went into the study, where you know she wasn't allowed—no one is. And while I forgave her for that, although I didn't say so, she humiliated me in front of half of the country of Tamin and half the country of Odsia. But you'll never believe that, will you? Because, like my brothers, you think she's perfect —sinless!" he hissed.

"How did she humiliate you?" Constance calmly asked.

Arlo frowned, simmering down just a little bit. "It's of no importance, and it's too late, anyway. If she wants to run off, that's fine, why should I care?" he asked. "I don't need her, she was Gladstone's idea."

❧

THOUGH IT WAS a gorgeous summer day at the Wilhelm Manor, it felt like one of the drearier days that were so common in the country. Elonnie sat at the desk in her bedroom, thinking of what to write in her diary. She couldn't come up with anything, as she was plagued with too many mixed feelings. It had been five days since she'd left Ravenhill and she knew deep down she missed the place, and she missed *him*.

Looking around her room, she could see it was exactly the same as she had left it—her family no doubt didn't have much time to change it. Or it could have been that they just missed her. She hoped so; it felt good to be missed.

"Elonnie?" Alex said, standing in her doorway.

She turned to him, smiling. "Yes, buddy?"

"I missed you," he said.

"I missed you too," she nodded, reaching her hands out, inviting him to come to her. When he approached her, she took him onto her lap and wrapped her arms around him.

"There was a letter for you," he said. "Nana said to give it to you." He gave her the small letter and with great excitement she took it from him.

Surely it was Arlo, requesting for her to come back to him; he missed her, he needed her, and was begging her for her forgiveness.

"The Tamin Académie of Ballet," she read the envelope. She frowned.

"Don't you love ballet?" Alex asked.

"Yes."

"Then why are you sad?"

"I'm not." She forced a smile. "I was just expecting something else."

"Oh." Alex leaped off of her lap and then started to the door. "Is Arlo going to come here soon?" he asked.

Elonnie swallowed before shaking her head. "Not anytime soon," she whispered.

"Then will you play the faerie princess?" he asked.

Elonnie thought for a moment. If the role was still available, then why shouldn't she take it? She only refrained from accepting because Arlo didn't want her to be away for so long, but if she was away anyway... She sat back in her chair. She still respected Arlo's place as her husband, and his issue was also with the handsome rogue who she'd be dancing alongside.

"I think someone else is better fit for it," she told Alex. "Besides, that's all nonsense, isn't it?" she grumbled. "At the end of the day, the angry rogue remains angry and the princess doesn't win."

Alex blinked, clearly saddened that she would say such a thing. This certainly wasn't the Elonnie he knew—the one who told him that every story would have a happy ending, the one who'd tell him countless tales that made him and the other little ones feel happy. "I—I love you, Elonnie," he said.

Elonnie's heart warmed. The little guy may not have understood what she was dealing with, but he knew she was hurt and he knew just what to say to make things somewhat better. It was nice to hear that after so long. "I love you too, Alex."

As he began out of the room, Elonnie glimpsed at the journal from Genevieve and her eyes teared up—she had made a promise to her in exchange for the priceless gift. "Alex!" she called, and the little boy turned back. "I never told you about the moon men I found in the attic at Ravenhill," she whispered a tad more excitedly.

The boy's eyes brightened as he ran back into her lap. "Will you tell me?" he gasped.

"Of course," Elonnie replied, offering the little one a small kiss on the head.

"Mail," Arlo snapped.

Constance pursed her lips annoyedly as she walked to him with the stack of letters and handed it to him. She raised her eyebrow, watching him shuffle through the mail. "Searching for something in particular?" she asked, folding her arms.

Arlo gave a disgruntled stare before handing her back the letters. "No," he said curtly.

"Just write her, Arlo. Or go to her," Constance implored him.

"This has nothing to do with her, Constance. Now, please, I have never asked you to back out of my affairs, but this once, I will. This is not your business. It's mine, and I intend to handle it myself."

"All right, young man; I will not get involved. But try not to run to me when your pain gets the best of you," she warned before readying to depart the room.

"Constance, I didn't mean that; I meant no harm by it," Arlo told her, stepping closer to her and taking her hand. "Please, don't take it to heart," he requested. Turning away from her, he took a deep breath and ran his hand through his hair as he walked around the entry hall. "I am not the enemy here, Constance," he protested. "I did nothing wrong, she had no issue shunning me, so I doubted it would bother her if I did the same to her."

"Sit down, Arlo," Constance instructed.

After a pause, he obeyed, sitting on the stairs, followed by the older lady.

"What did Elonnie do?"

"She made a fool of me," he said.

"How?"

"She practically threw herself at every man present! She danced with them, all of them, and not once did she ask me if I might want to dance with her. She acted as if I was invisible after she got that rush of fame from the guests," he explained, his skin turning crimson.

"I see." Constance pondered his words. "And did you desire to dance with your wife, Arlo?" she asked.

Arlo sat quietly. This was quite the predicament. Was he ready to admit to her that he did? He swallowed. "I—I should have been the first one she had a—"

"Did you want to dance with Elonnie?" Constance repeated.

Arlo twisted the ring around on his finger, scowling as he nodded his head.

"Why is it that you didn't request a dance from her?" she probed.

Keeping his focus on the tile flooring, Arlo couldn't think of a response; his pride had kept him sitting in that chair at the ball. Not only that, but something in him had wanted her to ask him. He wasn't sure why, but those were his feelings. "I don't know," he finally answered.

"It could be that she wanted to dance with you but, seeing as you often make it clear that the two of you are polar opposites, she figured you wouldn't want to dance with her. Perhaps she was apprehensive about how you might have reacted to her asking," she stated.

Arlo knew that was a reasonable thought. If she had asked him a few months ago, he possibly would have blown her off and told her he hated to dance and that was most likely Elonnie's fear. He lowered his head slightly, leaning his cheek into his hand, and Constance slid closer to him, placing a motherly arm around him. "Arlo?"

He turned to her.

"Do you love Elonnie?" she asked.

Again, turning away from Constance, he rubbed his hands together. "Elonnie and I were beginning to get along well, I believe, and I thought I made it clear to her that I was...oh, never mind all that," he sighed, standing.

Constance grabbed hold of his hand and peered up at him. "Arlo. Do you love Elonnie?" she asked firmly.

Arlo gulped as his heart raced> He knew he was being stubborn at this point. He missed the girl. Coming home every day to this estate and knowing she wouldn't be there to greet him was having an effect on him. He enjoyed having someone waiting for him—not only waiting, but eagerly anticipating his arrival. He missed having someone to kiss hello and goodbye, and hold all night. The smell of something new, like a pearberry candle or something sugary, like a Whim Wiffle, filling the home whenever he arrived. He missed that look of satisfaction in her eyes whenever he'd return home to her at the end of the day.

"I do," he whispered, now finally coming to terms with his feelings.

"I know," Constance nodded. "But you do an *awful* job at showing it, Arlo Darcy." She stood up and adjusted the button at the top of his collar. "I can only hope that you're not too late. Go tell her how you feel, honestly and in a manner that will assure her that you love her."

"She won't come back," Arlo sighed.

"Not if you don't ask her to."

"She's about as stubborn as I am; she won't come back to me. She hates me."

"That's far from the truth. Otherwise, I doubt she

would have run away," Constance said. "Before too much time has passed and the animosity grows, go to her, Arlo. Humble yourself and go to her." She took his face into her hands and looked him in the eyes. "And should she return to you, act like a husband. Not a business partner."

Arlo's eyes traveled down to the ground. "All right, then," he weakly said with a nod. "I will."

"And please, Arlo. Please tell her you love her," she begged.

Trente-un

When Gladstone opened the door, he saw his youngest brother standing there in the doorway, looking as pathetic as ever. "You have quite the nerve, showing your face here," he told him.

Arlo stepped inside the home and stood silently, twisting the ring around on his finger. "Gladstone?" he said at last, his voice cracking.

"Yes?" his brother replied, clearly not happy to see him there. "I hope you know that while I'm more upset with you for hurting that girl's feelings, you should also know that this defames the family name that you claim to care so much for."

"I didn't come here for a confrontation," Arlo told him.

"Then why are you here? To claim innocence?" He crossed his arms.

Arlo breathed deeply as he stepped closer to Gladstone and looked up at him. He readied to speak, but instead wrapped his arms around him in a hug.

Gladstone, surprised by the display of affection, took a moment to react. Finally, he hugged Arlo back, and couldn't refrain from allowing a small smile to creep onto his face. "You don't often give these out to just anyone," he finally said.

"I need your help," he told him, stepping back. "It was probably all a misunderstanding and I don't know what to say to make her come back to me."

"What are you requesting?"

"Tell Elonnie to come back to me, please. I never meant to harm her, Gladstone, honest. I just became so—so grossly jealous, and most likely for no reason at all. She's never going to forgive me. I know she won't, and all I ask is that you please, please request that she—"

"Steady on," Gladstone calmly commanded. "Are you telling me that you *want* to reconcile with Elonnie?"

Arlo nodded.

He sat down in the chair beside the fireplace and Arlo knew his brother was taking a minute to process his answer and thinking of a way to respond. "Arlo, I'm thrilled to hear that she's grown on you. And as much as I would love to fix the issue, I cannot. Only you can. If I go on your behalf, you and I both know that she'll only think you were too proud and arrogant to apologize to her yourself and she'll never go back."

"She doesn't want to see my face, I can assure you of that," Arlo sighed. "I don't even know what to say to her."

"'I'm sorry' is a good place to start," Gladstone stated. "You need to stop being so against apologizing, Arlo."

"But I—"

"You have to allow yourself to be humble. Suppose I do go and she decides to go back to you; the next time you have an argument—and you will have another one because you're both still very dissimilar—you're still going to need to say you're sorry."

"It's not that easy, Gladstone."

"You don't think I know that?" he chuckled. "I had to apologize to you all the time when I wasn't even guilty of doing anything to you. You'd bite if you didn't get your way and then I'd have to say sorry for striking you in return. You were a wretched little boy at times, do you not recall?"

"You're a..." Arlo grumbled.

"Now, now, you said you didn't want a confrontation, young man," Gladstone reminded him. He crossed his legs and looked over at him. "Does this mean you've fallen for her?"

Arlo turned his back to him, hiding his blushing cheeks. This should have been easy to discuss with his brother, surely easier than it had been with Constance. But it wasn't; it felt much tougher, perhaps due to the fact that he'd have to admit that he had ceased fighting against the choice his brothers had made for him and tell them that they had won. "I believe that's the case," he finally admitted.

Gladstone smiled. "Good," he said. "Grandmother knew she was the perfect choice."

"Grandmother?" Arlo asked, facing Gladstone.

"Yes. Believe it or not, this was not the scheme of Pritchard and I, but the matchmaking of Grandmother Genevieve. Of course, I still do think it was necessary due to your rather large blunder with your fortune, but when we thought of marriage, we had Meredith Marlowe in mind," he told him.

Arlo's nose turned up at the thought of the girl; beautiful, of course, with auburn hair and light brown eyes, but far duller than even Arlo himself.

"Grandmother suggested Elonnie."

"Why though?" Arlo asked.

"Because she didn't want you to end up like Pritchard and I," he laughed.

"But I've always wanted to be like you two, you know this."

Gladstone stood, pouring a drink for Arlo and then for himself. "Well, I'm afraid we're much too boring and uptight for Grandmother's taste," he shrugged. "As a child, you were always creative and fun, until you felt the need to walk in father's and our footsteps."

"Creative and fun never garnered me any attention from father," Arlo pouted. "I was always brushed off so he could ask you how your day was going."

Gladstone chuckled. "With your charming little drawings. Father adored you, Arlo, he just didn't know how to react to your... imagination," he said. "It was the same with Mother, so Grandmother says. Mother was lively and adventurous, until she started trying to fit into the mold of the Kensington family. She only hoped the same wouldn't happen to Elonnie, but that Elonnie would rub off on you."

Feeling somewhat hoodwinked, Arlo's brow puckered angrily, but slowly, it softened, as he recalled how his passion for art had rekindled—his desire to create. "Grandmother," he whispered. After placing the glass in his hand down, he started hurrying to the front door and Gladstone followed behind him. Arlo stopped running and jogged back to Gladstone. "If she doesn't take me back, promise me you'll try to convince her?" he begged.

"If all else fails, I will," Gladstone promised.

"Thank you," Arlo breathed.

ELONNIE SAT WITH BELLA, Alex, and Maddie with their feet in the fountain, this time telling them a story of a princess and a pirate—Maddie appreciated this one more, and Alex was content as he often had the chance to hear of the moon men. Bella was happy with anything; she held what remained of a dandelion in her hand and shook it around, hardly giving any attention to the story.

"But of course, you know the way of pirates," Elonnie related the story, "the treasure comes first, and then all else."

"Lookit!" Maddie pointed.

Elonnie turned in the direction she pointed and her eyes sparkled at seeing Arlo standing there; in the blink of an eye, her soft reaction faded, replaced by disdain.

"Go inside," she instructed the kids. Alex and Maddie leaped off of the fountain before assisting Bella off and running to the house. Elonnie stepped out of the fountain, looking Arlo up and down. "Lord Kensington," she said tersely.

"Elonnie," he softly started, walking closer to her. "Elonnie, I—I think we've been parted long enough, don't you?" he asked.

Rotating to face the fountain, Elonnie began dropping flower petals into the water. "I haven't noticed," she replied. Although she knew she had missed him, and each day she'd hoped he would do exactly as he had done today, come for her and ask her to go back to Ravenhill with him. But in her version, he also apologized.

"Elonnie, please don't do this," he requested, moving closer to her. "It's time to come home."

"Has gossip begun to spread about this? Is that why you suddenly feel the need for my return?" she questioned.

"I don't know of any gossip, I only know I wish you'd

come back home," he told her as he gently wrapped his arms around her waist and softly kissed her cheek.

"What do you think you're doing?" Elonnie hissed, pulling away.

"Will you please listen to me?"

"Now that you're finished snubbing me? I can see what you're trying to do and I won't be a fool for it," she told him. "You don't love me, you've made that awfully clear. I'll return to Ravenhill when I'm ready to!"

"Elonnie, please!"

"That's right, Arlie, you do the begging!" she snapped before taking off into the house. She locked the door behind her and rushed to the window to see what he might do next. He stood dejectedly in the garden for nearly three minutes, making her feel regretful. As he began walking away, Elonnie headed back to the door, grabbing hold of the knob and considering opening it.

She stopped herself; Arlo still hadn't said he was sorry, and he had been awfully comfortable speaking so disparagingly to her in front of all those people at the ball. *Let him wallow in his misery until he was ready to give an honest apology.*

"Where did he go?" Maddie asked, running to take Elonnie's hand.

"I don't know," Elonnie sighed.

"Is he coming back?"

Elonnie watched Arlo walking around and then picked Maddie up. "I hope so," she admitted.

Trente-deux

Waking up early the following morning to prepare to watch the kids, Elonnie walked around the manor. She was missing her family, as most of them happened to be out of town for the month preparing for the tour—this wasn't all bad, as she knew her aunts would persuade her to go back to Ravenhill immediately, as would her nana. She knew she did have to go back sooner or later, but that was easier said than done.

Strolling about her family's home, Elonnie realized that she had missed the glamour and bizarre elements of it. Not as much as she had missed the kids, who were clearly just as thrilled to see her. The little ones enjoyed the freedoms of not having a husband or a wife to worry about; they could tell nonsensical stories without worrying about criticism. They were happy because their lives were still very simple, and that was what made their company so precious.

They would be arriving soon, so she opened the door to sit on the porch and there she was greeted by Arlo. "Elonnie," he started.

She shut the door hastily and stepped back before

covering her mouth. She didn't mean to do such a rude and ugly thing to him—her reflexes had gotten the best of her. Taking a deep breath, she stepped closer to the door and opened it. "You startled me," she told him. "Can I help you?"

"Yes. Come back home."

"I am home," she said. "And I said I would come back to Ravenhill when I was ready."

"You yourself said that it was inappropriate for you to have a separate room from me and now you think this is all right?"

"I think it's inappropriate for you to ignore me and insult me publicly and never say what's bothering you, but rather leave me to try and read your mind."

"Can you allow me to explain what the issue was?" he asked.

Elonnie walked out of the house and passed Arlo. "I wish you would have explained when I asked you over and over again, but seeing as how I'm sure I'm the problem, as I always am in your narrative, I don't even want to hear it anymore," she told him. "The children will be here soon and I have no desire to argue with you in front of them."

"We don't have to argue. I'm not here to argue, Elonnie," he assured.

"Then you won't fight with me when I request that you take your leave." Reaching into her dress, she handed him a letter. "I've been contemplating whether to send it or not, but seeing as you're here, you may as well take it."

Arlo accepted the letter and looked down at it. "I'll read it," he told her. "And I will keep coming back until you decide to return home." He started down the porch steps and then once more looked at her before he stepped back onto the porch to kiss her head. "Farewell, Elonnie."

A<small>RLO DIDN'T GO FAR</small> from the manor, as his plan was to remain in the area until he could get Elonnie to return to Ravenhill with him. He was not going to leave the city without her. He watched as a couple walked past him, along with their Dalmatian, and considered if he should get Elonnie a puppy to persuade her.

That would surely do it. His eyes brightened. As the couple disappeared up the road, he slouched back on the bench he sat in and frowned. It wouldn't work—it would anger her that he thought a tangible present would suffice, as she had told him that she didn't want to be bought off every time she was angry with him.

Reaching into his pocket, he retrieved the letter that Elonnie had written for him. He swallowed, nervous to read it. It was a certificate of divorce. It just had to be. He put it down at his side and took a moment to rest his face in his hands before finding the strength to reach for the letter again and open it.

"*My darling Arlo,*" he read. That was a good start, to be not just "darling," but "*my* darling."

He continued reading.

"*I've struggled to write this for you because I know it will probably cause you to laugh at me as you take pleasure in doing. Nevertheless, I will, because I'm stronger than you give me credit for. I don't care if people should laugh at me.*

I want you to know one thing that's certain: I love you. And I'm almost sorry that I do, because that's what makes it so easy for you to have the control you have over me. You're very similar to the art of ballet; it can be so painful and strenuous, yet I can't seem to fall out of love with it. Only, ballet is good for me; it's healthy. I can't say the same for whatever is going on between you and I.

It didn't take too long for me to fall in love with you, although I wish it did. But something about you intrigued me and made me wonder who was hiding under that tedious young man, for I knew it was a more spirited man.

Something happened at the engagement ball that turned you into my enemy, and for that I'm sorry. I wasn't trying to hurt you with any of my actions yet it seems that I did—but I want you to see that I am willing to apologize to you, even when I don't know why I'm at fault.

As I have stated, I will return to Ravenhill when I'm ready. And by that time, I hope that you're far less arrogant and willing to apologize to me when necessary, even if you don't love me the way I love you.

Your wife until death,

Elonnie K."

"BUT I DO LOVE YOU, ELONNIE," he said weakly. He looked up from the letter which had turned out to make him tremendously optimistic and his eyes widened—he couldn't tell the air that he loved Elonnie. He needed to tell Elonnie. She hadn't heard the words from him once, even when he had started to feel himself weakening to her.

He wouldn't wait until the following day this time; he'd go back right now, and tell her how he felt, hard as that may be. And if she still didn't waver, he'd simply just toss her over his shoulder and take her back to Ravenhill. That wouldn't be too hard.

He stood up. *No, that would be too aggressive and only make her resent him more.* Perhaps he could write her a letter as she had written him. But he knew he lacked the skill to get the words down the way he desired to when it came to someone he cared about so deeply. He just had to go back and tell her not only that he loved her, but he was sorry, and he *needed* her to return.

He sighed heavily, swallowing his pride, and started back to the manor. But before that, there was one more thing he needed to do.

ELONNIE STOOD beside the fountain with Étienne, whom she was always pleased to see. At least now she could continue her French lessons, until of course it was time to go to Ravenhill. She read aloud from the fictional novel that Étienne gave her to practice from and tried her hardest not to giggle when she messed up. Looking up from the book after finishing the chapter, she met eyes with Arlo. Her shoulders dropped. "Mon Dieu, il est implacable," she complained.

"Voulez-vous que je me débarrasse de lui?" Étienne offered.

"I'll handle it," Elonnie sighed.

"Bon courage," Étienne smiled, then took her leave into the manor.

"Yes, Lord Kensington?" Elonnie asked.

"I haven't set foot out of Therondia yet," he told her. "I won't leave without you by my side."

"Well, I hope you have comfortable arrangements," Elonnie told him.

"Elonnie, I was jealous and that was foolish," he started. "I enjoyed every minute of your performance and I so desperately desired to dance with you after; and then I saw you choosing to dance with everyone else that wasn't me and I thought it was because you were hoping to upset me."

"Arlo, I wanted to dance with you!" Elonnie griped. "But why would I think you wanted to dance when you said that you hated it? I may be many things, but I would never use other men to make you feel hurt, and it hurts that you think I would! All I did was talk to them about you and tell them how badly I wished you danced, and that you'd swallow your pride and ask me to, but you didn't. And then you spent days letting anger fester instead of talking to me about it!"

"I know," Arlo said sadly.

"I thought you said farewell already," Elonnie groaned before she headed in the direction of the home.

"Ellie bear!" Arlo shouted.

Of course, that snatched the girl's attention, as did the sound of a splash— she turned back to Arlo to see the once so sophisticated young baron looking pitiable as he stood in the fountain, letting the water pour onto his head. She covered her mouth in shock as she held back laughter.

"I'm sorry," he told her. "I'm sorry I was cruel in Tamin, I'm sorry I didn't tell you about the paintings, I'm sorry I was cold and standoffish, and I'm sorry I never made you feel like a loved wife. I love you. I'm bewildered as to when it happened, but it did, and fast—and I do, Elonnie, I do!"

Elonnie stood speechless; her jaw quivered at the declaration. All of it looked and sounded sincere, from the tone of his voice to the afflicted look in his eyes. "Do you mean what you say?" she whimpered. "Do you promise?"

"On my life, I promise," he vowed, climbing out of the fountain and approaching her. "I didn't show much appreciation for anything, although I benefited from your presence in every way. I felt loved, Elonnie, even though I didn't make you feel the same way, and I'm sorry for that. I felt excited." He flashed a huge smile. The smile she loved. "Excited just thinking about the fact that you were there waiting for me, and I never paid much attention to it until it was gone. I felt comforted, too; you made Ravenhill a solace instead of a cold, dark estate, and I loved that. I love you, Elonnie Kensington. And I promise to never make you doubt that again."

No more was needed, Elonnie ran closer to him and leaped into his arms, offering him a long kiss. "I love you too, Arlie," she told him.

"One more thing," he whispered, putting her down. He kneeled onto the ground and reached into his pocket to take out a small velvet box, now a bit wet. "Perhaps I should have given it to you before the fountain," he nervously chuckled. "Long before that, actually," he said as he opened it, revealing a golden ring in the shape of a crown with diamonds encrusted in it. "Elonnie Kensington, will you do me the honor of... remaining my wife?" he asked.

"Arlo," Elonnie gasped, of course enthralled at the beautiful ring. "Yes, Arlo, absolutely, yes!" She nodded aggressively.

Pleased at her answer, he stood up and took her face in his hands, kissing her again.

"Before I forgive you for calling me a harlot in front of everyone," Elonnie began after she placed her finger on his lips. "You have to give me a reason to," she smirked.

"Did I not apologize?" he asked.

"Yes, but I want you to swim with me in the Malachi Brook."

"As you wish," he nodded, starting to kiss her again.

"And then," she interrupted. "I want you to teach me to paint a portrait like you can," she said.

His thumbs gently brushed her cheeks. "There is nothing that would give me greater pleasure," he said.

"Also, I want you to have dinner with me, in my ballet dress."

Arlo chuckled. "Of course. Elonnie, wear whatever you desire, whenever you wish, I don't care," he instructed before nestling his face into her neck.

"Not me, Arlo," she said, gently pushing him off. "Not me in the ballet dress." She shook her head.

Arlo's pupils shrunk as he looked down at her. "B...but?"

Elonnie smiled, biting her lip, her eyes focused in on his. "No buts about it," she told him.

Arlo sighed, peering down to the ground. "Just to give you solid proof that I meant everything I said to you, I'll do it," he hesitantly said. "Anything else?"

Elonnie gazed at the charming wedding ring on her finger and smiled. "That's all...for now," she told him.

Trente-trois

"Et, ainsi c-ommença le voyage du marquis dans un nouveau monde...."

Elonnie struggled with the novel which served as her French practice when she couldn't be with Étienne. "A beautiful language, but quite the struggle," she murmured. She placed the book upon the table and Arlo smiled at her as he reached for it.

He opened it up to the page she left off and, to her surprise, continued on reading from where she left off.

"Arlo Darcy, how are you doing that?" she whined.

"J'ai appris le Français en grandissant," he shrugged. "I thought you would have known that."

"What did you say?"

"Try and guess."

"J'ai appris...you learned French growing up?"

"Très bonne, Elonnie," he proudly applauded. "Yes, me and my brothers."

"But why didn't you tell me all this time?" she asked. Her brown eyes widened, mortified as she recalled all the rude things she had said about him in the language. "B-but that would mean...."

"Mm-hmm," he nodded. "Out of all the attacks, my favorite had to be 'miserable recluse;' it might have been the most fitting."

"Arlie, I'm sorry," Elonnie gasped.

"No need to be," he assured. "I do find it funny, though, how easily the insults trickle off of your tongue, but when it comes to reading simple passages you struggle." He laughed, handing her the book back and then kissing her cheek. "I have just a few more things to work on and then off to sleep. Don't wait up for me."

"Goodnight," Elonnie responded.

❧

It was nearly midnight when Elonnie wandered about the estate; she couldn't sleep knowing that Arlo was still awake—most likely stressing out over something work-related. She decided she'd bake him something sweet, as well as brew him a cup of Merry Berry tea to give him energy to achieve whatever he needed to.

She stood before the study door with the plate in her hand and knocked before she opened it. "It's almost twelve," she whispered to Arlo. She glanced down at the scattered papers along the floor and gave a look of confusion, remaining where she stood in the doorway. "What on earth are you doing?"

Arlo huffed. "Nothing I want to accomplish, that's for sure," he groused.

"I, erm, I figured you'd be working hard, so I made you a whim wiffle and some Merry Berry tea," she told him, glancing down at the treat. "Better not to stress yourself out,

Arlo; but if you really must, a little sugar always makes the pain disappear," she encouraged.

"Is that so?" Arlo managed a grin. He looked down at the blank paper in front of him and took a moment to breathe, leaning his cheek into his hand. Raising his eyes up to Elonnie, he softly smiled. "Come here," he requested.

"You mean I have permission to walk past the threshold of the confidential study?" she laughed.

"I beg that you do," he replied.

"If you wish it," she said with a nod. She walked over to Arlo and threw her arm around him as she placed the plate upon the desk. "Are you willing to try the treat?" she asked.

"It can't hurt," he succumbed.

Proudly, Elonnie perked up, sitting down on his lap and cutting a piece of the whim wiffle. She offered it to him and he ate, then tried his hardest to hide his disgust at the sweet dessert—his stiff grin appeared more as a grimace. "Do you like it?" she asked.

"Hmm? Erm...." He forced himself to swallow and no matter how hard he tried to smile, he could only offer her a grimace. "Have I told you I think you look beautiful today?" he asked.

"Yes," she nodded. "Do you like the whim wiffle?"

"I think you look pretty under the dim light of the candle."

Elonnie's lips formed a pout. "Do you like what I've worked so hard to make for you or not?" she pressed.

"Oh, never mind that," he brushed it off. "I desperately need your assistance with something."

Elonnie arched her eyebrow, annoyed that he wouldn't answer, but taking that as his way of saying he hated the snack. "What is it?" she asked.

"I want you to help me write a letter," he told her.

"A letter? To whom?"

"My father."

"Arlie?"

"I know, I know, it sounds awfully bizarre, but... I've tried to say it verbally nearly a thousand times; whenever I'd leave so early or stay out so late, it was usually because I was at his grave."

Elonnie sat on his lap and gave her attention to the paper on the desk. She certainly didn't judge Arlo for wanting to do such a thing, but now she just needed to figure out why. "I can try to help you, but I wish you'd explain to me why you feel the need to do it," she told him.

"To apologize," he said. "We both know I'm not so good at it."

"Apologize?" she asked weakly, shifting so that her eyes could meet his.

Arlo took a deep breath, looking away from her—the look cast on his face made it obvious that something heavy weighed upon his mind; regret, anguish and even frustration.

"Arlie? What happened?" Elonnie tried forcing a smile, although she couldn't hide the fact that she was becoming apprehensive.

Wrapping his arms around her, he found the courage to look her in the eye again. "Elonnie, when I was sixteen, I became very ill, with grandum fever—it's an awful sickness, sore throat, bleeding nose every now and then, even restricted breathing," he started.

"Oof, I know; I've had it," she stated with empathy.

"Father took the utmost care of me. And then he got it, but seeing as he was older and weaker..."

"He didn't recover," Elonnie realized.

"No."

"Arlo, don't be mad, but you had me frightened," she breathed. "I thought maybe you had.... But that isn't the case," she shook her head. Now wouldn't be a good time for her to tell him she thought he had murdered his father—after all, that was already what the man was thinking. "Arlo, you understand that this isn't your fault, yes?"

Arlo didn't answer immediately; she knew he felt at fault and always would. "If I didn't get it, he wouldn't have."

"How do you know?" she asked. Again, leaving him in silence. "Nevertheless," she continued, then proceeded to dip the pen into the ink and hand it to him. "Dearest Father," she started. "Is that what you called him? Father?" she asked.

Arlo nodded. "Most of the time."

"Hmm...use Papa, instead," she encouraged. "It's more endearing."

Arlo was ready to dispute, but he only laughed softly and wrote it down.

"I am writing this letter to you because there is something I must get off of my mind," Elonnie went on. "It weighs heavily upon my heart, like a massive boulder's crushing weight upon an ant. I understand that, as a loving father, nothing could have prevented you from caring for me the way you did before you fell ill. And so, even though I am not at fault for your heartbreaking loss, I feel as though I am...."

Elonnie's eyes wandered over to Arlo. "You stopped writing," she said. She stroked his cheek. "Write it down, it's true. You're not at fault."

Arlo breathed heavily and finally did as she said; as he wrote the words down, he felt as if the pressure was being lifted off of him.

"And, therefore, I find it necessary to tell you I am sorry.

And I love you, and I'd give anything just to have one more day with you. But as I know that's not possible, I will promise you that I won't go on hurting this way forever, because I know how much you loved me and would want me to be happy." Elonnie frowned. "Arlie, you stopped again."

She looked at him; his eyes were wetter than usual. "Would you like to cry?" she asked.

"No, never," he shook his head, blinking.

"You don't want to write 'I love you?'"

"Well, he didn't say it often. That's not to say I didn't feel that he did, I just—"

"Write it," she persuaded. She kissed his temple and then laid her head down on his shoulder before repeating herself from, 'And I love you' until Arlo finished writing the letter. "There. Now breathe deep, and tomorrow we'll take it to the grave," she said.

Arlo obeyed, breathing deeply and then smiling at her. "Mrs. Kensington?"

"Yes, darling?"

"I think you're the best thing that's ever happened to me."

FIN.

A Happily Ever After...

"Elonnie Mary," Arlo called. "Elonnie?"

Elonnie raced down the stairs almost in a panic at hearing his calls. "What is it? Is everything all right?" she asked.

"Yes. The library, go into the library!" he directed.

Elonnie smirked. What was it? A fort? The cozy chocolate drinks from Grandmother Genevieve?

She hurried into the library and it was as it normally was, leaving her in a baffled state of mind.

"Arlo, why did...." She froze, her question interrupted by the cutest little yips.

Looking down, she saw two little puppies at her feet, a golden retriever and a boxer, both no older than four months. "Arlie!" she squealed, nearly ready to pass out.

"I fell for their eyes and I figured you would just the same," Arlo laughed, entering the library. "Especially this guy," he said, kneeling down before the boxer.

Elonnie's features shifted into a bragging smirk as she kneeled along with Arlo. "I knew you would cave," she boasted. "I knew you would end up getting me a puppy; and to my surprise, it's not one, but two."

Arlo frowned at her before he shook his head, laughing. "Ah, come on and kiss me, Kate," he told her.

Dear Reader

I hope you had a bunch of fun reading Au Contraire! If you would like to know more about "Siren Pirates" or even see where life took Dorian and Elandra, be sure to check out Pirates of the Withering Coast and A Peculiar Royal!

Love,
 Alonna.

Also by Alonna Williams

Pirates of the Withering Coast: The Siren's Call

A Peculiar Royal

Deadly Midnight